THE
WOODHOUSE
CHRONICLE

by

Neil Cawtheray

Grosvenor House
Publishing Limited

The right of Neil Cawtheray to be identified as the author of this
work has been asserted by him in accordance with Section 78
of the Copyright, Designs and Patents Act 1988

The book cover picture is copyright to Jennifer Cawtheray

This book is published by
Grosvenor House Publishing Ltd
28-30 High Street, Guildford, Surrey, GU1 3EL.
www.grosvenorhousepublishing.co.uk

A CIP record for this book
is available from the British Library

ISBN 978-1-78148-839-3

This one is for the Woodhouse Junior School class of 1950/51. I remember them all with great affection.

I would also like to express my heartfelt thanks to my dear wife Jennifer for her patience and understanding.

CHAPTER ONE

It was bitterly cold as Billy and I walked the short distance from our homes to Woodhouse Junior School. It was still early January and the previous day had been the last one of the Christmas and New Year break. As we passed the entrance to the Electra Picture House my thoughts immediately returned to the last day of term and, as I recalled that sublime moment that Susan Brown and I had sheltered in the cinema doorway after having triumphed together in the Christmas quiz instigated by Mr. Rawcliffe, the headmaster, I felt a warm glow engulf me despite the extremely cold weather. My companion and closest friend, however, soon brought me back to reality.

"I don't think I can stand much more of this," he complained while blowing huge puffs of cold air. "I'm freezing."

"Well at least you haven't got a hole in one of your gloves," I said, holding out my index finger for his perusal which clearly showed the tip protruding through the material. "It stings something rotten."

"That always happens if you wear those knitted ones long enough. You can't even make proper snowballs either."

"Yes, I know. The snow just sticks to them. I think I might as well take them off anyway and put my hands in my pockets."

"Not much point now, Neil. Everyone's moving into assembly."

As we vaulted the low wall into the schoolyard I could see that Billy's statement was correct. The two neatly formed lines, girls to the left and boys to the right, were being led into the school premises by the formidable figure of Miss Hazlehirst. Her pet subject was Nature Studies and she had taken various classes on educational rambles onto Woodhouse Ridge, though it was true to say that they did not, from her point of view, always have the desired conclusion. In fact the previous one, during the autumn, had caused much embarrassment for her in particular, though her pupils had taken an entirely different view of the proceedings. Nevertheless, she strode purposely on and it wasn't long before we were all safely gathered in the assembly hall.

"Where's Old Rawcliffe?" Asked Billy as quietly as possible, not wanting to repeat an earlier mistake when he had been singled out by the teacher who had just accompanied us for making some derogatory remark loud enough for her to hear.

I had noticed myself that the only other tutor in the room was Mr. Barnes, who was also our rugby coach. It was certainly unusual for the headmaster not to be present on the first day of term. It was his favourite assembly and always lasted longer than the others as he attempted to explain, in a long drawn-out manner, the advantages of school attendance, and how all the pupils of today were much more fortunate than the children of a hundred years ago when so many of them received no education at all. It certainly seemed that on this occasion we were going to be spared the customary lecture.

Mr. Barnes was beginning to speak. "I am sure that none of you have failed to notice that the headmaster is not with us today, and I am sorry to have to inform you that he has suffered a serious accident and is unlikely to take charge again for several weeks. He injured his back when he fell from a ladder while decorating in his home. The situation, therefore, is that there remains only Miss Hazlehirst and me to take the lessons until a new, temporary, headmaster is appointed in a few days time. Obviously, two teachers cannot cover three classrooms, so it will be necessary to disperse some pupils until he is fit again to resume. Are there any questions on this subject before we move on?"

Though there was a lot of muttering among everyone gathered in the hall no one actually spoke out aloud, though Billy did whisper in my ear. "I bet he got his foot stuck through the wallpaper." Shamefully, we both laughed at the mental image that this statement produced.

Realising that no further questions were forthcoming Mr. Barnes gave a brief speech about the coming term, paying particular attention to the fact that it was now 1951 and that it was important for each individual in the country to make sure that the second half of the century, which had just begun, was a vast improvement on the first half. We were then asked to sing the obligatory hymn which always preceded dismissal to our various classrooms. On this occasion, however, our release from assembly was delayed in order for us to be told the details of how the amended classes would be constructed. It was decided that half of Standard 2 would be joining Standard Three, taken by Mr. Barnes and that the other half would move into Standard One, taken by Miss Hazlehirst.

After much activity, which consisted mainly of the moving of desks and chairs between classrooms, Billy and I took the opportunity to sit next to each other as our normal places had disappeared in the upheaval caused by the increase of pupils to a total exceeding forty. I took a good luck at my surroundings and I soon realised that the boys in the class greatly outnumbered the girls.

"You know what Barnesy's done, don't you?" I whispered to Billy. "He's brought all the lads from Standard Two here, which means he's got everyone that's played in the rugby team together."

"You're right, Neil," said Billy looking round. "There are only about ten girls in the room. I bet the lads from Standard One who are with Miss Hazlehirst and all those girls aren't very pleased about it."

I couldn't help noticing that Susan Brown, my favourite girl in the whole school, was one of those relegated to the other class and I just hoped that the new headmaster didn't take too long too make an appearance. It soon became obvious why Mr. Barnes had made sure that his rugby players were all in the same class when he began to address the pupils.

"Before we begin this morning's lesson," he announced, "I'd just like to say a few words to all those boys who have played, or have expressed a desire to play, for the school's rugby league team. I know that the results so far in the handful of games in which we have been engaged have not gone in quite the way that we had hoped."

I thought this was rather an understatement considering that we had lost them all, which included two by quite a heavy margin, and said so to Billy. Our coach continued speaking.

"I would like to point out to you all that we are nowhere near halfway through the season yet, as you will no doubt recall that two of our games had to be postponed, one because of fog and the other when one member of the team broke his arm. We have, therefore, plenty of time to turn this season around. With this aim in view I am looking for ways to increase the amount of time we can take from school for training purposes. I am hoping that we might be able to arrange to finish half an hour early on three days of the week instead of just the one."

The player who had broken his arm was Nicky Whitehead. Nicky lived in our street but, being a year younger, was normally in Standard Two. Today was his first day back at school after the accident. The announcement by our coach brought cheers from all the boys in the class. Mr. Barnes waited for the noise to subside before continuing.

"I had discussed this with the headmaster just before Christmas and he was quite keen for this to go ahead as he fully understood the need for the school's sporting activities to be portrayed in a better light. I had hoped to begin this immediately at the beginning of the new term but because of Mr. Rawcliffe's unfortunate accident I feel it is only right and proper that I broach the subject with the new headmaster when he takes over in a few days time. You will all be informed of the decision then."

As he finished speaking the pupils settled down to the first lesson of the new term, as much as that was possible taking into account the increased size of the class. Perhaps it was the strangeness of this new set-up that was responsible for the remainder of the day, at least in my mind, passing so quickly and as Billy and I walked home together in the still freezing conditions, we were eager to discuss the main issue that had arisen.

"I wonder what the new headmaster will be like Billy, what do you think?" I asked.

"I don't know, but anyway he'll probably only be here for a few weeks," he replied.

"I hope when he does arrive that we'll go back to three classes instead of two."

"I know why you're saying that, Neil. It's because you don't want Susan Brown to be in the other class."

I didn't make any reply to what he said but continued walking in silence. A few weeks ago Billy's statement would have caused my cheeks to burn, but since that afternoon when Susan and I had sheltered from the hailstones in the Electra doorway I no longer seemed to care about my feelings being exposed in this manner. As we walked past the lavatory yard and approached our respective houses in Cross Speedwell Street and I said farewell to my companion the first to greet me was Nell, a scruffy-looking mongrel that had been a member of my family ever since the end of the Second World War almost six years previously. She had been sitting on the doorstep in a silent protest at being left outside on such a bitterly cold day. The expression on her face said 'It's about time you showed up. Nobody's taking any notice of me.' I opened the door and we walked in together, Nell immediately taking up her accustomed place on the clip rug in front of the fire while casting accusing glances at my mother who had just entered from the adjoining room.

Ours was a modest terrace house with a front and a back room, two bedrooms and a cellar. I was currently living alone with my parents as my older brother Tim was performing his National Service duties. My father worked in a leather manufacturing factory in Meanwood Road and usually arrived home just after six o'clock.

"Don't bother taking your coat off," said my mother before I had time to make myself comfortable and join Nell in the vicinity of the glowing coal fire, "I want you to pop round the corner to Doughty's. We need some more bread before your dad comes home and you might as well ask Mr. Senior if there's anything you can get for him. He can't really get about properly in this sort of weather and I don't want him falling down and hurting himself."

The person in question was elderly and lived a couple of doors away, though when he was younger he'd led a very active life in the merchant navy. As I knocked on his door and then opened it the strong scent emanating from his pipe filled my nostrils. I always regarded tobacco smoke as an extremely pleasant aroma wherever I encountered it as it always reminded me of the fascinating sea stories that he had entertained Billy and me with on numerous occasions.

"Come on in, lad," he said, beckoning me inside. "Come on in."

"Would you like me to bring you anything from Doughty's shop, Mr. Senior?" I asked. "I'm just going for my mam."

"Well, that's very nice of you to ask. As a matter of fact there is. I could do with some more baccy for a start. I'll write it down for you, which one to get. Get the wrong one, do you see, and I have trouble smoking it."

He handed me a list, which contained a couple of other items, and a small notebook similar to the one that my mother had given me before I left the house. These were generally known as 'Tick Books', and were frequently used by many of the households in Woodhouse. The local shop would itemise each item bought and enter the price at the side. At the end of the week, when the breadwinner of the family received his wages, the book would again be taken to the shop for settling up and the final total would receive a large tick to indicate that the correct amount had been duly paid. Everyone seemed highly satisfied with this arrangement. My only concern now was to make sure that the right purchases were entered into the correct book, and as I opened the door to leave Mr. Senior called out. "There'll be a glass of Tizer for you lad, when you get back."

As I left the shop, after acquiring all the requested items and ensuring that the 'Tick Book' procedure had been carried out satisfactorily, I spied a familiar figure just turning the corner from Melville Road.

"Hiya, Johnny," I said, "What do you think the new headmaster will be like?"

Johnny Jackson was one of the boys in my class and also a member of the school rugby team.

"I don't know," he replied, "But I hope we get this extra time off school. We need a lot more practice if we're going to win a game soon, don't we? I'm getting fed up with losing all the time."

"So am I. Surely we can't go the rest of the season losing every game. I hate having to tell my dad the score every time I get back from playing. I'm running out of excuses now."

We continued to discuss the misfortunes of the team and what the prospects might be for the remainder of the term, before I decided I'd better return to Mr. Senior's house with his shopping, the glass of Tizer that he'd promised being foremost in my mind. When I arrived it was already poured out and waiting for me on the table.

"You took your time, lad," he said. "I thought something must have happened to you. Still, you're here now, so never mind, eh"

I left after a few minutes, but not without finishing the soothing drink and hearing the enthralling story of how he and a former shipmate, while still in their twenties, became lost after visiting a seedy, outdoor market in Tangiers and almost missed returning to their boat before it sailed.

When I entered our house the familiar, but quite nauseating smell of wet clothes drying in front of the fire engulfed me. For about nine months of the year my mother's wash day routine did not give me this problem, as there was a line stretching right across the road. In the winter months, however, this was not a viable solution to the drying of clothes. On a really cold day, like the current one, they would be frozen solid, thus giving the impression of having already been ironed, an illusion that quickly disappeared the moment they were brought into the house. So, as I grew, winter wash days became a favourite hate of mine. It would be fair to say that Nell was not too happy with the situation either. Today, she had voluntarily left her comfort zone on the clip rug in front of the fire and moved as far away from the offending articles as she could, but not without casting accusing glances at anyone who approached her, especially my mother. This situation would rapidly change as soon as the ingredients of the stew that she was currently preparing from the remains of the Sunday joint made its presence known by heating up and wafting a tempting aroma around the room, at which time she would be quickly restored, at least in my canine companion's eyes, to her rightful position as head of the household.

By the time my father had arrived and changed out of his work clothes the dinner was ready and laid out on the table where my mother and I were already seated and awaiting his presence.

"We're getting a new headmaster, dad," I informed him the moment he sat down.

"Why, what was wrong with the old one?" he responded.

"He fell off a ladder and injured his back while he was decorating."

"He'll be coming back when he's better though, won't he?"

"Yes, Mr. Barnes said he'll be back in a few weeks. He also said that we should be getting a bit more time off school for rugby practice."

"Well, that's a good thing. Isn't it? You can't keep losing games like you have been."

My father was a very keen Rugby League fan. As a child he had played for Buslingthorpe National School which, according to him, was constantly winning awards for the sport. When he began his working life he had joined Buslingthorpe Vale, a quite well-known amateur team in the area and played for them for several years before a cartilage operation ended his sporting career and I knew it pained him to hear about the dismal performances of my team, although his remarks to me were never less than encouraging. We continued to discuss this subject for a couple more minutes before my mother decided to make an input into the conversation.

"There'll be plenty of time for talking later," she admonished after watching me picking at my food instead of eagerly devouring it. I've spent a lot of time making that stew and I want to see you eat every mouthful,"

We had the same fare every Monday, made from what was left of the previous day's joint of meat. It was a meal I never looked forward to and, shamefully, I never really appreciated my mother's efforts on what, for her, was always the busiest day of the week.

The freezing cold weather and the dark winter night were sufficient reasons for me to spend most of the evening indoors reading a comic or listening to the wireless. The one exception to this was when my mother's stew, having worked its way through my stomach, beckoned me into making the short journey from our house to the lavatory yard. On this particular occasion it seemed to me that this is how Captain Scott must have felt when he trudged with his companions to the South Pole. I was only allowed to light one match when entering the cubicle and one when leaving and to make sure that this rule was adhered to there were always only four matches in the box, two being allowed for emergencies, and as I sat in the total blackness, hoping that no one had forgotten to place some square pieces of newspaper on the nail in the door in front of me I couldn't help wondering where the spiders were or whether there were any mice running around and also hoping that my bottom didn't freeze to the seat. At least no one had seen a rat since just after the end of the war, the unfortunate observer being Mrs. Wormley who made sure, in no uncertain manner, that everyone knew about it.

After having survived the ordeal I entered the house to find that my mother had decided that the temperature for this particular night merited my being allowed to take a hot oven plate wrapped in a cloth with me when I went to bed. Whatever system my mother used for granting this favour I was never able to work out as there seemed to be no consistency to her decisions.

As I climbed the stairs leading to the bedroom while carrying my trophy I knew that there was just one more task to perform before I could snuggle under the warmth of the blankets. I took from the drawer a large notebook with a plain grey cover and the words 'THE WOODHOUSE CHRONICLE' emblazoned across it in large, bold letters. Opening it at to the page marked by the red ribbon that Susan Brown had dropped when we had sheltered in the Electra doorway, I began to write all the happenings of the day. 'On this day,' I began, 'We heard that we would be getting a new headmaster.' I went on to complete the remainder of the entry before climbing into bed and falling asleep almost immediately.

CHAPTER TWO

After having endured a second day without a headmaster, and being told that he would undoubtedly arrive on the day following, both Billy and I found ourselves in the unusual position of looking forward to Wednesday's school assembly. As we entered the hall, however, the only teachers present were Mr. Barnes and Miss Hazlehirst. There were a lot of mutterings among the pupils as we awaited an explanation as to what had gone wrong. It was not long in coming.

"I know you were all expecting to see the new head this morning," began our team coach, "But I'm afraid you will all have to wait until this afternoon for an explanation as I don't have any details myself at the moment. We will, therefore, continue with the same procedure that has been in place since we began the term on Monday. I know it is not ideal but I firmly believe that it has not had too detrimental an effect on your education."

"Will we still be getting the extra rugger practice, sir?" asked Tucker Lane, the toughest boy in the school and also one of the best players, though he could on occasions be quite menacing. His favourite pastime, apart from rugby was trying to arrange a fight with someone in the schoolyard, or a good scrap as he called it. As far as I know, no pupil in our school had ever beaten him.

"I don't see why not, Tommy," replied our coach. Tucker winced; he hated being called by his given name. "However, no decision will be made until I have confirmed it with our new headmaster when he arrives."

So that was that. Despite the disappointment of not having the matter resolved, the remainder of the morning was very similar to that of the two previous days, with the boys again outnumbering the girls by a ratio of about three to one. Mr. Barnes did his best to make his geography lesson as interesting as possible to his enlarged and, on this occasion, rather disruptive class. Several pupils had to be singled out for not paying sufficient attention and I think the girls, in particular, were finding the reduction in female company rather irksome.

As Billy and I returned to school for the afternoon session, both of us being fortunate in having mothers who were prepared and able to provide their offspring with some form of sustenance and therefore avoid having the weekly pay packet reduced by the necessity of paying for school meals, we looked forward to hearing what Mr. Barnes had to say regarding the failure of the new headmaster to make an appearance. We were all taken aback, however, by his explanation.

"The person who had been selected to take over from Mr. Rawcliffe," he announced as we all took our places again in the assembly hall, "Has unfortunately met with an accident. After leaving his house yesterday, he tripped over something and broke his foot. He will, therefore, be unable to return to work for several days. This, of course, means that another temporary head will have to be appointed and I do not now expect that to take place until the beginning of next week."

A stunned silence followed as the pupils attempted to take in this new information, and I wondered if this was some sort of epidemic, where headmasters of all the schools in the country were suddenly becoming the victims of accidents. I immediately abandoned the thought as Billy was whispering in my ear.

"If it keeps going on like this, Neil, it'll be Easter before we get a new headmaster and you know what that means, don't you? Your lady love will be in the other class all that time."

I hadn't really had the opportunity to speak to Susan since I discovered that she knew that I had used the red ribbon that she had lost as a good luck token when Billy and I had completed The Long Sledge together just after Christmas, the reason being that I just didn't know what to say or what her reaction might be. I decided not to make any comment regarding Billy's statement, but as the afternoon wore on I realised just how much I wanted the headmaster situation to be resolved quickly and Standard Three to return to how it was before we broke up at the end of the previous term.

It was already dark with a considerable amount of fog when we left school and the street gas lamps were not very effective in penetrating the gloomy atmosphere. However, just as we were about to pass the Electra Billy paused and looked towards the ginnel opposite, which sloped down towards Craven Road.

"It's nearly all iced over," he informed me. "I noticed it on the way to school. If we'd have had a bit more time before assembly we could have gone sliding down there, but we can still do it now, can't we?"

I strained my eyes in the direction he was looking, but was unable to verify his observation. "It's dark, Billy, and if we can't see anything, how on earth are we going to be able to even stand up on it?"

"It'll be more fun that way. It'll be a lot more exciting."

I suddenly had a vivid recollection of his saying something remarkably similar the previous November when, after our scheduled rugby game on Bedford's Field had been abandoned because of thick fog, he had decided that it would prove to be more thrilling if we got lost on purpose on Woodhouse Ridge and attempted to find our way home. Despite the unexpected satisfactory conclusion to the escapade, we had both found it very daunting and decidedly unpleasant for most of the time. Although I was unwilling to trust Billy's judgement again I found myself slowly walking towards the top of the ginnel. The faint light that was attempting to shine through the mist did nothing at all to ease my misgivings.

"I'll go first," declared Billy, noticing my reluctance. "If we stay near the fence on the left-hand side, we can always grab hold of it if we think we're going to fall. I bet we'll be able to slide right to the bottom."

I watched as he stepped onto the ice, and with his right foot forward he set off down the slope. He got about a third of the way down before desperately reaching out for the fence to avoid falling. Struggling to remain on his feet he held onto the fence as he inched his way back up the slope.

"You didn't get very far," I chided.

"I bet you can't do any better," he said

"Well, I could get further than that."

"All right, go on then if you think you can do it. I bet you don't get half as far."

I hadn't really wanted to step onto the ice in the first place. Unfortunately, Billy's challenge meant that I would have to go through with it if I didn't want to lose face.

"I'll tell you what then," I said. "I'll do it without sliding near the fence like you did. I'll go right down the middle."

"You'll be flat on your back in the first few yards if you do that," he replied.

Attempting to present a sense of bravado that I really didn't feel I took up my position on the ice, right foot forward just like my companion, but directly in the centre of the ginnel. I rapidly lost interest, however, in whether I went beyond the distance that he had achieved as I was rapidly losing the struggle to maintain my balance, and the inevitable conclusion occurred. I fell heavily after hitting a large stone, that was covered in ice, and which I had been unable to see in the dark. I fell forward rather than backward, and am still unsure whether that was fortunate or unfortunate. I knew immediately, however, that I had a large cut on my forehead as blood was streaming down my face and getting into my eyes. Somehow Billy managed to get to me without suffering the same misfortune, and helped me to my feet and over to the fence. "Are you all right?" he asked, his question not really meriting an answer as the evidence that I wasn't all right was plainly visible on my face. "It was a bit daft Neil, trying to slide down the middle like that," he added, unsympathetically.

"I didn't want to do this in the first place," I said, trying to keep the flow of blood from my eyes. "It was your stupid idea, don't forget."

Rather than let the war of words continue, my companion realised that the wound could, indeed, be serious and we tentatively made our way back up the slope while holding onto the fence. When we entered the house and my mother saw the extent of the blood her expression was one of panic, but after wiping my forehead with a damp cloth she suspected that the injury was not, perhaps, as bad as it looked. When she had calmed down, of course, her immediate reaction was to discover how it had happened and then berate me for doing something so irresponsible as to slide down the ginnel in darkness. Even Billy was left feeling a victim of my mother's wrath. Nell, however, after initially walking over to see what all the excitement was about, decided there was nothing to make a fuss over and settled back down again on the clip rug in front of the fire wondering, no doubt, why she had been disturbed in the first place.

"I'm not taking any chances, announced my mother. "Don't bother taking your coat off because we're going straight round to the dispensary. That cut might need some stitches in it. I'll leave a note for your dad to read when he comes home and we'll have our tea later." This latter statement caused Nell to raise her head again and give what I could only describe as a disapproving look.

A few minutes later saw us on the number eight tram heading towards town. The flow of blood had slowed down, but the gash on my forehead did appear to be a considerable one. As our chosen mode of transport rattled along Meanwood Road and then North Street it suddenly occurred to me that inserting stitches into a wound might hurt. Up to that point I had not been too despondent over this change to routine, but I was now fully aware that it might have its disadvantages and by the time we had disembarked from the tram, walked across the road to the dispensary, gone through the door marked ACCIDENTS and had a look around the waiting room my apparently calm demeanour had changed completely. I gazed at the various individuals gathered there and attempted to ascertain the seriousness of their injuries with a view to determining how long it would be before I was taken into one of the three cubicles for treatment. Without reaching any valid conclusion my mind suddenly became focussed on one particular conversation. A middle-aged man who kept holding his neck as if it was about to detach itself from the remainder of his body was speaking to the patient next to him in a voice loud enough to be heard.

"I was seated on the front seat on the top deck of the bus that was taking me to work," he said in a commanding tone, "When, completely without warning, the driver slammed on the brakes so hard that I nearly crashed through the window. My head was then jerked sharply back and I suffered severe whiplash. I just wish I could get my hands on the idiot youth who ran in front of the bus like that. If I had him in my school he'd suffer for it, I can tell you."

"Are you a teacher then?" asked the person sitting next to him.

"That's right," he replied, "I'm the headmaster at Beeston Primary school."

So there it was then. It was an epidemic. Headmasters all over the country were becoming victims of accidents or, perhaps even worse, could it be some sinister communist plot to deprive the children of this country from receiving a proper education?

My thoughts were interrupted as a very small boy with his hand heavily bandaged emerged from a cubicle with a very attractive lady who I assumed was his mother. What struck me and made me feel rather ashamed of my earlier apprehension that my forthcoming examination might prove to be painful was the fact that the child, who couldn't have been more than four, was smiling and was contentedly chewing on what presumably was some sort of sweet offering from the consultant for being a brave little boy. I did not harbour any pretensions, however, that any similar reward would be offered to me.

When my turn did eventually arrive the ordeal was nothing like the one that I had imagined. I was still relieved, however, that it was all over.

"I'm glad we came," announced my mother, as we walked along the corridor to the exit which led into North Street. "I was right about it needing a few stitches, but at least the nurse said it wasn't anything too serious. You'll even be able to go back to school tomorrow, but we'll have to come back in a few days to have them taken out."

I had been hoping that I might have been able to brag to Billy about having a few days off school, but at least now I'd be able to keep up with the situation regarding the new headmaster. I couldn't wait to tell him my suspicions about a communist plot aimed at depriving all the schools in the country of their head teacher.

However, the first person I saw on entering our street wasn't Billy, but Nicky Whitehead standing under the faint glow of the street lamp and gazing longingly into Mrs. Ormond's sweet shop window. It was obvious from his opening comment that he had been unaware of my recent mishap.

"What's been happening to you?" he asked, evaluating the evidence of my accident. "Did you walk into a wall or something?"

"Don't be too long before you come in, Neil," said my mother in a commanding voice, as she made to continue along the street leaving me to talk to Nicky. "None of us have had our tea yet, remember."

As I watched her go I explained to Nicky the circumstances which had led up to my current predicament and went on to inform him that one of the patients was the headmaster of a school in Beeston. I was pleased that his reaction was a similar one to mine.

"Not another one," he said. "What's happening to them all?"

I spent a few minutes explaining my theory of a communist plot before we both decided to discuss in a more serious manner the prospect of a new headmaster arriving in a few days time.

"I hope he's better than Old Rawcliffe," suggested Nicky. "He always seems so grumpy."

"Well at least you didn't get him for nearly every lesson," I replied. "I hardly dared ask him anything half the time. You've usually had Barnesy taking your class. I bet he used to spend half the time talking about the rugby team. Anyway, whoever we get, at least we'll be able to split into three classes again."

I was already resenting the fact that Susan Brown was sitting in a different room all day.

"Won't your mam let you stay off school because of that cut on your forehead?" asked my companion. "When I broke my arm during the rugby game before Christmas I was off for ages. It was great."

"No chance, Nicky, but I'll have to be off sometime during the week so that I can go have the stitches out."

Obeying my mother's instructions about not having a long conversation was easy to do as my stomach was already reminding me that it was a long time since I had last eaten and I entered the house just in time to see the egg and chips being placed onto my plate. My father was already seated with Nell by his side awaiting the occasional offering that was held out for her whenever my mother wasn't looking. My canine friend had long been accustomed to this procedure and would never contemplate sitting anywhere else at meal times. The fact that the location of her own bowl was at the top of the cellar steps, the contents of which had only recently been eagerly devoured was never, in her mind, a consideration. My father's reaction to my injury was that it was self-inflicted and that there would be little sympathy coming from his direction. Nell, always finding it more beneficial to share his viewpoint, especially when food was on the table, stared at me with a disapproving look that indicated that she was totally in agreement with his analysis of the situation.

During the remainder of the evening I did not suffer any real discomfort as the painful throbbing on my forehead had lessened to such a degree that I was almost able to forget that the injury existed and as I lay in bed after having completed the Chronicle's daily entry I reflected on all that had taken place on that day. The prospect of encountering a new headmaster remained uppermost in my thoughts. Would he be grumpy and disagreeable like Old Rawcliffe, or perhaps a little less strict and easy-going? Only time would tell. However, as I attempted to settle down for the night I discovered another question demanding an answer. How on earth were we going to prevent him from having an accident on his first day?

CHAPTER THREE

"We're going to see your Grandad Miller this morning," announced my mother. "He'll need someone to do a bit of shopping today. He won't be able to go out, not in this weather. We'll go for the tram as soon as you've finished your breakfast."

Every morning in winter when I drew back the curtains in my bedroom it was with an eager anticipation that I might witness a heavy snowfall. On this occasion, however, I had been greeted by freezing fog and I had barely been able to make out the lighted windows in the houses opposite. Just the act of gazing out of the window had seemed to make the temperature in the room fall by several degrees.

Despite it being a Saturday my mother had been downstairs for well over an hour, making sure that yesterday's ashes had been raked out of the fireplace and despatched to the midden at the end of the lavatory yard before making preparations by laying firewood in the grate on top of pieces of newspaper. She would then have lit the paper and gone down into the cellar, returning with a shovel full of coal to remain on the hearth until the fire had taken hold properly. My father, by this time, would have already arrived at the leather factory in Meanwood Road where he was employed. On this one day of the week, however, he felt himself fortunate in only having to work until midday.

With breakfast over we set off, suitably attired for the extreme conditions, taking the usual route to my grandfather's house which was via the number five or number eight tram to the Corn Exchange in town, followed by a number ten to a terminus at Compton Road in Harehills. This left us with a five minute uphill walk to the upper flat of a two-storey building in Foundry Approach in which he had lived since my grandmother had died a few years earlier. Grandad Miller was a postman who was rapidly approaching retirement age, but hadn't returned to work since he almost lost his life during a chronic attack of asthma a few weeks before Christmas and everybody considered it extremely unlikely that he would be delivering mail again before he collected his hard-earned pension in a few months time. When we entered his abode, however, it was to find him in his usual cheerful mood.

"I thought you might be showing up this morning," he said, his words seemingly directed at me. "I suppose you think your old grandad is too frail to go to the shops in this sort of weather."

"Well, it's very cold, grandad," I responded, "And you can't see very far in this fog. You might fall on the ice and then we'd have to get an ambulance."

"Aye, lad, well there's something in what you say, I suppose."

After this initial exchange of words my mother took decided to take charge of the conversation.

"There's no need for you to go out at all today," she said rather forcefully. I knew she was remembering how he had almost died in the Infirmary only a few short weeks earlier. "If there's anything you want from the shops Neil will be able to get it for you, providing it's not too heavy."

"Nay, lass, all I need are a loaf of bread and a jar of Bramble Seedless jam. Oh, and if they've any sticks of celery I'll have a couple of them. I'm very partial to it as you well know."

My grandfather always enjoyed sprinkling salt onto the table cloth before dipping a piece of celery into it and then biting a chunk off. I had witnessed this ritual on many occasions.

"I don't think there's anything else I need," he went on. "I've plenty of stuff in the pantry."

"Don't take your coat off," said my mother, turning towards me, "You can go for them now. Then your grandad might give you a glass of Tizer when you come back."

"It'll have to be Dandelion and Burdock," said my grandfather. "I know there's plenty of that left, because I've only just opened the bottle." He suddenly noticed the plaster on my forehead. "What on earth's been happening to you?" he went on. "Did you walk into a lamp post or something?"

I explained to him in detail exactly how my injury had occurred.

"Here you are telling me that I might slip on the ice, and you've already done the same thing," he said, aghast.

"Yes, but he brought it on himself, didn't you?" said my mother, showing no signs of sympathy and turning her head to address the last two words directly to me. "So you'd better be careful how you go this time, hadn't you?"

The nearest parade of shops to my grandfather's house was about three hundred yards away, mostly downhill. The journey did not present me with many problems. It was very slippery underfoot, though the fog was beginning to ease slightly. I trod very carefully having no intention whatsoever of attempting to slide down the pathway and repeat the mishap that had befallen me a few days previously. What concerned me the most, however, was the freezing weather and by the time I returned with the items that Grandad Miller had asked for, I was so cold that my mother immediately bundled me in front of the warm fire. I made sure that my temperature had risen sufficiently before I attempted to drink the Dandelion and Burdock that was placed on the dining table behind me.

"Right, dad," announced my mother, "I'm just going into the kitchen to do a bit of tidying up. Now, don't let Neil be tiring you out."

"By heck, lad," said my grandfather, addressing his remarks to me as my mother moved into the other room, "she means well, especially with me not being long out of hospital and all that, but I don't reckon I'm at death's door just yet."

I decided to make no comment on his remarks, but I knew full well that he had almost died when he was in the Infirmary and I knew that he knew it too. Still, he had looked a lot better lately.

My thoughts were interrupted when my mother returned almost immediately. "I found this, dad," she said, holding up a smooth-looking stone, which measured about four inches across. "It was at the back of the cupboard where you keep your pans. I've no idea where it came from or how it got there. Shall I just throw it away? I mean you can't be keeping it for any reason, surely."

I had heard of people who started doing strange things as they entered old age and I could sense that she was hoping this wasn't the case with my grandfather, though he certainly was, at least in my eyes, in total command of his faculties.

"Just leave it with me, lass," he said, holding out his hand to take it from her. "I'll see to it."

As she handed it over, I could see that my grandfather's eyes as he gazed down at it were looking a little misty.

"What is it, grandad?" I asked, wondering why he wasn't just throwing it into the waste bin.

"This, lad, this is the Lucy Stone. At least, that's what I've called it for the past fifty years or so."

My interest was immediately aroused. "Why do you call it the Lucy Stone?"

He seemed deep in thought for a few seconds before beginning to speak, and I knew that I was about to hear another of his fascinating stories.

"It was the year that the old queen died," he began, "So I reckon that would be 1901, and we were experiencing one of those hot summers that just seemed to go on forever. Now, my family was very poor, you understand, and I think it's true to say that all the mill workers in Hunslet were, but there was one advantage I did have over most of the other lads in the area and I know for a fact that my best mate, Harry Crabtree, was very jealous of it, and that was the fact that I had an uncle and aunt who lived there lives in a caravan, just like those Romany gypsies do. Now at the beginning of August in that year, and I wasn't much older than you are now, my father surprised me and my younger brother by announcing that we were all going to spend a week on the east coast with my Uncle Fred and Auntie Emily.

I can't begin to tell you how excited we all were. Me and my brother had never even seen the sea before and I think my mam and dad had only been a couple of times, and then only on a day's outing."

"Where was this caravan?" I asked, interrupting his narrative. "Was it in Scarborough?"

"You're very impatient, lad," responded my grandfather, frowning. "If you'll stop interrupting for a few minutes I'll tell you all about it."

"Sorry, grandad," I mumbled. I wanted to tell him that it was because I was so interested in what he was relating, but I thought it best to remain silent.

"Well, in answer to your question," he continued, after gathering his thoughts and returning to his story, "It wasn't Scarborough but a little place a few miles north of there and just south of Whitby called Robin Hood's Bay; and before you cut in again I'll tell you that as far as I know it has no connection whatsoever to the famous outlaw."

It was as if he were reading my thoughts because I would indeed have asked that particular question as Billy and I had always been very interested in the legend.

He continued speaking. "Now, the village itself, because that's all it is really, consists of two narrow streets that slope down, quite steeply, to the sea, but Uncle Fred had parked his caravan in a field at the top of the cliff alongside several others, some of which, judging by the style and shape of them, were probably owned by more orthodox gypsies. We had a great time and me and my brother Jimmy spent most of the first couple of days on the beach at the bottom of the steep hill, though it was always a bit of a bind having to climb all the way back up again when we started to feel hungry. Anyway, on the third day Jimmy came down with this stomach bug and had to stay inside, which virtually left me to my own devices." He paused for a moment and it seemed his eyes became a little misty again as he gathered his thoughts.

"Are you all right, grandad?" I asked.

He took off his glasses and wiped them on his pocket handkerchief. I heard him utter a little sniff before restoring them to their rightful place. He peered down at me through them.

"Aye, lad, I'm as right as I'll ever be. I'm just remembering, that's all, just remembering."

He paused for a moment. "Anyway," he went on, "I decided that I wasn't going to let my brother's misfortune prevent me from enjoying my excursions to the beach, and what a beach it was. Admittedly there was only a narrow strip of sand but it made up for that with an abundance of rock pools and you could just about guarantee to find something of interest in each one. The best time was when the tide was out and you could walk along a rocky outcrop that seemed to stretch forever. The fun part was waiting until the tide turned and watching the sea cover the parts where you had been standing just a few minutes earlier as you retreated back along the hazardous causeway. I knew that my parents would have been horrified if they knew I was engaged in what could be quite a dangerous activity, and I had heard that people had been cut off by the tide on numerous occasions. I was aware, however, that on this particular morning the tide was already on its way in and it seemed much more perilous when I didn't have my brother accompanying me even though he was a couple of years younger. So I deliberately chose not to linger too long. As

I approached the much safer area close to the lifeboat slipway I realised just how much I was missing Jimmy. I pondered over whether to climb back up the hill to see if dinner was ready or to hang about a little longer, but my mind was suddenly made up for me.

'Do you want to see a crab?' said a female voice from behind me. 'I'll show you one if you like.'

Startled, I turned around to be confronted by a very pretty girl of about my own age. She had shiny, black hair which stretched down to her shoulders, but it was her dishevelled appearance and the wildness in her eyes that led me to believe that she was a true Romany.

'Follow me,' she said and began to clamber, barefoot, among the rocks, never doubting for a moment that I would set off in pursuit. She was so adept in what she was doing that I was having difficulty keeping up. I was conscious of the fact that the tide was still coming in but I was intrigued by this strange and alluring creature. Eventually she stopped by a large pool and placed her hand into the icy water. How she managed to extract the crustacean in such a way that she managed to avoid the sharp claws was a total mystery. That moment was the beginning of the most wonderful few days I had ever experienced. We met every morning on the beach and, though I had never paid much regard to girls in the past I was beginning to look at them in an entirely different way. Lucy, for that's what she told me her name was, seemed to have a strange hold on me and I was totally under her spell. She said that she lived in a caravan with her ma and pa, but she would never tell me where it was. I tried following her up the hill once but she ran so swiftly that it was impossible for me to keep her in sight."

"It couldn't have been a very steep hill then, grandad, if she could run up it," I interrupted.

"Don't you believe it, lad. It was all I could do to walk to the top and yet she took that hill in her bare feet as if it was no effort at all. Anyway, when it came to the final day before we had to return home I realised that I had enjoyed her company so much that I felt devastated that I might never see her again. By that time I was reasonably sure that she had the same feelings for me that I had for her and as we waded in one of the larger pools, hoping that there was nothing in it to bite our toes, Lucy suddenly pulled out this beautiful stone, or large pebble if you like, and showed it to me. As we both stared at it, fascinated by the beautiful colours running through it, it somehow slipped through our fingers, crashed onto the rock and broke into two pieces. What was remarkable, however, was the fact that the break was so clean that the stone seemed to consist of two almost equal halves. It was as if our two minds had merged into one as we each picked up one half of the stone and vowed to each other to keep it forever, so that if we never met again we would always be able to recall, by gazing at the stone, the wonderful time that we had both shared, and as we parted for the last time she kissed me. That heartfelt kiss was the first I had ever had. When I got back to the caravan I felt heartbroken. Jimmy had just about recovered from his stomach ailment sufficiently to enable us to travel on the following morning, but the journey home provided me with perhaps the most miserable few hours I had ever spent."

Did you never see her again then, grandad?" I asked, once again enthralled by his story.

"No lad, I never did, and I've no idea what happened to her but as long as I kept my half of the stone I knew that I would never forget."

"I've finished in the kitchen, dad," announced my mother, disturbing the atmosphere as she emerged into the living room. "I'll just do a bit of dusting in here if that's all right."

"Aye, lass, that'll be fine, thank you very much." He picked up the Lucy Stone and beckoned me to follow. "I'd like to show you something," he said, directing his words to me. I accompanied him to the kitchen where he filled a bowl with clear, cold water and placed the object of his narrative inside. I watched, fascinated, as the hitherto dull appearance of the stone was magically transformed into one containing bright, shiny colours and I immediately understood his fascination with it.

"Aren't you going to tell my mam that you're going to keep it?" I asked him.

"Nay, lad, she wouldn't understand. She'd just think I was being silly. I'll wait until she's gone and find a different home for it."

It seemed a pity, yet the more I thought about it, the more his reasoning seemed to make sense. We left shortly afterwards so that we would be in time to be home when my father returned from work, but I remained deep in thought during the entire journey, contemplating the events that my grandfather had related for his story had made a very deep impression on me.

We arrived home to a frenzied barking from Nell, whose bed for the times when she was left alone in the house was located on the wide top step behind the cellar door, as the most likely route for a burglar to take was via the cellar grate. This enabled her to leap into action at the first indication of a disturbance. Whether she realised that this was her main function was another matter and she had not so far had the opportunity to demonstrate her prowess in such a situation.

"I think we'll have fish and chips for dinner," announced my mother, a statement which caused Nell to become even more excitable as she contemplated receiving a few delicacies from the hand of my father when he was not being observed.

The nearest fish and chip shop was the one around the corner opposite Doughty's off-licence, but my mother never wanted me to go there, always preferring Jubilee Fisheries which was much further for me to walk, being opposite the far end of my school. As I passed the Electra Billy was gazing at the notice board. We usually went to the pictures on Friday evenings, but the previous day was an exception as neither of us had fancied the film. It appeared to be what Billy usually described as a sloppy film, in other words a love story.

"Why won't they let us go to the Woodhouse Street pictures?" asked Billy after I had announced my arrival. "I mean it's not that far away, is it? I don't know what's on but it could be George Formby or Abbott and Costello."

Billy had a point. While my mother was quite content for us to go the few yards to our local cinema, she was very reluctant to allow us to travel further afield on dark, winter nights. I thought about the last occasion that I'd been to a different one, which was a few months earlier when I had accompanied Grandad Miller to the Capitol at Meanwood. This thought immediately brought to the forefront of my mind his story about the Lucy Stone and I related the whole episode to Billy.

"It all sounds a bit soppy to me," he offered, after listening patiently. "I wouldn't mind meeting a real gypsy though."

I found Billy's dismissal of any sense of adventure in the story very disappointing and I was well aware that there were still some things that we were unable to look at in the same way. I left him still gazing at the poster as he had already indicated that he had no desire to accompany me to the fish and chip shop as it would make him feel hungry, having been dissatisfied with the fare that he had been offered at home.

When I had collected the Saturday dinner and re-entered the house my father had arrived and had just changed out of his work clothes. Nell was already seated at the side of his chair, knowing that any food offerings would be coming from that direction. This, of course, was in addition to the dog food which she had eagerly devoured a few minutes earlier. I thought about telling him about the Lucy Stone, but I feared that his reaction might have been similar to my mother's. It seemed to me to be something that should remain personal to my grandfather. I could not help but remember the misty look in his eyes as he related its meaning and I felt privileged that he had considered me a worthy recipient for it.

When I went to bed the first thing that I did was take out the Chronicle and record most of what my grandfather had told me. I gazed at Susan's red ribbon. Would that be like the Lucy Stone for me? Would I always have it with me? The answers wouldn't come but I knew that the situation wasn't the same, as Susan had nothing of mine as a keepsake. I remained in a pensive mood before finally falling asleep.

CHAPTER FOUR

"Why does tracing paper always smell of polish?" I asked my companion as we approached the end of the geography lesson being taken by Mr. Barnes on the first morning of a new school week. We had been asked to trace the outline of a map of South America and to place the names of each country in the appropriate section, though most of the pupils appeared to be working half-heartedly while awaiting the bell that would herald the end of the morning's activities. Despite my not being happy with the necessity of reducing three classes into two and the temporary transfer of Susan Brown into the other one it did have one advantage. Because of the enforced increase in the number of pupils there was no strict rule in force regarding seating arrangements. This meant that Billy and I had always been successful in occupying desks next to each other.

My closest friend decided to give the offending article a big sniff before attempting an answer to my question. "I've no idea, Neil, but it does pong a bit, doesn't it?"

I knew we were both having difficulty concentrating, as were most of the other pupils in the room, on the task at hand. We had all been told in morning assembly that the new temporary headmaster would be calling in to see us during the morning lessons. No name had been mentioned and none of us had the faintest idea what he might be like. We just hoped that he might prove to be a little less strict than the previous one, and as I half-heartedly attempted to produce an acceptable image of the South American continent my thoughts were firmly fixed on the event which was to take place immediately after the dinnertime break. They were eventually dragged back to the present by a voice at the other side of me.

"What did you do to your forehead?" asked Phillip Thatcher.

I was astonished that there was still anyone in the class who had not heard of my recent mishap for I had lost count of the number of times I had been forced to relate it. However, I managed to get through yet another explanation without displaying any outward sign of annoyance. I had been told that I would be able to have Wednesday morning free from school in order to have the stitches removed from the wound, and had decided that I would prefer there to be a visible scar that I could brag about, providing it wasn't too big and would eventually disappear.

"That big one's Brazil, isn't it?" asked Billy, as he gazed down at the country he'd outlined onto the paper. "At first I thought it might be Argentina, but I think that's further down, isn't it?"

Before I had time to answer him I bent down in order to retrieve the ruler that I had inadvertently knocked under the desk. What I saw as I picked it up took me by surprise. "I can see Eva Bentley's knickers," I whispered. "Her dress has risen up against the chair." Billy put his head under the desk to see for himself. We both sat upright again to make sure that we hadn't been seen. Satisfied to observe that Mr. Barnes was busy writing something on the blackboard we got into a huddle again.

"I bet if you put the end of the ruler just above the elastic, Neil, you could pull them down and we could see her bum."

"Why me?" I whispered. "Why can't you do it?"

"Because you can reach better. She's right in front of you isn't she?"

"Well, I'm not getting into trouble. You know she's always giggling. There's no way we can do it without her knowing. Anyway, we can just bend down every so often and have a look."

The matter was resolved without the necessity of further discussion on our part as the person responsible for our education, and also the safeguarding of our morals, chose that moment to notice that two of the pupils who had been in his charge only a couple of minutes previously had miraculously vanished. Immediately accepting that abduction by aliens was not a viable option he successfully concluded that the only possible explanation was that only the top halves of our bodies were missing and that the lower halves, therefore, remained undisturbed.

"You two boys," he shouted, "What are you doing under your desks?"

Startled, I regained my posture on the seat. Billy, however, was less fortunate. In attempting to complete the same manoeuvre he banged his forehead on the underside of his desk.

"Well," persisted Mr. Barnes. "I'm waiting for an explanation."

"I dropped my ruler, sir," I eventually managed to get out and Billy Mathieson was helping me to find it." It was fortunate for me that our intended victim remained unaware of what we had been attempting to achieve.

"And how long was this ruler, boy?"

"How long, sir?" I asked with a baffled tone.

"Yes, how long was it? Can't you understand simple English?"

I was aware now that everyone else in the class seemed to find the situation amusing. "Twelve inches, sir," I replied, undoubtedly portraying a puzzled expression.

"Then perhaps you might care to explain to me why it might take two people to locate an object which is twelve inches long in a confined area. Well, Master Cawson, do you have an explanation?"

"No sir," I mumbled, knowing I was well and truly beaten." As I wondered how Billy and I were going to get ourselves out of this dilemma while still retaining a shred of dignity, fortune chose that moment to come to our aid. The door opened and a well-dressed lady who appeared to be about thirty-five walked into the room.

"I'd like you all to stand and welcome the new temporary head teacher of Woodhouse School," announced Mr. Barnes, immediately abandoning his reprimand of Billy and me.

All eyes were focussed on the door as everyone wondered why the new headmaster had brought his wife along. It was several seconds before the penny dropped.

"This is Mrs. McIntyre, your new headmistress," he went on.

His introduction was met with complete silence as we all rose to our feet, and the majority of the pupils stood open-mouthed with eyes wide open. It would have been patently obvious to any observer that his announcement had been totally unexpected. It was a girl's voice that brought the class back to life.

"Does this mean that we'll be having all boy and all girl classes, sir?" asked Jenny Unsworth.

This was a possible consequence that had not occurred to me.

"I shouldn't think so," he replied, turning towards the school's newest arrival, "But I think the best person to answer your question satisfactorily would be your new head teacher"

Everyone stared directly ahead as she began to speak with a soft, yet pleasing, Scottish accent. "I'm sure you are all really surprised to be getting a headmistress instead of a headmaster and to be truthful I wasn't expecting to be awarded this temporary position myself. As you will no doubt be aware from my accent I am Scottish, but I have been living in Leeds for a couple of years now, ever since my husband, who is a school inspector, came to work in this area. Actually, it's only by good fortune that I'm here at all. Had it not been for someone shouting a warning I would have fallen into a publican's cellar. It seems the flaps had been left open after a delivery of beer barrels had taken place. Anyway, I'm here now, so it's best not to dwell on what might have happened, I suppose."

Billy and I exchanged knowing looks as Mrs. McIntyre continued speaking.

"I am not going to say much more to you all at the moment as I intend to address the entire school this afternoon in the assembly hall and I will answer the question that has just been raised at that point. So I will leave you in the charge of Mr. Barnes so that you can continue with the remainder of your lesson."

Very shortly after she had left, the bell sounded the end of the morning's activities. My earlier indiscretion was not referred to again and as Billy and I strode out of the classroom we found ourselves accompanied by Tucker Lane.

"She's going to be dead easy," he remarked. "You watch. She'll be a pushover. I bet I can even get her to start calling me Tucker instead of Tommy like the other teachers do. This is going to be great, a woman in charge. I'll be able to get her to do anything I want, you'll see."

"Do you think he's right, Neil?" asked Billy as we watched him head home, full of enthusiasm, while we walked in the opposite direction.

"I'm not so sure. We've never had a headmistress before, have we? She might be worse than Miss Hazlehirst and she's quite strict isn't she?"

Immediately after we had returned to school for the afternoon session all the pupils were hustled into the assembly hall and I found myself standing between Billy and Tucker. Our new headmistress was already on the platform, accompanied by the other two senior teachers. She addressed the class for about ten or fifteen minutes without really saying anything that the class hadn't already heard from the sort of assemblies that Mr. Rawcliffe presided over before moving onto something that really was different.

"I firmly believe in pupils having a say in things and expressing what's on their minds, so are there any questions that anyone would like to put forward?"

Tucker Lane got in first. "Will we be getting extra rugby practice, miss?"

Mr. Barnes turned towards the headmistress and whispered something in her ear.

"It's Tommy Lane, isn't it? She asked her interrogator.

Tucker grimaced. "Yes, miss, but I don't like being called Tommy."

"And I couldn't agree with you more." Too many people are having their names abbreviated these days. It is a trend I have always taken exception to. Thomas Lane you were Christened and Thomas Lane you will be called. I hope everyone understands this," she announced, addressing the gathering. From now on I don't want to hear this pupil being addressed by any other name than Thomas. Is that completely understood?"

"Yes, miss," was the response. I could see that several of the lads in particular were struggling to avoid laughing out loud.

"She's got to go," snarled Master Thomas Lane in my ear, with a look of sheer horror on his face.

Our new headmistress hadn't finished speaking. "In answer to your question, Thomas, Mr. Barnes has already raised the subject of extra rugby practice with me and I promise to give the matter some thought."

There were no further questions from any of the pupils and the remainder of Mrs. McIntyre's verbal communication was remarkably similar to that conveyed by Mr. Rawcliffe with regular monotony.

At the end of school Billy and I hung back for a while, as did several of the other pupils, because of the blizzard raging outside which seemed to have begun while we were all in the assembly hall. The howling wind was causing the heavy snowfall to blow almost horizontally.

We discussed the unexpected prospect of a headmistress being in charge and the general consensus was that she might be an improvement on the previous incumbent, though the one person who we knew for sure did not subscribe to that view had decided not to stay behind but to stride manfully out of the building, head held high in defiance, as he dared the elements to do their worst. Eventually, when the fierce weather showed no sign of abating, Billy and I, accompanied by Nicky Whitehead and Johnny Jackson, decided to make a dash for it. Without making any effort, in the terrible conditions, to speak to any of my companions I reached the shelter of home and stepped inside with a huge sigh of relief. Nell took one look of disgust at my dripping clothes and immediately decided to stretch out as far as she could on the clip rug in front of the fire in order to make any extra space as small as possible knowing that it would be my first port of call. She was certainly correct with regard to my intentions, but she needn't have worried about being disturbed as my mother had other ideas for my immediate future.

"Don't take your coat off, yet," she announced, just in time to prevent that very action from being carried out. "I've got an errand for you. Mr. Senior's run out of bread and I told him you'd call at the shop for him when you came home from school. You might as well go now before you dry out. I can't see much point in you getting wet twice."

Nell visibly relaxed her position, safe in the knowledge that her favourite territory was no longer in danger of immediate invasion.

"I'm freezing, mam," was all I could muster to explain the obvious reluctance etched on my face.

"Well, you'll feel all the better for it when you get back in," she replied, in a way that suggested it would be futile to protest any further.

Nell stopped witnessing the one-sided dispute when she realised it had been resolved to her satisfaction, and decided to settle down for a snooze.

As I left the house I was reminded of the film Scott Of The Antarctic which had so impressed Billy and me when we saw it at the Electra and I had difficulty in stopping myself from saying, "I'm just stepping outside. I may be some time."

When I arrived at Doughty's shop I was not surprised to find it empty. It occurred to me that I was probably the only person in Woodhouse having to brave the horrendous conditions. I took off my gloves and placed them on the counter, blew onto my hands, handed over a shilling and asked for a loaf of bread. With the required object safely in my hands I was eager to get out of the shop and hurry home where I was determined to claim my rightful place in front of the fire, by virtue of the established pecking order, and therefore relegate my canine companion to the perimeter of the clip rug. My eagerness to escape, however, was to receive a temporary setback.

"Don't go without your gloves, lad," cried out the owner of the establishment. "You'll need them when you step outside."

This assertion was only partly true, as the hole in the tip of one finger always caused a painful stinging in the exposed area. Nevertheless, I decided it would still be beneficial to retrieve them rather than to place myself in the dubious position where I would have to invent a reason for their disappearance. After collecting them and calling on Mr. Senior, while not giving him time to say much more than a muttered 'Thank you', I returned to the warmth of my house. Once the outside door had been closed, and the extreme conditions safely left behind it, I breathed a huge sigh of relief and dealt with the most immediate task of Nell and I negotiating pride of place in the fireplace area, most successfully from my point of view I might add and, having eventually thawed, out I was allowed to take my customary seat at the table for the evening meal.

I had hoped not to venture outside again but the inevitable, unpleasant journey to the lavatory yard prevented my intention from being realised. At least, given the unpleasant conditions, there wasn't much chance of Mary Pearson arriving on the scene. This fact provided very light relief, however, as I was still faced with the problem of how to prevent the four matches that I had been allocated from going soggy.

Before retiring for the night, as I was entering in the chronicle about my mother's insistence that I prolonged my exposure to the elements immediately after returning from school, I recollected Mrs. Doughty informing me that I had left my gloves on the counter. With Grandad Miller's story about the Lucy Stone in mind I couldn't help wondering whether, if I had lost them in the vicinity of Susan Brown, then she might have retained them as a keepsake. It was an interesting thought to have on my mind as I drifted into sleep.

CHAPTER FIVE

The next three days were completely uninformative with regard to how the new regime at school would be taking shape and the pupils were beginning to get restless. We were all still crammed into two classes instead of three and absolutely nothing had been heard about the possibility of extra rugby practice. The only good thing was that the foul weather had now abated, though there was still a firm covering of snow. I had been given a couple of hours off on the Thursday so that I could go to Leeds Dispensary to have the stitches removed from my forehead leaving behind just a slight scar, though I hadn't yet decided whether I was proud of it or not. Now that I was rejoining my fellow classmates on the following morning it was with the hope that some announcement would be made during the course of that day.

Nothing was forthcoming during the assembly period and the same pupils were ushered into the same classrooms that they had occupied since the beginning of term.

"I'm getting fed up with this, now," said Billy as we took up our seats. "Why hasn't she said anything?"

"Do you know what I think?" suggested Ernie Peyton from the row behind. "I bet she doesn't know how to teach properly. I bet she's going to spend all her time sitting in the office pretending to do some paperwork."

"That doesn't make any sense." I said, though I was beginning to wonder if there was some merit in his suggestion. "I mean, if she can't teach properly, how did she get to be a headmistress?"

"I bet I know," said Billy. "I bet she's only been to all-girl schools and she's only taught things like needlework and cookery."

"And netball," added Ernie Peyton.

We were all laughing now.

"Even if that were true," I said, after the laughing had died down, "It shouldn't stop her from letting us do extra rugby practice, should it?"

We all stopped speaking the moment Mr. Barnes entered the room.

"He doesn't look too happy, does he?" I whispered to Billy after noticing the expression on his face.

The reason for my observation soon became obvious as Tucker asked the question he had asked several times during the week. "Will we be having extra rugby practice then, sir?"

The teacher thought for a while before speaking. "Well, in response to your question, boy, all I can say is that it has not gone entirely the way I planned. So the only valid answer I can you give is YES and NO."

"How do you mean, sir?" asked Philip Thatcher.

"You'll have to wait a little while longer to find out, I'm afraid. Mrs. McIntyre will be speaking to all of you later today. Now, I suggest we all get down to some work."

"What do you think's happening?" whispered Billy.

"I haven't the faintest idea," I said. "We'll just have to wait to find out, won't we?"

As it happened we didn't have to wait very long. Immediately after the mid-morning break we were all summoned into the assembly hall. Mrs. McIntyre was standing on the platform with Miss Hazlehirst and Mr. Barnes just behind her. Everyone eagerly waited for her to speak.

"Now that I have been at this school for a full week," she began, "I have had plenty of time to assess one or two things, and I think that the time has now arrived for us to revert to the original three classes. On Monday I will be taking charge of the senior class of ten to eleven years old while Mr. Barnes will take over Standard Two again and likewise Miss Hazlehirst will be in charge of Standard One."

I waited for Tucker to ask his usual question about extra rugby practice but he was surprisingly quiet. I suppose he didn't want to suffer the embarrassment of being called Thomas again.

Mrs. McIntyre continued speaking. "Mr. Barnes has suggested to me that we should introduce extra rugby practice for some of the boys which would include an extra hour off school for this to take place. I have thought long and hard about this suggestion and one thing that struck me quite forcibly is that there seemed little of this sort of activity for the girls. Now I'm not, of course, suggesting that they all should start playing rugby."

This caused a ripple of laughter around the room, though perhaps not as much as there otherwise might have been as everyone was waiting to hear what came next.

"However, I have decided to introduce something new in which they can take part. Immediately after the afternoon break on Monday everyone in the top two classes will re-assemble in the hall. I have allocated forty minutes for rugby practice in the schoolyard providing the weather is suitable. If it is not suitable then the practice will take place on the following day, and so on."

I was disappointed that we wouldn't be given the full hour asked for, but it was better than nothing. Our head teacher hadn't finished, however.

"As I said, I want to do something for the girls. Prior to the rugby activities I am going to introduce some Scottish dancing, which will also last for a period of forty minutes. Mrs Greenop from the infants' class has kindly agreed to play the piano for us."

That sounded quite fair to me if it was the only way we were going to get any extra practice. Having music playing in the background while we were engaged in our lessons should prove to be quite a novelty. Unfortunately, it transpired that that situation was not what she had in mind at all.

"The boys and girls will line up on opposite sides of the hall and will select a partner," she went on. "They will retain that same partner for each of the dances, and don't worry about having two left feet, because you will soon pick it up."

This statement was greeted with complete silence by all the boys who seemed numb with shock, though a few girly giggles broke the stillness. Tucker could remain silent no longer.

"You mean all the boys have to dance as well miss?" he said, incredulously. "With the girls?"

"Now then, Thomas," said Mrs. McIntyre, "It seems to me that you must be quite a shy boy and that the idea of dancing with girls must be causing you some embarrassment, but perhaps this is just what you need to get over your shyness."

Tucker tried to say something else, but he just couldn't get the words out. If there was a hole somewhere where he could hide I feel sure he would have climbed in.

"Are there any more questions?" asked his tormentor.

"Yes, miss," replied Lorna Gale, her hand being the only one raised. I knew that Lorna would never miss an opportunity to speak. Unfortunately, she never knew when to stop. I still had horrible memories of when she tried to claim me for a boyfriend. My sympathies were with anyone who had to partner her.

"I think it's a great idea, miss," she went on. "My Auntie Jean went to Scotland once. She doesn't go to Scotland very often, but I know she went once because I remember her saying that the weather wasn't very nice when she was there. She said they had a dance there that was like a barn dance, but they called it something else. Now, what was it called? It sounds like that sweet that you can buy called Kaylie; you know, the one that you get in a bag. You dip your finger in and it's like a powder, but it tastes all fruity. Sometimes it gets up your nose though and makes you sneeze. I got some once, and when I got home I dropped the bag and it went all over the floor. It took my mam ages to sweep it all up. Anyway, I think the name of the dance was something like that. I hope that we won't have to dance over swords, though. I've seen them do that at the pictures. It's very clever, isn't it? I don't think I'd be able to do that, though. So, I hope I don't have to."

"You won't have to dance over swords, silly girl," declared Mrs. McIntyre deciding to take charge again, "And the name you're thinking of is a ceilidh, though

I don't expect you to be able to spell it. It is a traditional social gathering in Scotland where people go to hear folk music and to dance. I think, perhaps, we'll dispense with any more questions for now and it has just occurred to me that it might be better if you decided in advance who you are going to partner as it will save time."

As she made a closing remark and walked back into the office I looked across at Susan Brown to see if she was looking at me. She wasn't.

We made our way back into the classroom and I noticed that Tucker remained in the hall, talking to Mr. Barnes. He appeared to be pleading.

"There's nothing I can do about it, lad," I heard him say. "I only wish there was."

When we were all seated back in the classroom our rugby coach did his best to explain that, though he was disappointed with the head teacher's decision, it was a situation that we would have to put up with until Mr. Rawcliffe made a welcome return. At least we would be getting forty minutes extra rugby practice and anyway, a little spell of Scottish dancing should help us all to keep fit.

The rest of the day remains a blur. None of the lads were appreciative of this new activity that had been thrust upon us and it certainly affected everyone's ability to knuckle down to schoolwork. As we left the premises at the end of lessons Tucker called a few of us over.

"There's no way I'm going to be prancing about the hall with some girl," he declared, protecting his reputation as cock of the school. "We'll have to do something about it."

"I don't see what we can do," said Phillip Thatcher. "We can't just refuse to take part. If I did that I'd be sent home from school and my dad would give me a right towelling."

"You'd probably get the cane first, as well," I added, helpfully.

"One of us should see Mrs. Haggis and tell her that we're not happy about it," said Tucker, using her new name, which had crept into use by some of the pupils over the past week. "Look, she'll be coming out in a minute. We can't let her see us all standing here talking about it. Let's go round the back."

The little group, consisting of myself, Billy, Tucker Lane, Philip Thatcher, and Ken Stacey walked behind the school building to the old air raid shelter which had still not been demolished despite the war being over for nearly six years. We were joined there by Nicky Whitehead and Ernie Peyton, who had obviously decided that something interesting was taking place. We almost became eight when Lorna Gale, emerging from the girls' lavatories began walking towards us, no doubt wondering what was going on.

"Get lost," said Tucker, with his usual charm, not giving her the chance to begin exercising her powerful vocal cords. We watched her depart.

"Right," he went on, no one wanting to challenge his assumption of leadership, "We need to make sure she knows that we're just not having it and if she won't take any notice we'll go on strike like those workers in factories do when they can't get enough money."

I wasn't too happy with the direction in which he appeared to be taking us and I could tell by the expressions on the rest of the faces that all the others gathered there were horrified of the consequences if they did as he asked.

"We could all play truant," suggested Tucker, obviously warming to his theme, "And in addition to that, I don't think we should be talking to any of the girls either until after we've got what we want."

He seemed unaware that if we all bunked off school together there wouldn't be any girls to speak to anyway.

"I don't think that would work," challenged Ken Stacey, rather bravely I thought. "I mean if I stayed away I know my dad would find out and give me a beating and apart from that we wouldn't get any rugby practice at all, would we?"

Tucker appeared to be weighing up this unforeseen consequence of his master plan of action.

"I'll have to think about that one over the weekend," he said. "Anyway, it'll still be a good idea for someone to tell her on Monday that we don't think it's a good idea. Maybe we can get Barnesy to have a word with her as well. He didn't look very happy about it, did he?"

"I think he's already done that," I told him. "He said there was nothing he could do about it, didn't he?"

"Right then, lads," said our accepted leader," We still need to find out who's going to speak to Mrs. Haggis on behalf of the team."

We all looked at him as we'd assumed he would be the one to take on the task, especially as it was his suggestion. Tucker had other ideas, however.

"I'd do it myself but she'd call me Thomas and then I'd get angry. No, it needs to be someone who might be better at putting our objections across."

I wasn't entirely sure exactly what our objections were, except that none of us fancied dancing with girls and I didn't think that would be a valid one from her point of view, anyway.

"I know," he decided. "We'll do 'Spuds Up' and the last boy standing can talk to her first thing on Monday before the start of the lesson. Then we'll decide what to do after that."

The procedure he had mentioned was the generally accepted way among the lads in Woodhouse to decide who would be the one who had to close his eyes and count to a hundred while everyone else disappeared in a game of Hide And Seek, or Hiddy as it was known locally. The process involved all the participants forming a circle. Each boy would make his hands into fists and hold them out at arms length. One of them would then go around the circle hitting each fist with his own while chanting 'One potato, two potato, three potato, four; five potato, six potato, seven potato, more'. The person whose fist he landed on at the end of the sequence would then place it behind his back. The process would then start again commencing with the next fist in the circle. Eventually there would be only one boy remaining with an arm outstretched and he would be the chosen one. I could always work out how it would end up providing I began the process, but only when up to four people were involved. In this case there were six, Tucker having conveniently opted out, and I certainly didn't want to end up being the one who had to approach Mrs. McIntyre.

Things were about to change, however.

"Just a minute," announced Tucker, "I don't think this is going to work."

It was baffling why it took him longer to work out what everybody else seemed to know.

"Right," he went on. "I want you all to have a think about this over the weekend and see if you can come up with a way to get out of it and I'll see what I can think of. I'm going home now."

The rest of us couldn't think of any reason to hang about and as Billy and I made our way along the street, accompanied by Nicky Whitehead, it became obvious to me that we were in for an extremely cold weekend. The hard snow was crunching underfoot.

"Well if we have to do it," said Billy," At least it's Scottish dancing. It can't be as bad as the waltz or anything like that, can it?"

"I'm not sure about that," challenged Nicky. "I mean the music's probably a bit faster but I think you still have to part your arm around the girl."

"Eergh!" said Billy, a look of disgust on his face. "I'd never live it down."

"It could be a lot worse," I suggested. "Mrs. Haggis said that we'd be picking our own partners. I can't see how that would work. I mean all the boys will be going for the best-looking girls, and if you're not quick enough you could end up dancing with Sophie Morton."

Nicky tried to emulate the look on Billy's face. "That would be awful," he said. "No one would want to dance with her. If it was me I'd pretend to start coughing and collapse on the floor."

All three of us started laughing, despite the fact that we were dreading going to school on the following Monday.

"I might come out again after tea," said Billy. I fancy sliding down the ginnel. The snow's all crispy and sparkly."

"After what happened to me last time, Billy, I don't think I'll be joining you." Having to have stitches in my forehead hadn't exactly put me off the activity but my mother had made such a fuss that I wanted to give her a bit of time to forget what happened before doing it again.

I said goodnight to both of them and entered the house, taking my coat off immediately before my mother had a chance to tell me not to. I'd no need to have bothered, however, as I could hear her performing some sort of household duty in one of the bedrooms. I settled onto the armchair near the fire, which would otherwise remain unoccupied until my father returned from work, and Nell came and rested her head on my lap. I couldn't think of any way of avoiding this Scottish dancing lark and wondered if there was anything at all I could do to make sure that my partner would be Susan Brown.

CHAPTER SIX

The following day was every bit as cold as I had expected. On Saturday mornings, with my father at work and my mother often on a shopping trip to town I was usually left at home to do as I pleased. My mother felt quite safe with this arrangement as my Auntie Molly, her sister, lived next door and if I was engaged in anything that was deemed unacceptable she would certainly hear about it. The door was rarely locked as everybody was very neighbourly and they always looked out for one other. On this occasion, however, my mother had other ideas.

"I'm taking you into town with me, this morning," she announced. "You're just about wearing out the seat of those trousers. I'm going to have to get you some more. I was hoping they'd last you until Whitsuntide but there'll be a hole in them long before then." Whitsuntide was the one time of the year when, due to tradition among the working classes, just about every child in Woodhouse would be presented with a completely new set of clothes.

It certainly wasn't how I'd intended to pass the time as I would much have preferred to have gone sledging with Billy and Nicky, and I could think of nothing more boring than being dragged around a clothing shop. I was aware, though, knowing my mother's tenacity, that there was no possible way of avoiding it once she had declared her intention. So I didn't bother to try. The thing to do was to get the wretched morning over with and call on Billy after dinner.

"We'll go on the tram," she declared. "There's less likelihood of it getting stuck in the snow."

That made a lot of sense to me. Running on lines was a lot easier than having the whole width of the road to find a hazard. Trams were renowned for reaching their destination whatever the weather, even in thick fog and I much preferred travelling by tram, anyway. It wasn't just the fact that you could turn the seats to face the other way, something I always took a delight in doing whenever the number six tram arrived at the terminus at Meanwood, but I just liked the noise they made, a sort of clangy sound as they rattled along. One aspect of my earliest recollection of trams, which was wartime, concerned the windows, which were always blacked out in order to confuse air raid pilots and there was only a tiny peephole available for each passenger to determine where to disembark. Being born at the beginning of the conflict, the war seemed to be something that had always existed and it was a source of wonder to me when it ended and all the windows reverted to their former state.

The conditions were treacherous as we made our way down the hill towards Meanwood Road, and I found myself clinging to the hope that my mother might have second thoughts and decide to call a halt to the outing and head back home. I decided to encourage her.

"It's very slippery, mam. Do you think we're doing the right thing? It won't do any good if we fall and break our necks, will it?"

"Don't be silly. I've purposely put on sensible shoes today. Anyway, when we get into town it'll be much easier to walk. It always is where there are lots of people treading the pavements."

So that was that. With my mother in such a determined mood I knew from experience that it would be useless to pursue the matter any further. I resigned myself to what I expected would be a totally miserable morning.

We arrived at the tram stop outside the Primrose Public House without any mishap. There was no one else in the queue which was hardly surprising given the conditions underfoot. It occurred to me that there might not be as many shoppers treading the pavements in town as she had imagined. One thing she had been right about, however, was the fact that the trams were having no difficulty whatsoever in coping with the snow and ice, for we had waited no more than three or four minutes before one came rattling along, proudly displaying on its destination board 'Number 8 - Elland Road'.

There weren't many passengers inside and within seconds we were on our way. When the tram reached the next stop, which was at the Junction Public House opposite Buslingthorpe School, three women got on. One of them was quite large, one quite small and one of average size. I knew two of them. The large lady was called Edna, and she was always complaining about her husband's wandering eye to the small one, who was called Phyllis. The third lady I did not know, but it was obvious that they were travelling together as soon as they took up their seats. Phyllis was squashed up against the window by her somewhat larger companion, while the one that I didn't know sat opposite them at the other side of the aisle. It occurred to me that they could have arranged the seating much better by Edna swapping with her, as it would have allowed her to overlap onto the second seat, thus allowing the long-suffering Phyllis to have a little more room. They were soon in conversation.

"I'll get the tickets," declared the average-sized lady, opening her purse.

"Put it away, Dorothy," said Edna. "I've got it here."

"But you paid last time."

"It doesn't matter, and anyway I think you're wrong."

"Don't be silly, Edna." I'm sure it's my turn."

"Turns have got nothing to do with it where friends are concerned."

"I'll pay if you like," piped up Phyllis in a rather subdued voice.

"You will not," commanded Edna, with a touch of menace in her tone. "I'm not taking your money. You know you can't afford it."

Phyllis looked rather hurt but didn't attempt to play any further part in the proceedings.

"Quite right," added Dorothy. "Anyway, look, I've already got the coins in my hand."

"Well you can just put them back in your purse again. "I'm paying and that's that."

"Tickets please," said the conductor who had just reached our part of the tram.

"Two to the Corn Exchange and one to the dispensary," stated Edna quite firmly, making sure that she spoke before anyone else could get in.

"It's the same," said the man with the ticket machine.

"How do you mean it's the same?" asked Edna. "It's the same as what?"

"The Corn Exchange and the dispensary are the same. That's what I mean."

"Are you telling me the Corn Exchange is now a hospital like the dispensary?"

"I mean the fares are the same." he said exasperatedly.

"Oh! Well you'd better give me three then."

My mother seemed to be totally oblivious to the conversation that had taken place and bought one and a half tickets to the West Yorkshire bus station in Vicar Lane. I tried to ignore the remainder of the conversation which took place after the ticket situation had been resolved to Edna's satisfaction, but after Dorothy departed at the stop near the dispensary I couldn't help overhearing Edna's comment.

"She never pays, you know, Phyllis."

"It's a real shame is that, Edna," replied her companion. I'm afraid there are a lot of people like that these days."

As my mother and I stepped off the tram outside the bus station I could see that the pavements were not as hazardous as they were back home. Even though there were less shoppers in town than there would have been on a normal Saturday morning enough people had been walking about to turn the icy conditions into slush. Knowing my mother's method of shopping, my main concern was that I would probably be dragged around several shops instead of just the one. I suddenly thought about the dreaded prospect of Scottish dancing on the horizon when we returned to school in two days time. I was glad I hadn't mentioned it to my mother or she could have ended up buying me a kilt instead of a pair of trousers. I was surprised to find myself smiling at the thought. I suppose things could have been a lot worse, however. We only had to visit two shops, before my became satisfied with a pair of trousers from Hitchens in Briggate. I knew it would make no difference whatsoever what I thought of them and she never asked. This store always seemed to have a unique way of accepting payment. After the money was handed over the assistant would put it into a metal container which was then place inside a pipe. The container would then begin to move at a rapid pace along the pipe which hugged the walls of the shop before disappearing into what I assumed was an office. The sound it made as it progressed was very noticeable. A few minutes later it would return to its starting point. The container was then opened and the required amount of change was handed over to the purchaser. This whole process was always a sense of fascination to me.

We made the inevitable visits to Woolworth's and Marks and Spencer before she realised that we needed to be setting off back, in time to arrive home before my father.

"Why are they called trousers, mam?" I asked.

"What do you mean? Why shouldn't they be called trousers?"

"Because there's only one item. Why is it plural?" That was a word that I had learnt in school just a few months previously, though I wasn't quite sure that my mother knew the word's meaning.

"It's because they have two legs," she answered, feeling that she had solved the question satisfactorily. I wasn't satisfied, however.

"So is something with only one leg called a trouser?" I persisted.

"I don't think you can buy anything with only one leg," she said, "

"So, what's a trouser then?"

"I don't think there is anything called a trouser."

"Well, how can you have more than one, then?"

"Now, stop asking all these silly questions," admonished my mother, finally accepting defeat.

I remained quiet for a couple of minutes as we walked down County Arcade towards the tram stop before I decided to break the silence.

"Mam?"

"Now, what do you want?"

"If you dismantle something and then change your mind, would you have to mantle it again?"

"Stop it now," she said, beginning to get annoyed. I shan't tell you again."

I decided not to antagonize her any further. We were back home around twelve o'clock and I knew this would almost certainly mean a visit to the fish and chip shop. My mother was not long in affirming this.

"I want you to bring some fish and chips for Raymond as well as for us. Nell pricked up her ears at the mention of her favourite food, though she only ever received small offerings, and then only from the hand of my father, given to her under the table in such a way that my mother invariably failed to notice. My Cousin Raymond lived next door with his mother, my Auntie Molly, who was my mother's sister. Despite being six years older than I he always seemed to have plenty of time for me and I probably learnt more from him during my childhood than from anyone else I knew.

"Your Auntie Molly's had to go out today so Raymond is having to see to his own dinner," she went on," And I told him we'd bring him some fish and chips."

"Why do you always tell me not to go to the one round the corner opposite Doughty's?" I asked, which was something that had always puzzled me as it was certainly the nearest one.

"Because we prefer them from Jubilee Fisheries, that's why" was her reply.

"So if one day they're closed is at all right if I go to the one round the corner then?"

"No, because there wouldn't be any need. You could go to the one in Craven Road," she said, pausing for a while before adding, "Anyway, there's another one up near Ganton Steps somewhere."

As I arrived at my mother's preferred establishment I was surprised to see Billy just leaving. "Where have you been all morning?" he asked.

"When I mentioned to my mother about the Scottish Dancing lessons, she decided to take me into town to buy me a kilt," I told him.

He just stared at me open-mouthed for several seconds. "Aw, you're kidding me," he finally managed to say. "You'd never get me to wear one of those things." It'd be just like wearing a frock."

"Me neither," I laughed, "Even if I had a dagger stuck down my sock like we've seen at the pictures."

As there was only a small queue he waited until I'd got my bundle of fish and chips and we started to walk back home together.

"I saw Ken Stacey this morning," he said, "And he told me that he and a few other lads had been on the ridge this morning and that they had found a pond that was all frozen over. He said they'd been playing on it all morning."

"That sounds great," I said. "Did he tell you where it was?"

"He said it was down near the beck, near where Miss Hazlehirst and Leonard Horsey got stuck in the bog." This was an incident that had occurred on a nature ramble the previous autumn and it was a great source of merriment to all the pupils of the junior school. It had been frequently discussed in the playground, which had invariably put everyone in a jolly mood, and it had only recently fallen out of favour as a subject of mirth.

Playing around on a frozen pond was exactly the sort of activity to brighten up a dull afternoon, and my interest was immediately excited.

"Why don't we go down there after dinner, Billy?" I suggested.

"I can't Neil. I have to go with my mam to see my Auntie Emily. She lives at Kirkstall. Can't you wait until tomorrow morning, and we can both go down then?"

I immediately fell in with his suggestion as I always enjoyed this sort of adventure more if Billy was enjoying it with me.

"I know," I said, "I'll see if Nicky can go with us."

When I arrived home the first thing my mother did was to tell me to take Raymond his dinner.

"I'm just ready for those," he announced, as I stepped over the threshold. "When you're as hungry as I am there are times when only fish and chips will do, and this is one of those times. By the way, where did you go for them? It wasn't from round the corner opposite Doughty's, was it?"

"No, they're from Jubilee Fisheries."

"Oh, that's all right then." "They certainly smell great, don't they?"

I knew immediately what Raymond meant. There was nothing to beat the smell of fish and chips when you were really hungry.

"Who's Baldy Hogan?" I asked him, rather intrigued by the title of a story in the Adventure comic that was open on the table, which Raymond had obviously just been reading. The title read 'They've Kicked Out Baldy Hogan'.

"Baldy Hogan," he told me, "Is the manager of Burhill United, or I should say he was the manager, because he's just been sacked."

He went on to explain that all the football teams mentioned in the story were imagined ones as proper names were never used.

"Why did he get the sack?" I asked. "Was the team losing every game?"

"No, it was nothing like that. He'd just been accused by a member of the board of directors of being dishonest. They're the people who own the club. He's well liked by all the players and they're talking about going on strike to try to get him his job back."

I thought about Tucker's suggestion regarding strike action to get Mrs. McIntyre to change her mind about Scottish Dancing lessons and asked Raymond what he thought of the idea.

"It doesn't seem to be the right way of going about things to me," he mumbled as he began to eat his dinner straight out of the newspaper they were wrapped in, while offering me a chip at the same time, which I eagerly devoured. "I'll have a think about your problem and see what I can come up with."

I went back home and saw that my mother was just placing our mid-day meal onto the table, having taken the fish and chips out of the newspaper and placed them onto three plates, which had been warming on top of the oven at the side of the fire. My father arrived from work just as she was finishing.

"Those smell good," he said. "I'm absolutely famished."

I thought about telling him about our head teacher's plans for us on Monday, but I was reluctant to do so. I was embarrassed by it all, and I wasn't sure whether I had done the right thing in mentioning it to my cousin. Of one thing I was reasonably certain. I would prefer it if no one else knew. I decided to forget it for a while and hope that nothing prevented me from enjoying an interesting trip to a frozen pond on Woodhouse Ridge with Billy and Nicky.

CHAPTER SEVEN

When I gazed out of my bedroom window on the following morning I was pleased to see that the weather conditions had not changed. There was still a covering of hard, crunchy snow, though it did not appear that any more had fallen during the night. I dressed hurriedly and went down to breakfast. It was to find my mother busily scraping the ashes out of the fire grate. On occasions, if he was up early enough, this task would be performed by my father. However, Sunday was the one day of the week when my mother ensured that he had a little lie-in and she always performed the chore herself. As soon as she had completed this task she placed strips of newspaper into the grate and laid some wooden chips on top of them. As she was doing this I went into the cellar and returned with a shovel full of coal. This would not be put in place until the fire had taken hold. As my mother struck a match and lit the newspaper Nell looked on with eager approval, waiting for her to complete the task before taking up her favourite position on the clip rug.

"I thought I'd go with Billy and Nicky onto the ridge this morning, mam?" I said. "I want to see what it looks like with all this snow." I purposely made sure that I made no mention of a frozen pond as I knew what her reaction would be.

"Make sure you're back by dinnertime then, and you'd better see to it that you're wrapped up properly.

It's very cold out there this morning. Don't take the sledge up there though. I don't want you ending up in the beck."

I knew that she wasn't planning on visiting some relative today, which was quite a common occurrence on a Sunday. However, I was still relieved that she wasn't making any serious objections. I hadn't intended taking the sledge anyway.

Immediately after breakfast I called round to see Billy. I wanted to make sure that he hadn't changed his mind. I had no need to worry. "Let's go see if Nicky wants to come with us," he suggested. "I haven't seen him to tell him about the pond yet. Have you?"

"No, but I think once he hears about it, he'll want to go."

We walked along the street and knocked on the door of the house next to Mrs. Ormond's sweet shop. Mrs. Whitehead opened the door.

"Is it all right if we have a word with Nicky?" asked Billy.

"He's only just started his breakfast," she replied. Do you think you can call back in half an hour?"

"We might as well get ready, Billy" I said, as we made our way back home. "I know I'm going to be made to wear all sorts of stuff with it being so cold. Did you tell your mam about the frozen pond?"

"Don't be daft. If I'd have told her about that she probably wouldn't have let me go."

I was right about my mother's insistence on attiring me in clothing which would have been eminently suitable for an Antarctic explorer, though she failed to consider its restrictive powers with regard to the kind of mobility that an eleven year old boy would require on the sort of adventure that we had planned for this particular morning. However, I could always discard some of it when we arrived at the pond and make sure that everything was back in place when I returned home.

With Billy clothed in a similar fashion we made our way back along the street.

When we explained to Nicky the nature of our venture his enthusiasm was the same as ours, as I knew it would be, and a few minutes later the three of us were heading up the hill towards Woodhouse Ridge.

"I hope the area's not full of other kids," I said, as we left the street and walked down the few steps which led to the uppermost concrete path. "It'll be a lot better if we're the only ones there. I bet Ken Stacy's told loads of people about it."

"You're probably right," agreed Billy, "But it's a bit quiet up this end, isn't it?"

We continued along the sturdy path as quickly as we could. It was very slippery underfoot, but fortunately we were all wearing sensible boots for the wintry conditions. It was very cold and I began to feel thankful that my mother had insisted on my wearing so many layers of clothing. Unfortunately, however, there was still a hole in one of my woollen gloves and the tip of my finger was throbbing painfully.

"Where exactly is this pond?" asked Nicky, after we had been walking for several minutes.

"I'm not sure exactly," replied Billy. "Ken Stacey said it was near the area where Leonard Horsey and Miss Hazlehirst were stuck in the bog, but you weren't with us on that day, were you?"

"No, but I had a good laugh when I heard about it."

"Well, I remember we went down towards the beck from the Monkey Tree," I said, "So it's bound to be somewhere near there, isn't it?"

To tell the truth, I was beginning to feel a little anxious. A white mist seemed to be settling in and we hadn't come across another soul. The whole of the ridge seemed to be totally deserted. As we passed the place known locally as Death Valley just below Table Top, where we had all played on numerous occasions, the January conditions gave it a threatening appearance, causing me to shiver.

"I think it's getting even colder," complained Nicky. "I'm freezing. Are we nearly there?"

I was beginning to wonder whether anyone was thinking of abandoning the escapade, yet I knew that none of us would admit it.

"I think we're probably in the right area," announced Billy, who seemed to be taking charge of the expedition. "Let's head down towards the beck."

We carefully made our way down the slope, trying not to slip and travel the rest of the way on our backsides. We were all painfully aware, however, that the mist would probably be much thicker nearer the water. After reaching the bottom path we made our way along it, listening for any sounds that would indicate other children in the vicinity. In contrast to my earlier mood I was now beginning to think that it might not be a bad idea if there were, but the silence remained overpowering. I couldn't even hear the sound of running water coming from the beck. It occurred to me that maybe that was iced over as well.

"Look, that must be it," shouted Billy, disturbing my thoughts.

I looked to where he was pointing and saw a clearing that did, indeed, have the appearance of a frozen pond.

"I've been down here many a time," said Nicky, "But I've never seen a pond down here."

"I didn't know there was a bog either," I told him, "But at least that has to be frozen over as well, so we're not likely to get stuck in it."

It was quite a small pond, as ponds go, circular in shape and about fifteen feet across. It was also quite shallow as there was a tree in the middle of it, with icicles dangling from the branches. Because of the mist and the gnarled appearance of the tree the whole atmosphere seemed to hold a threat of menace. Now that we had arrived no one was quite sure what to do.

"I wonder if we could reach the tree," suggested Billy, with more bravado than we all felt. "If we could get across to the bottom of it, the branches look low enough for us to climb up."

Well, at least that gave us something to think about.

"Did Ken Stacey and the other lads climb the tree?" asked Nicky.

"I've no idea," Billy responded. "He never said anything about a tree. He just said that they'd been playing there all morning."

"It was sunny yesterday," I said, "Even if it was cold. I bet they wouldn't think it looked as interesting today."

"I know what we could do," said Billy, enthusiastically, "Let's all pee on the ice together in the same spot and see if it melts."

"That's a daft idea, Billy" I chided. "There's no way I'm getting my willy out in this weather. It's freezing. Besides, it'd mean I'd have to take my gloves off as well."

"I don't think I could squeeze more than a few drops out anyway," protested Nicky. "I went to the lavatory just before you called round."

"I'm going to see if I can walk over to that tree," said Billy, thinking better of his earlier suggestion about trying to melt the ice.

"Better be careful, Billy," said Nicky. "That ice might be thin."

"It doesn't look thin," I said. "Let's all throw stones on it to see if it cracks."

We all accepted the challenge but it made no impact whatsoever on the frozen surface. Billy stepped gingerly onto the ice. As he carefully made his way towards the centre of the pond I happened to glance to my left. The mist was still fairly thick but it didn't prevent me from detecting an elderly man walking towards us. He was heavily attired and was wearing a flat cap. A dog strolled along by his side. It was the first sign of life I had witnessed since we had all stepped onto the ridge.

"Look, there's someone coming Billy," I said, as he was about to grasp hold of the tree.

As he turned around to look at me his feet gave way and he fell quite heavily onto the ice.

"What did you do that for?" he admonished. "I wouldn't have slipped if you hadn't shouted."

"As we haven't seen anyone else all morning, I thought you might like to know that there's a man out walking his dog," I explained.

"Where is he?" asked Nicky. "I can't see anybody."

"Over there," I indicated, pointing to the left. The expression on my face must have been one of amazement. No matter how hard I stared I could see no sign of the pair, yet only a few seconds could have elapsed.

"Where have they gone?" I asked, speaking to no one in particular. "They haven't had time to go anywhere."

"Maybe they turned round and went back the other way," suggested Nicky.

"No, that can't be right," I said. "I would still have seen them."

"I don't think you saw anybody at all," said Billy. "I think you just shouted to see if I'd fall." He started to walk back across the ice, making sure he was more careful than before.

"I did see someone, I tell you. Look, I'll prove it. Come with me and I'll show you the footprints."

Billy stepped off the ice and we all set off to cover the thirty or forty yards to the spot where I had seen the emerging couple. I knew that on this part of the ridge the snow would be much thicker than on the concrete paths and that what footprints there were would be bound to be deep. However, when we arrived in the vicinity the snow was so smooth it had obviously not been disturbed since it had fallen. I scratched my head in bewilderment. I knew what I had seen and what I was looking at now seemed an impossible situation.

"Are you sure this is where you saw them?" said Nicky, trying to be helpful.

"He didn't see anything at all," announced Billy, venomously. "He just shouted so that I'd fall."

"I know what I saw," I told him, "And if you don't want to believe me then we're not friends anymore."

I could tell Billy was thinking this over. I was becoming very disillusioned with the entire morning's events. I was extremely cold and I was beginning to find the mist very threatening. Most of all I wanted to be in the warmth and comfort of my own home before trying to make sense of what had occurred. I came to a decision.

"I'm going back home," I said. "If neither of you want to come back with me, I'm not bothered."

I could see that both of them were feeling just as uncomfortable as I was and I tried to lessen the antagonism that was beginning to dominate our activities.

"Look," I said. "I swear to you that I saw a man and a dog walking towards us, and I haven't a clue what happened to them, but I think it would be a good idea if we all go home and get out of the cold and talk about it tomorrow, because it'll probably take me all afternoon to warm up again."

It didn't take them long to come to the same agreement, and I could sense that Billy was regretting speaking so harshly. He had gone very quiet. Eventually, as we regained the uppermost path, he broke his silence.

"Do you know what I think, Neil?" he said. "If you're so sure you saw something, then it might have been a ghost."

"Don't say that," said Nicky. "I don't like talking about ghosts. My uncle told me that he'd seen one once. It was just before I went to bed and I had nightmares for ages."

All I was prepared to believe at that point was that it was a mystery, and as I said farewell to my companions and entered my house the aroma of hot, roast beef charmed my nostrils, which immediately relegated the morning's events to the back of my mind. I hadn't realised it was so close to dinnertime. On Sunday, and I feel sure that went for just about every family in our street, we always had a roast joint. This was invariably preceded by Yorkshire Pudding, which was always a large one covered with onion gravy, and which filled the whole plate. It seemed to me that Nell, with her enhanced sense of smell, was experiencing the same feeling as I, if not more so, as she kept glancing at the oven with an expression of expectation on her face as if to say 'How much longer will it be?'

By the time I had finished eating my dinner I had warmed up considerably quicker than I had expected and I decided to call next door to see Raymond as I remembered he had said that he might be able to find a solution to the dreaded Scottish dancing problem which had now promoted itself to the top of my anxieties. I found him in the back room.

"I've been thinking about your problem," he said, before I had a chance to raise the subject, "And I've decided that going on strike or playing truant is definitely not the answer. That would only make things much worse and just think of the possible consequences when your dad found out."

I had already thought of that but I didn't say anything.

"I suppose I can understand why you hate the idea," he went on, "Especially with your rugby team not doing so well and your needing extra practice."

He went silent for about half a minute, with a thoughtful expression upon his face, before continuing.

Is it just the top class that will be involved?"

I explained to him about how the three top classes had been temporarily merged into two, and that from the following day we were to revert to how things had been before the Christmas holiday, but only Standard Three and Standard Two would be taking part in the Scottish dancing lessons.

"And where will the music be coming from?" he asked. "You won't be able to dance without music."

"Mrs. Greenop from the infants' class will be playing the piano."

"Good heavens!" he said, with a look of astonishment. "Is she still there? She taught me when I was about five and that's twelve years ago. She must be about ninety by now."

I couldn't help laughing at his overstatement.

I waited for him to continue.

"So children will still be working in Standard One and in the infant classes," he said. "It's going to get very noisy then. I think the answer is to make as much noise as possible. You've got to get your teacher to realise that it isn't a good idea, and get her to cancel it."

I thought about this, but my cousin hadn't finished.

"By what I've heard about ceilidhs there always seems to be a lot of yelling and shouting going on. You can do some of that, pretend you're getting into the swing of it all. Do you think you can keep bumping into Mrs. Greenop without knocking her off the piano stool? I mean, with two classes prancing about there can't be much room for manoeuvre, can there? Maybe, some of you can keep bumping into each other or falling down."

What I was being told was beginning to make sense and I realised that if we did what he suggested it couldn't be long before one of the teachers in the other classes complained. I thanked him and told him that I'd have a word with some of the other lads about doing what he suggested. I thought about going round to see Billy and telling him straight away, but the doubt he had expressed about what I claimed to have seen on the ridge was uppermost in my mind and I didn't want to get drawn into another argument. I decided to tell him tomorrow on the way to school.

When I entered the house my mother presented me with three buns, which I knew were part of a tray full that she had baked on the previous afternoon.

"I want you to give these to Mr. Senior," she said. "I know he likes them. He told me so the last time you took some round."

It occurred to me that he probably dared not say any other, but I kept my mouth shut. I had to admit, though, that my mother's baking was nearly always first class.

As I entered Mr. Senior's house and presented him with my mother's offering the expression on his face was very welcoming.

"By heck, lad," he exclaimed. "I must say those look absolutely delicious. Thank you very much. I'll have one of those straight after my tea. Now then, sit yourself down for a few minutes and I'll bring you a glass of American Cream Soda."

I did as he asked while he poured out my drink.

"Now, what have you been up to today?" he asked. "Not much, I reckon, not with the weather being like it is. I can't get out much myself these days, do you see, and winters always seem to last a lot longer than when I was a lad."

I told him about our expedition to the frozen pond but did not mention how it had ended.

"You must have been either very brave or very foolhardy trudging down there in this freezing fog. It brings to mind the story of old Jack Armitage."

"Why, what did he do?" I asked, fascinated and expecting to be told another of Mr. Senior's naval stories. What I got, though, was a story of an entirely different nature and one that was to keep me awake for much of the night.

"Old Jack Armitage lived in a cottage at the top end of Woodhouse Ridge and the story I'm going to tell you happened, now let me see, about twenty years ago. I was on leave from the merchant navy at the time, and I remember it really well. Now the reason that brought it to mind, do you see, is the fact that the weather at the time was almost exactly as it has been today, icy under foot and freezing fog."

I was really enthralled by what he was attempting to relate as it was obviously a local story and not something that happened thousands of miles away. I waited for him to continue as he gathered his thoughts.

"Now old Jack lived alone with only his dog for company, Chip I think its name was, and he was absolutely devoted to it and I'm quite sure, do you see, that it was exactly the same the other way round. The pair of them used to walk along the ridge at the same time every morning whatever the weather, and on the sort of day it has been today they could quite possibly find themselves the only ones in the vicinity."

He paused and lit himself a pipe of tobacco as he warmed to his narrative.

"Anyway," he went on, "It soon transpired that several of his neighbours realised that they hadn't seen either of them for three days and they got in touch with the police who, receiving no response to their shouting at his front door, decided to break in. There was no sign of either of them, though everything in the cottage was left in such a way that it seemed they had just gone out for their usual walk and intended to return. With the wintry conditions still being very severe, do you see, a search was made in the area where they usually took their morning exercise. Eventually, old Jack was found down near the beck, face down in the snow and it was obvious that his life had expired, possibly from some reaction to the extreme cold, I suppose. They reckoned he'd been dead for at least two days, possibly longer. What was strange, however, was the fact that Chip had remained by his side all that time. Though the dog was still alive, his breathing was very shallow. Jack's faithful companion did recover, however, and one of his neighbours took him in. He spent his remaining days there, though I heard it said that he never barked again."

Mr. Senior finished his story with a sigh and went quiet for a while. I made no mention of what I had seen but a shiver ran right through me.

That night I made the longest entry so far in the chronicle and when I went to bed I could picture in my mind's eye what I had witnessed that morning down by the pond, the man and his companion walking towards me. The image that stayed with me was one of the dog opening and closing its mouth as if barking and yet, despite the eerie stillness of the morning, no sound was coming forth.

CHAPTER EIGHT

When I awoke on the morning following our visit to the frozen pond I immediately decided not to mention to either Billy or Nicky any details of Mr. Senior's story about old Jack Armitage and his dog Chip, at least not until I had had time to think about it a bit more. I found myself, surprisingly, not minding the possibility that I might have seen a ghostly apparition. After all, they were not the kind of ghosts that could fill a child's mind with a sense of doom. In fact I had found the entire story quite warming in a way and I couldn't help wondering if Nell would have stayed by my side for three days in freezing fog given similar circumstances. I decided that the fact that the period would include several meal times made the supposition an extremely unlikely one, especially as there would be one less person challenging for space in front of the fire at home.

I called on Billy on my way to school and decided to direct the conversation towards my Cousin Raymond's possible solution to the Scottish dancing problem. After I had explained it to him I could tell immediately that he was quite excited about the prospect of disrupting the event in the manner suggested.

"I think it might work, Neil," he said, enthusiastically. "I mean, how could the other classes do their lessons properly with all that noise going on? Mrs. Haggis will probably have a fit, but I bet she'll have to back down and cancel it."

"I bet Mrs. Greenop won't be too happy about it either if we keep bumping into her while she's trying to play the piano."

I knew that the activity that all the lads had been dreading, though it was fair to say that the majority of the girls did not feel the same way, would not be taking place until the afternoon. So we had plenty of time to allow the planned line of action to take root in the minds of our fellow conspirators.

"All the lasses will just have to put up with it," observed Billy with a shrug of his shoulders. "Imagine what it would be like having to dance with Sophie Morton."

"Eergh!" I exclaimed at the thought, while putting on an exaggerated facial expression of horror at the thought, just for Billy's benefit.

However, as the boys and girls lined up alongside each other in the schoolyard while waiting to be called into assembly, and I found myself, standing next to Susan Brown, a different thought entirely struck me. If, by chance, I found myself whirling around the floor with her in my arms, could I then bring myself to join in the disruption that we were hopefully about to plan? I immediately dismissed the thought as the possibility that she might be my partner was extremely unlikely. Billy and I had decided to bring up the subject with as many of the other lads as we could during the morning break. I looked along both lines of pupils and it did seem that the girls outnumbered the boys. Was there some truancy involved? Or was it more likely that a few imaginary illnesses were being aimed at unsuspecting mothers? Surprisingly, I noticed that Tucker was not one of those missing, though he did have a grim expression on his face.

"I'm really looking forward to the Scottish dancing, Neil," came an instantly recognisable voice from beside me, "Aren't you?"

"I looked to my left at the exquisite face on which was that same cute smile that always turned my knees to jelly."

"Yes, Susan," was all I managed to splutter out as I gazed into her eyes.

Phillip Thatcher, who was standing in front of me turned round and stared with an angry look on his face. Billy, however, at the other side of me, was grinning profusely. He obviously thought my predicament was hilarious.

We all entered assembly and, though nothing was mentioned about the afternoon activity that half of the two senior classes were dreading, I knew that there was no possibility that our new headmistress would change her mind. What did surprise me was the fact that, although we had reverted to the original three classes that had existed before we broke up for the summer holidays, Mr. Barnes appeared to be still in charge of Standard Three, with Mrs. McIntyre taking Standard Two. Our teacher explained that this was because she had indicated that she wanted to get to know the pupils in that class prior to taking charge of our class on the following day.

When we were all dismissed for the morning break the first person I searched for was Tucker Lane. I caught up with him just as he was entering the playground and hurriedly explained the action that my cousin Raymond had suggested, being aware of the fact that there would be precious little time to let all the other lads know what we were planning to do without any of the girls finding out.

"That sounds like a great idea to me," he said. "If we do as much yelling and shouting as we can she'll have to cancel it eventually. Quick, let's get as many of the lads together as we can."

We spread the word and about a dozen of us made our way to the abandoned air raid shelter at the back of the school, which seemed to have become the accepted venue for a meeting place. When he considered he had a sufficient number of pupils on hand, our unelected leader began to speak.

"I told you on Friday," he began, "That I'd think of a way out of our predicament by today and I've come up with a brilliant plan that I'm sure is bound to work."

He refused to engage in eye contact with me as he spoke and Billy flashed me a knowing look

He went on to explain the action we needed to take and, despite his accepting the plan as his own, I had to admit that he was analysing it in exactly the way that Raymond had suggested without adding any foolish ideas of his own. There were a few questions from one or two of the lads but the consensus was that it was better than anything else we'd come up with. There weren't many details to work out. It was just a question of being as noisy and unruly as possible while appearing to act in the spirit of the thing. At the very least, it seemed to me that there was a very good chance that this Scottish dancing lesson could be the last as well as the first. I certainly hoped so.

When, a few minutes later, as we all trudged into the classroom, everyone who had been at the meeting knew exactly what was expected of them, and I was pleased to note that all of them were in favour of executing the plan. As we took up our places for the remainder of the morning's lessons we tried our utmost to enlighten all those lads who hadn't heard what transpired in the playground. Then Mr. Barnes made an announcement.

"It's fairly obvious," he began, "That the extreme wintry conditions that exist today mean we will be unable to get the extra rugby practice we had been promised, and we have to face the fact that the poor weather looks set to continue for the remainder of the week."

This statement was met with mixed feelings by most of the male pupils in the class. Everyone wanted to ask the same question, but Tucker Lane was the first to raise his hand.

Does that mean that we won't be doing the Scottish dancing as well, sir?" he asked, with an eager expression on his face.

"No lad," said our team coach with a scowl, "I think it's more likely to mean that you'll get a double session, and there's not a thing I can do about it."

An assortment of groans from most of the lads in the classroom greeted his words, and Tucker looked shell-shocked. It was now obvious to me that our plan just had to work.

It was mid-afternoon before we became fully aware that Mr. Barnes's supposition was about to be realised as the lads and lasses of Standard Two and Standard Three were called into the assembly hall immediately after the afternoon break, which was a full eighty minutes before lessons were due to end for the day. As we trudged out of our classrooms which many had begun to regard as sanctuary, we could all see the plump form of Mrs. Greenop on the piano stool, already flexing her fingers in anticipation. I always imagined Scottish dances to be accompanied by the sounds of bagpipes, accordions and fiddles. Just having a piano for accompaniment didn't seem appropriate. We were made to form a circle around the room with boys and girls in alternating positions, having been told by our dancing teacher that her earlier plan of boys selecting their partner had been abandoned as being virtually unworkable. I made a point of ensuring that I was not standing next to Susan Brown as I knew I would find it too much of a distraction bearing in mind what we were planning to do. I just hoped that I had done it in such a way that she did not realise it was intentional. I also made sure, of course, that I wasn't next to Sophie Morton or Lorna Gale.

"Now there are many types of dancing in Scotland," began our instructor, "But first of all I want to show you a few basic steps and I have chosen Thomas to be my partner for this demonstration. So, come on, Thomas. There's no need to be shy."

I wanted to laugh out loud, but surprisingly I felt sorry for him. For someone who had for so long been number one in the pecking order, being cast as teacher's pet in such humiliating circumstances was surely more than body and soul could bear. As I watched him grudgingly accept his fate, at least I knew that he was already plotting his revenge.

My partner proved to be Dorothy Steedman, who had been standing to the left of me, but I had no idea what dance our instructor was attempting to show us or what dances we attempted to perform afterwards, but I have to admit that our performance, at least from our point of view, was worthy of the highest award, though I found the annoying looks that I kept receiving from my partner a little off-putting. Once we had got into the swing of things it seemed so natural to yell and shout at the top of our voices. After all, weren't we only behaving in the same way that dancers at a ceilidh do, albeit a bit more so? Even some of the girls began to join in once they became aware of the fun factor. Tucker, once he had extracted himself from his original partner, was swirling around like a man possessed and almost knocked Mrs. Greenop from her stool on two occasions. Mrs. McIntyre desperately tried to inject a modicum of dignity into the proceedings but soon became aware that she was fighting a losing battle. I can't recall exactly how long things continued in this fashion. It may have been twenty minutes. It may have been half an hour. What I do remember is that a halt was called to the fiasco when Miss Hazlehirst came out of her classroom to complain that she was finding it impossible under the circumstances to get her pupils in Standard One to get down to any serious work.

"You sounded as if you all enjoyed that," said Mr. Barnes, with a grin on his face, after we had all retaken our seats in the classroom. It occurred to me that I could hardly recall him smiling before, let alone grinning. It soon became obvious, however, that the cause of his good humour was not only what we all supposed was his reaction to the way the Scottish dancing lesson had turned out, but also to another matter entirely.

"I have received a letter from Mr. Rawcliffe today," he began, "And I'm sure you will all be pleased to hear that his injuries have healed more quickly than he expected and that he will be able to resume his duties as headmaster next Monday."

A cheer went up from the class, though it would be fair to say that its composition was made up mostly from the boys. I couldn't help thinking that if someone had suggested to me before we started the new term that the headmaster would be missing for several weeks and that we would cheer when we heard he was returning I wouldn't have believed them, and I couldn't help wondering if, perhaps, we had judged our headmistress a little too early now that the thing we had dreaded most was at an end. After all, she hadn't even been in charge of a lesson yet.

Mr. Barnes hadn't finished speaking. "I would like to point out to you, however, that from what I have seen Mrs. McIntyre is a very good teacher despite her rather unusual ideas regarding the sort of physical activity that the rugby players of this school should be engaged in."

"Look at Tucker Lane," whispered Billy in my ear. I looked in the direction he was indicating and I have to admit that I had never seen the self-proclaimed leader of the class looking more pleased with himself. The expression on his face was one of pure delight.

"Tomorrow," continued Mr. Barnes, "The temporary headmistress will be taking charge of this class until the end of the week and I expect all of you to be extremely well-behaved and to give her all the support you can. Is that understood?"

"Yes, sir," came the unanimous reply. I felt sure, given the way that things had turned out, that we were more than capable of doing that.

When I arrived home the first thing I did was to call next door to congratulate my cousin Raymond on the success of his plan.

"So, you made quite a bit of noise then, did you? I thought it would work. I remember Miss Hazlehirst from when I went to your school and I know she always liked silence during her lessons. With all that piano playing, dancing and yelling it must have been impossible for her to bear. I bet the girls in your class were disappointed though. I bet they were looking forward to it."

I must admit that, once the dancing had started, I hadn't even considered that possibility. I was so obsessed by what we were trying to achieve. Raymond's remark was starting to make me feel guilty. Could it be possible that Susan Brown had been looking forward to dancing with me? After all, wasn't that what she had indirectly indicated when she spoke to me before we entered school? Unfortunately, it seemed that that was something I would never find out.

I went back home happy in the knowledge that Mr. Rawcliffe would shortly be returning and, hopefully, things would soon get back to normal. The month of January was drawing to a close and lighter evenings were beckoning. I went to bed very pleased with the way things had gone and the entry I made in the chronicle was quite a cheerful one.

CHAPTER NINE

The final week of Mrs. McIntyre's tenure went remarkably well as all the male pupils visibly relaxed at the prospect of Mr. Rawcliffe taking up office again at the beginning of the following week, and I think it was true to say that our temporary headmistress was not too disheartened either that it was coming to an end. To be fair, her lessons were well presented and she had to deal with no unpleasant incidents from any member of the class. There was very little improvement in the weather and the first rugby game that we were scheduled to play, which was at the end of January against a school from Chapeltown, had to be postponed. There was of course no chance of any outdoor rugby practice either, though we did manage some passing movements in the hall. Mr. Rawcliffe's welcome return heralded the beginning of February and it became considerably warmer as the snow underfoot turned into a messy slush. One of the headmaster's first actions was to agree to Mr. Barnes's request for extra rugby practice. In fact he allocated half an hour more than had been asked for as he could certainly see the need for it and the fact that the weather had become less severe enabled us to get on with it straight away. We did not know when the postponed game would be re-arranged for, but we knew we had a game scheduled for the middle of the month and we were all keen to present a more determined performance when it took place.

"Look, it's not dark anymore," observed Billy as we made our way home from school on the Friday of the headmaster's first week back in charge.

I had also noticed that it was indeed the first time we had not gone home in the dark since well before Christmas.

"That's great," I said. "It'll get a bit lighter every day now."

On most Friday evenings we went to the pictures together but we were both conscious of the fact that on the two previous occasions the film that had been on offer did not look sufficiently interesting to tempt us to brave the extreme weather conditions as the Electra Picture House was by no means as warm and as comfortable as sitting at home in front of a blazing fire while listening to the wireless. We had even missed the last two episodes of Nyoka, The Jungle Girl, which was the serial that had replaced Superman in October. I knew a new fifteen part serial was due to begin at the weekend and we were both anxious to discover what it was about. We paused outside the cinema and gazed at the poster. The title of the film had not altered from two days earlier when we had first perused it. It was the word 'Love' in the middle of it that had put us off. It was accompanied by a picture of a man and woman in evening dress kissing on a sofa.

"Why don't they show proper films any more?" asked Billy, with a look of disgust on his face. The fact that the picture was certified a 'U', which meant that anyone under sixteen could view it without being accompanied by an adult, did nothing whatsoever to encourage us.

"What's the point in giving it a 'U' certificate"? I asked. "Nobody under sixteen is going to want to see it, anyway?"

"Some girls might," suggested Billy. "They seem to like sloppy pictures, don't they?

"Well, I don't. I think it would be dead boring."

"Me neither. I'd rather listen to the wireless."

Our eyes were suddenly drawn to a rather insignificant little poster which seemed to have only appeared on that day and which contained a very short message which read 'The Scarlet Horseman' begins here this weekend.

"That must be the name of the new serial," explained Billy, excitedly.

"I don't think it would be worth having to sit through the big picture for though," I told him. I mean the serial's only on for fifteen minutes, isn't it?"

I could see from Billy's expression that he was agreeing with me. "I wonder what it's about, though," he said. "Do you think it's a cowboy picture?"

"It sounds like it," I replied. "Anyway, we can probably find out next week. They can't keep putting these sloppy films on forever, can they? I haven't seen a Tarzan picture for ages."

Just as we were about to leave Johnny Jackson came up behind us. "You're not thinking about going to see that, are you?" he asked, with a surprised expression on his face.

"Don't be daft," said Billy quickly. "We were just wondering about the new serial, that's all. It's called 'The Scarlet Horseman'"

"Sounds like a cowboy picture then," he said, echoing Billy's thoughts about it earlier. "My mam and dad are taking me and my brother to the Woodhouse Street Picture House tomorrow."

"I think it's called the Astra now," I told him.

"Is it? I didn't know that. Anyway, that's where we're going."

"What's on there?" enquired Billy

"It's the Bowery Boys," he said, "And there's a serial on there as well, you know. I think it's called 'Superman Versus Atom Man'. Anyway, I think I'd better be getting home. I'll see you both on Monday."

"Bye Johnny," we said in unison as we watched him walk along the street.

"I like the Bowery Boys," I said to Billy. "Why couldn't they have had that on at the Electra?"

I was beginning to regret the fact that my mother refused to let me visit a cinema that was further away than the end of our street.

"Do you think your mother would let you go to the Woodhouse Street Picture House?" asked Billy. "I mean the Astra."

"No chance Billy, I asked her just before Christmas."

"She let us go to Woodhouse Feast by ourselves though, didn't she? And that's even further."

"Yes, but I had to be back home by nine o'clock, didn't I? We can't get back by that time from the pictures can we?"

"We can ask though, can't we?"

"Waste of time, Billy. I know what the answer would be."

We stood there contemplating the situation before Billy broke the silence. "My mam doesn't like me going to a different picture house either, but what if we go without telling anybody. Just let them think we're going to the Electra."

I thought about his suggestion. I had never deceived my mother in this way before, but after all I was now eleven and I couldn't think of any reason why I shouldn't be allowed to walk back from halfway up Woodhouse Street at ten o'clock.

I made my decision. "Let's do it," I said. "I'll tell her we're going to the Electra."

When I entered the house my mother had left a note stating that she had gone to see Grandad Miller and that she might not be back until five o'clock. The fire in the grate was burning very low and the first thing I did was to release Nell from behind the cellar door. Her eyes had an accusing look, as if to say 'why do they keep doing this to me?' I brought up a shovelful of coal and moved away the fireguard. As I emptied the contents of the shovel into the fire grate Nell's eyes now began to show a look of approval and I allowed her to settle down on the clip rug having first replaced the fireguard. Having opened the cupboard door and taken out a digestive biscuit, I broke a piece off and handed it Nell and then seated myself on the armchair to the left of the fire. This particular piece of furniture would only remain available until my father returned home from work at about twenty to six. He always finished half an hour early on a Friday.

"Me and Billy are going to the Woodhouse Street pictures tonight," I said, addressing my remarks to my canine friend. "But I'm not telling anybody else."

She gazed up at me with a disapproving look and begged for another piece of biscuit. With a strange feeling that I was being blackmailed, I returned to the cupboard, took another one, and gave her half just to be on the safe side. With our bargain now sealed I switched on the wireless and sat down again to await my mother's arrival.

She arrived at ten minutes past five complaining about the slushy conditions underfoot.

"I was just walking up Speedwell Street," she said, "When Mrs. Round-The-Other-Side fell over and started sliding down the hill. It was all I could do to stop myself from falling when I helped her get back to her feet."

My mother's method of getting around her difficulty in remembering people's names did not always work. On this occasion I had no idea who she was talking about. I decided not to ask any questions on the matter.

"Mam, is it all right for me to go to the Electra with Billy tonight?" I asked her.

"You won't like it tonight," she replied with a surprised look on her face. She knew I was usually aware of what was on offer at our local cinema several days in advance. "It's a romantic film."

I thought hard about what to say. I feared that if I asked to go to the one in Woodhouse Street I would be met with a prompt refusal.

"There's a new serial starting tonight. It's called 'The Scarlet Horseman', and anyway, the Three Stooges might be on."

"Well I'll tell you what then. Me and your dad were thinking of going tomorrow. We can take you with us if you like. In fact it's nice to know that you'd like to see a sensible picture instead of those violent cowboy ones that you always want to see."

I was wondering what to say next that might in some way extract me from the pit I was digging myself into and I couldn't help noticing that Nell was glancing at the cupboard where the biscuit tin was located. I was considering confessing my intentions when I was saved by Billy's knock on the door.

"Is it all right if Neil goes to the Electra with me, Mrs. Cawson?" he asked, before he even had time to step inside.

"Aw, let me go with Billy, mam," I said, now that my closest friend had opened the window of opportunity. "It's much better when we see it together."

"All right! You can go today," she said, realising I think that if I went with her and my father I would almost certainly get bored, bearing in mind the nature of the film, and spoil it for them. "But make sure you come home as soon as the picture has finished or there'll be trouble," she added. I know it finishes at twenty to ten because I saw them all coming out last night.

"Thanks mam," I said. "I'll just play out with Billy for a while until the tea's ready."

"Well make sure you don't get yourself too dirty or you just might end up having a bath instead of going to the pictures."

"She wasn't going to let me go until you knocked on the door," I said to him as soon as we were outside. "She said I could go with them tomorrow instead."

"Crikey!" That would have been worse still," he said. "I bet they'd have made you keep quiet all through the film."

I thought about climbing onto the lavatory yard roof via the open midden to see if it was still icy on top but my mother's warning about not getting dirty made me think better of it. As we stood at the entrance to it Mary Pearson stepped out of one of the cubicles. She was two years older than Billy and me but had an annoying habit of pushing the lavatory door open if she thought it was occupied by an unsuspecting lad. I suppose she would eventually grow out of it but it hadn't happened yet. We both looked down to make sure that our trouser buttons were fastened.

After she had entered her house Billy and I began to discuss our plans for the evening.

"Do you know what time it starts?" I asked. "I haven't been to that picture house for ages. Do you think it'll be seven o'clock like it is at the Electra?"

"I suppose so, but it'll take us ten minutes longer to get there, won't it?"

"Right, so we'll have to leave at about twenty to seven then. My mam'll want to know why I'm going so early."

Tea was over by six-thirty and my mother, surprisingly, did not raise any objections to my leaving immediately afterwards. Billy was ready when I called round for him and we set off towards the end of Melville Road before turning up Woodhouse Street.

"Have you any idea what the picture's about?" I asked him.

"Johnny Jackson just said it was called 'Blues Busters'," he replied, "But that doesn't really tell us anything, does it? It should be good, though. I like Satch best. I think he's funny."

"I wonder why they call him Satch. Because his real name's supposed to be Horace Debussy Jones, isn't it?"

"If my name was Horace Debussy Jones I think I'd rather be called Satch as well, Neil"

We both laughed.

"The main one" I said, "The one who's called Slip, is really called Terence Aloysius Mahoney. I think that's just as bad, don't you?"

We were both having hysterics as we continued up the hill towards the Astra Picture House, which was now just coming into view and we just had time, before we joined the queue, to make the comment that we wished we had somewhere to go like Louis Dumbrowski's sweet shop which always featured in Bowery Boys films. As we entered the cinema and settled into our seats all thoughts about possible repercussions if I was late home left my mind altogether. Johnny Jackson was right. There was a serial on called 'Superman Versus Atom Man' and both Billy and I thought it was great. Unfortunately, it was getting close to the end of its fifteen episodes so there seemed little chance of us catching any more. We contented ourselves with the thought that it might eventually come to the Electra. The main picture was even better. The plot revolved around Satch developing an exceptional singing voice after having an operation on his tonsils and Louis' sweet shop being turned into a night club as a result. We found it all very funny and as we got up to leave I knew that I was glad that I had taken the decision to defy my mother by not telling her where I was going. However, as we re-entered the ticket office hallway that led into the street my feeling turned to one of panic as I glanced at the clock on the wall.

"It's ten to ten, Billy" I said, the expression on my face indicating dismay. "It's finished ten minutes later than the Electra and we've got further to walk."

"That's not our only problem," announced my companion. "Look at the weather."

I gazed outside at the torrential rain making the already slushy condition of the pavements much worse.

"We'll be soaked to the skin when we get home," I said "And my mam's bound to know that we haven't just been to the end of the street. Anyway, everybody that went to the Electra will be home by now."

"Not all of them," said Billy, rather pointlessly. "Some of them call at the fish and chip shop first."

I glared at him. "Well they're not likely to do it in this weather, are they?"

I looked again at the teeming rain. Would it be more beneficial from my point of view if we rushed home soaking wet or if we waited a while in the hope that the rain might stop and get home much later, but remain dry?

"What do you think, Billy?" I asked him. "Have we to hang back a while and see if it eases off?"

It seemed to me that that was what most of the patrons were doing anyway as the small hallway was very crowded with few people being prepared to step outside to brave the elements.

"Let's just wait fifteen minutes and see," he suggested.

As it was we were unable to wait any longer anyway as the owner of the cinema was anxious to lock up and the temporary inhabitants had been gradually dispersing. Eventually, with only about a dozen individuals remaining, we were all forced to leave the premises. I glanced at the clock again. It was almost ten minutes past ten. The conditions outside had not improved. If anything, they had worsened as a biting wind had arrived which blew the rain directly into our faces as we stepped outside.

We set off running down Woodhouse Street in the horrendous conditions. Thoughts of what would happen when I arrived home refused to surface in my mind. I only knew that I wanted to be through the door and warming myself in front of the fire as soon as possible. It was almost half past ten when I opened the door and presented myself to my mother in my dishevelled state. I hadn't even paused to say farewell to Billy.

What followed was nothing like as bad as I had been expecting. My mother's immediate expression was one of concern rather than of anger, the torrential rain having elevated it to her list of priorities. I was made to dry off and put on some pyjamas which had been warming on the oven top at the side of the fire. There was of course still some explaining to do and I still had to face my father.

When my mother considered I was sufficiently dry I began to face the music.

"Don't tell me you went to the Electra," she said, "Because I won't believe it."

I decided my best option was to come clean. I could think of no other explanation that she would accept. The only part that I made up was that we had only decided to go to a different cinema after we had left the house.

"After I called round for Billy we met Johnny Jackson from our school," I explained, "And he told us that the Bowery Boys were on at the Woodhouse Street picture house. We thought we'd be back in time and we didn't know it was going to rain."

Nell gave me a knowing look and I was glad, not for the first time, that she was unable to speak, as I had confided in her many times before.

"I knew you didn't really want to see the one at the Electra," she said. "Why didn't you tell me you might be going to the other one?"

"Why mam, would you have let me go?"

"Well I'd certainly rather give you permission than to see you go wandering off without telling me. I want you to promise me that you will never do that again, and if you do go to a different picture house at night it had better be no further than the one you've just been to or the Royal in Meanwood Road."

I promised, relieved that I hadn't received a longer telling-off. My father, surprisingly, had little to say on the subject.

All in all I was very happy with the way things had turned out. I came to regard that day as my first coming of age and as I made the evening's entry in the chronicle before retiring I emphasised that fact by marking it with three stars at the bottom.

CHAPTER TEN

After one of the most miserable Saturdays I had ever spent I awoke on Sunday morning at least secure in the knowledge that this day could hardly be worse. Saturday was usually my favourite day of the week, but on this particular one the heavy rain of the previous day had continued unabated. Everyone had been confined to the house and by midday it was so dark that we had had to switch on the lights. There had been nothing to do but listen to the wireless for hours at a time. My father hadn't even had that option, being forced to go to work until dinnertime. That would, as often as not, mean fish and chips but my mother, realising that the only establishment that would give anyone a chance of returning home without being soaked to the skin was the one round the corner opposite Doughty's, had decided to manage without them on this occasion and we had had to make do with some cold polony and some pikelets. What I had hated most was the fact that I hadn't seen Billy for the entire day.

As I gazed out of my bedroom window I could see that this day was going to be different and my spirits lifted immediately. The rain had ceased and, despite the fact that it was still dark, I had a strong feeling that the sun might eventually make an appearance. The clock on the wall was showing almost half past seven and I practically ran down the stairs. The first thing I did was to open the cellar door and rescue Nell from her night time incarceration at the top of the cellar steps. She walked over to the fireplace, saw that there was no fire and gave me a reproving look. I could hear my mother moving about upstairs. I knew who it was immediately as this was the one day in the week when my father was able to stay in bed a while longer. I decided to go into the cellar for a shovelful of coal. Nell accompanied me just to make sure that I knew where it was. When we returned my mother was already poking about among the ashes.

"You're up early," she said. "I thought you'd be staying in bed a bit longer with not having to go to school."

"Well it looks like a better day today, mam. I hated having to stay in all day yesterday."

"It might look inviting outside, but it's still very cold, don't forget. You're not going out unless you wrap up well and, if you do go out, don't forget that I asked your grandad to come over for his dinner today if the weather was suitable. So make sure you're back inside in plenty of time. I don't want to be standing at the door shouting for you."

There was no way that I could possibly forget that Grandad Miller was calling round, especially in view of the fact that my mother had never told me about it. Still, I always looked forward to his visits which, unfortunately, had been all too few after his recent spell in hospital. With the weather having improved somewhat I supposed it meant that he was able to walk to and from the tram stops unaided.

As soon as I had finished eating my breakfast I called round to see Billy after having first accepted my mother's conditions.

"Did you get into bother for getting home late and being soaked to the skin?" were his first words of greeting.

"It wasn't as bad as I thought it would be Billy and, do you know what? My mam said it would be all right for me to go to the Astra or the Royal as long as I tell her about it first. I can hardly believe it."

"My mam wasn't too bad about it either," said my companion, "But she didn't actually say it would be all right for me to do it again."

"Do you know what I think, Billy? I bet that if you promised her that you'd tell her before you go every time, without sneaking off, then it might be all right."

"I'll find out. It'd be great wouldn't it? It would mean that we'd have a choice of three picture houses every time and we'd probably never have to see a sloppy love picture again. Anyway, what do you want to do, Neil? I don't have to go anywhere today."

"I'm not sure, Billy, but we'd better do something interesting because yesterday was the worst Saturday I can remember."

"What, worse than last October when Lorna Gale decided she wanted you for a boy friend when you were on the tram going to Meanwood?"

That was certainly a Saturday that I would never forget and it had certainly ruined my whole weekend, yet eventually things had turned out okay and I could now look back on it with some amusement.

"Well it was certainly terrible at the time, but yesterday was definitely the most boring."

"Let's go down to the Dammy," suggested Billy. "After all this rain it might have flooded its banks."

The Dammy was the beck that flowed along the bottom of Sugarwell Hill which was on the far side of Meanwood Road and complemented Woodhouse Ridge on the opposite side. It was really just an extension of Meanwood Beck and no one really knew why it had acquired a different name.

"We'd better go straight away then," I said. "It might start raining again this afternoon."

With our minds made up and without informing our parents where we were going we made our way towards the end of Cross Speedwell Street. As we were about to pass Nicky Whitehead's house Billy suggested that we ask him if he wanted to come with us.

"I'm glad you two have called," he said, after having joined us outside, "I was dead bored yesterday. I had to stay in all day."

"So were we," I told him. "So let's make the most of today. It could start raining again anytime."

We set off down the hill and, on reaching the bottom, crossed over Meanwood Road to enter Buslingthorpe Lane. As we crossed over the bridge we could tell from the sound of the water beneath that it was running much faster than on the previous time we had been down there. We turned left and walked down to the bank.

"I bet you don't fancy sitting in it today, Nicky," said Billy, remembering the previous October when our companion had taken quite a tumble.

No one made any comment. I think we were all taken aback by how fierce the current was as the stream continued on its way to discharge itself into the river Aire in the town centre. The water had not yet encroached onto the bank but its surface was virtually level to it. We stared at it in fascination.

"Why don't we follow it up upstream to where it goes under Meanwood Road to the bottom of the ridge?" suggested Nicky. "It might have broken the banks farther on."

"Good idea," I said, and Billy voiced his agreement.

We walked along the path in the direction indicated which seemed to grow muddier the further we went. By the time we reached the crossover point the mud was up to our ankles. The beck, however, remained level with its natural boundary.

"What do you think?" I said. "Shall we cross over the road and pick it up again at the bottom of the ridge?"

"We might as well," said Billy, "But we'll have to be getting back home soon. It must be nearly dinnertime."

I knew Billy was right. Sunday dinner was different to other days of the week and my mother was very particular that we were all seated at the dining table at least five minutes before the Yorkshire puddings were taken out of the oven and the fact that Grandad Miller would be arriving made me eager to get home.

When we arrived at the other side of the road the conditions underfoot were even worse and I knew that we were not far from the boggy area which had caused such problems on the school's nature ramble the previous autumn.

We decided to set off for home, being a little disappointed at not having been able to witness the Dammy in full flood. We had gone no more than about a hundred or so yards before Billy broke the silence caused by our despondent mood.

"This is about where you said that you saw a man the other day walking his dog, isn't it Neil?" he said, with a hint of mischief in his voice. I hoped we were not going to repeat the argument we had had previously. However, I wasn't going to let his comment go unanswered

"Yes, and I did see them Billy," I said, indignantly, "And I can even tell you who they were. It was old Jack Armitage and his dog, Chip." As soon as I had got the words out I began to regret it. How on earth was I going to explain that I had seen a couple of ghosts without being ridiculed? However, I knew there was no turning back.

"Who are they?" was Nicky's rather obvious reaction.

"It's not who they are," I replied. "It's more a question of who they were, because they're both dead."

"How do you know that?" asked Billy. "It's only a few days since you said that you saw them."

I decided, reluctantly, to tell them the story exactly as it was related to me.

"I don't believe all that," said Billy, as soon as I had completed the narrative. "I don't believe in ghosts."

"Then why didn't we see any footprints?" I said to both of them in a forceful manner."

I felt we were back to where we had been on the day of the encounter with each of them beginning to doubt again that I had seen anything at all. I had to admit to myself that if it was one of them who had claimed to have seen the apparitions I would have had difficulty accepting the validity of their statement as well, for I had hitherto never believed in ghosts either, which was precisely why I had never mentioned it to anyone else.

As we slowly made our way back home I could tell that neither of my companions was prepared to accept my explanation of what had occurred on that particular morning. I decided not to pursue the matter and we walked home in comparative silence.

As I entered the house the aroma of Sunday dinner made its presence felt on my nostrils and I could see immediately that my grandfather was already seated on the armchair close to the fire, my father having kindly vacated it for his older guest.

"Now then, lad," he addressed me as I began to divest myself of the significant outer garments that my mother had insisted on my wearing, "What have you been doing this morning, then?"

"I went with Billy and Nicky down to the Dammy," I told him. "We wanted to see if its banks had been broken after the heavy rain."

I immediately realised my mistake.

"You didn't tell me you were going down there," scolded my mother. "What if you'd fallen in? The water might have been flowing too fast for you to clamber out again."

"What's the Dammy?" asked Grandad Miller, before I had the chance to attempt to justify my actions to my accuser.

"It's the beck at the bottom of Sugarwell Hill," I answered.

"Well, blow me! I've never heard it called that before. Are you sure you're not kidding me?"

"No grandad, everybody calls it that, but before it crosses over Meanwood Road it's just called Meanwood beck."

"Well, I can't see any sense in that. Anyway, what your mother said is right. It could be very dangerous"

"Yes, grandad," I acknowledged.

"And had it burst its banks?" he added as an afterthought.

"No, but the water was just about level with them. We walked farther along the path, but it stayed the same."

My mother began taking the Yorkshire puddings from the oven and we all sat at the table eagerly waiting to be served, with Nell taking up her usual place beside my father's chair.

After a very satisfying and fulfilling Sunday dinner my mother walked over to the sink and began to wash the pots, my father sat in the armchair and opened his copy of the 'Empire News' and Nell settled on the clip rug in front of the fire and immediately fell asleep. My grandfather was already making his way into the other downstairs room after having thanked my mother for the excellent meal and having announced that he was just going for a short nap. Normally, I would have gone straight round to see Billy, but on this occasion I decided to accompany Grandad Miller as there was something I was keen to ask him before he succumbed to his forty winks.

When he had seated himself on the sofa he noticed that I had followed him into the room.

"I want to ask you something, grandad," I got in, before he had time to close his eyes and pretend there was no one there.

"What's that then, lad?" he asked, perhaps just a little irritated that I was threatening to disturb his after-dinner relaxation.

"I just wondered grandad. Have you ever seen a ghost?"

"Now, what sort of a question is that? Are you hoping that I'll have nightmares as soon as I close my eyes, because I'm afraid you'll be disappointed if you are?"

"No, grandad, I just wondered, that's all." I wanted to tell him about the two apparitions that I believed I had seen, but thought it better not to, at least until I knew what his feelings were on the subject.

He didn't answer for a few seconds as if deciding whether to allow me to disrupt his repose or whether to merit my question with an answer. He finally came to a decision.

"Well, lad, if you must have an answer to your question, all I can tell you is that I'm not sure."

"How do you mean, grandad?" I asked rather puzzled by his response, but also a little intrigued regarding what he might be about to relate.

"Well," he said, "I'll explain it all to you and then, when I've finished, I'll let you decide whether or not I have experienced a ghostly encounter. Now, I have to go back over fifty years to recollect all this, you understand, for I was just about your age when it happened."

I joined him on the sofa with an eager expression on my face, as I just knew I was going to be told something fascinating. I waited for him to gather his thoughts before continuing.

"Now," he said, "Around the turn of the century my best mate was called Harry Crabtree and around Hunslet way we were known as ---"

"The tearaway twins," I finished for him.

"Now how on earth did you know that?" He said, with a surprised look on his face.

"Because you've told me before, grandad." As a matter of fact he'd told me several times before, but I didn't tell him that.

"Well, it just goes to show how old age can creep up on you all unexpected like. I suppose your memory stops being quite as reliable as you get older. I admit to sometimes being unable to remember what I was doing on the previous day, yet I can recall events from way back very clearly, and that applies to the story I'm about to tell you. So perhaps if you won't interrupt again, I'll get on with it."

"Sorry, grandad."

"Anyway, as I was saying, when I was about your age my best mate was called Harry Crabtree. Just like you and that friend of yours along the street, me and Harry didn't stay in much if we could be outside larking about and yes, getting into mischief occasionally. Anyway, I remember that this particular day was a Saturday, so there was no school to worry about. It was a sunny day at the beginning of spring when we found ourselves wandering along a back street close to Hunslet Lane. Neither of us had anything planned, but the weather for the time of year was very pleasant and we were in a jolly mood. We had it in mind just to wander towards a piece of spare ground where we'd played on many occasions and just do whatever took our fancy, which would probably mean finding something to kick around, such as an old tin can. There were always plenty of things of that nature lying about. We also hoped that there might be several other lads of our age, also with nothing particular to do, which would make it more interesting with the possibility of engaging in something a bit more exciting. By the time we arrived, however, we found ourselves to be the only ones there and the weather had taken a dramatic turn for the worse. The sun had gone in and it seemed to have taken all the light with it. It was only mid afternoon yet it had become so dark that you could easily believe that it was early evening. The air was very oppressive and the impression that we got was that we could quite easily find ourselves caught in a thunderstorm. We were both convinced that a downpour was imminent and we immediately looked around for some shelter. Neither of us thought we would be able to make it back home before it started to rain. Harry knew of an old deserted factory about a hundred yards beyond the far side of the open area where we were currently standing and, as we saw the first flash of lightning followed a few seconds later by a loud peal of thunder, we set off running as fast as we could."

Grandad Miller's story was getting really interesting, but it was interrupted by my mother entering the room with a cup of tea for him.

"I thought you might like a cup of tea dad before you have your nap," she said. Her next remarks were addressed to me. "I didn't know you were in here. I thought you'd gone outside. You know your grandad likes to rest after he's had his dinner."

"Nay, the lad's all right," said my grandfather. "We're just having a bit of a chat for a few minutes."

"Well, don't stay talking too long, Neil and come back in as soon as your grandad's finished his cup of tea."

"Yes, mam," I said.

As my Grandad Miller took his first sup of tea and my mother re-entered the kitchen, I noticed that Nell, having awoken from her dog-nap, had joined us. She looked up as if she sensed that something interesting might be taking place and wanted to ensure that she became part of it.

My grandfather resumed his narrative, unmoved by the fact that there were now two listeners instead of one.

"The building we were racing towards," he continued, "Had been empty for years and we were not entirely sure as to what type of product had been manufactured there, though we believed it to have been some sort of clothing factory. The first heavy drops of rain had begun to fall just as we arrived, and we knew immediately that there was no sign of any other form of shelter in the immediate vicinity. Fortunately, we could see that there would be no problem entering the place as most of the windows had been shattered. We were a little apprehensive, however, about the few shards of glass that remained around the edges and almost certainly on the floor inside. Staying where we were was not really an option, so Harry took one window while I took the other, both of us being careful where we put our feet when we landed. The light inside was very dim, brightened only occasionally by a flash of lightning. As we began to explore our surroundings, by making our way to towards the far side of the building, our attention was drawn to a closed door. What startled us, however, was the message that someone had scrawled across it. It read: BE WARNED. DO NOT ENTER THIS ROOM. IT IS HAUNTED."

Nell, who had been lying in front of me, got up and moved behind the sofa while my grandfather continued his story.

"Now neither Harry nor me had ever believed in ghosts and I would like to tell you that we laughed at the idea of that room being haunted, but if you'd been there in that eerie atmosphere with thunder and lightning going on all around you, I'm sure you'd have been just as frightened as me and Harry were. Nevertheless, we felt we were being compelled to open that door and step inside."

At this point I felt like joining Nell behind the sofa, but I hardly dared move. I was dying to know what happened next. My grandfather continued speaking.

"When we entered the first thing that we noticed was a strong, musty sort of smell, which we put down to the fact that the door had probably been closed for a long time and there was no outside window. It was a small room and seemed to have been used as some sort of storage cupboard as there were empty shelves all around the walls. We must have just stood there for two or three minutes looking around while we could still hear the storm raging outside. We could see nothing at all that could justify the words that had been scrawled on the door. We couldn't see much point in remaining, but just as we were about to leave we both heard what seemed like someone breathing behind us. It was quite loud and it gave us the fright of our lives, for we felt that something, though we couldn't see it, was between us and the door, thus blocking our escape route. However, when we eventually turned to face whatever was making the sound that was so terrifying us, there was no one to be seen. The sound of breathing then became both louder and quicker and as we ran out of that room as fast as our legs would carry us we heard what I could only describe as a long moan of despair. As we slammed the door closed it was only at that point that we could no longer hear the sound. We decided not to hang around, however, and climbed out of the windows to face the elements outside, which we both considered to be the lesser of two evils. When we arrived home we were both soaked to the skin and received quite a telling-off from our parents. We never made any mention to them of our visit to the old factory and what had occurred inside, and both Harry and me stayed well away from the area for months afterwards. So, all I can say in answer to your question is that, although I've never seen a ghost, I certainly believe that I've heard one. Now, I'm going to lie on the sofa for a little nap and if you have any notions of creeping up on me and doing some loud breathing for my benefit you can forget it."

"Yes, grandad," I said, and left him to it. Nell followed me out of the room, probably wishing she'd never gone in there in the first place.

I didn't make an entry in the chronicle that night, deciding to leave it until the following morning, and as I climbed into bed, somehow I forgot to turn out the light.

CHAPTER ELEVEN

On the Tuesday following Grandad Miller's visit, disaster struck the Woodhouse Junior School Rugby League team. During a practice session in the schoolyard Tucker Lane, one of our two best players, injured his foot after falling heavily. I knew that if Tucker winced with pain then the cause of it must be really serious as he usually just leaped to his feet as if nothing had happened and carried on playing, as if to do otherwise would put the macho image that he had carefully built up over the years in jeopardy. It wasn't until the following morning, however, that we learnt the full extent of his injury. Mr. Barnes told us that, at the very least, he had badly sprained his ankle, which had swollen so much that he was unable to place his foot on the floor, and at the worst it was possible that he might have broken a bone, which would be verified after the results of an x-ray became known.

"We've got a game on Saturday," said Billy to me as we entered the classroom immediately after assembly. "We're not going to have much chance of winning it now, are we?"

I knew what he meant. No matter what our views were on Tucker's general behaviour and attitude, we both knew that his absence from the team lessened our chances considerably of putting in a decent performance.

"There's not much we can do about it, Billy, is there? We'll just have to do our best."

The game would be against a school at Beeston and we would be playing on their own ground.

"Right, everybody," said Mr. Rawcliffe with his usual scowl which, not surprisingly after Mrs. McIntyre's tenure, had now become to us more of an acceptable feature, "Let's get down to some work."

Everyone stopped speaking and began to pay attention.

I'm going to test you on some dates in English history," he announced, "But before we do that, who can tell me what date it will be one week from now?"

Leonard Horsey was first up with the answer. "February the fourteenth, sir," he stated, confidently.

"That's quite correct boy, but can you tell me the significance of that date?"

"No sir," he replied, with a puzzled expression on his face.

"I'll give you all a clue then. It's the day when we celebrate a famous saint. Does anyone know who it is?"

"I think I know, sir?" came a girl's voice from the back row. I couldn't see who it was. "Is it St. Valentine?"

"Well done, girl," said Mr. Rawcliffe. "That is absolutely correct. Now, can anyone tell me what custom we observe on St. Valentine's Day?"

"It's the day when sweethearts send cards to each other," volunteered Pauline Dixon, enthusiastically, "And it's very romantic, because the card usually has a heart on the front or a bunch of roses."

"Yukk!' exclaimed Billy while pulling a face to indicate his disgust.

"Well done," said the headmaster, "That's quite correct."

I couldn't understand why he was speaking about such a soppy subject. It wasn't like him at all. Fortunately, he soon came to his senses.

"I'm only mentioning this," he said, "To point out to you all that dates and the events associated with them are very important in life. I'm not suggesting that you all suddenly start sending each other Valentine cards."

"No, sir," said several male voices.

Just as Billy and I were beginning to accept that the subject was closed and looking forward to something more interesting Lorna Gale decided to offer some thoughts of her own.

"I think it would be a great idea, sir," she offered, "For us to send cards out on St. Valentine's Day. We could all make our own and then decide who we wanted to send them to. I know my Cousin Doreen had one once from a boy at her school. She's my Auntie Jean's daughter and they live at Meanwood. Auntie Jean wasn't too pleased about it because she thought she was too young to be getting a card from a boyfriend. Anyway, I don't think she ever found out who it was from, my cousin Doreen I mean, because the person who sends it isn't supposed to put his name on it, is he? I think that's a bit silly myself, because if I got one I'd want to know who sent it to me then I could decide whether I wanted to send him one next year. I wonder if it would be all right to send one to more than one person because sometimes I think I like one boy best and then sometimes I think I like someone else. Anyway, I bet you got a lot of them when you were younger didn't you, sir?"

"I think we've exhausted this subject now, Miss Gale," said the headmaster, no doubt wishing he'd never mentioned St. Valentine's Day. "It's time we got onto some serious work. I want you to open your history books to page eighty-six."

"I thought she said she'd gone off boys," I whispered turning towards Billy. "I wish he hadn't put the idea into her head. I hope she doesn't send me one. I'd never live it down."

There was no more talk of Valentine cards and we all knuckled down to Mr. Rawcliffe's history lesson, but an idea was already forming in my mind.

At the end of school Billy and I were joined by Nicky Whitehead and Johnny Jackson as we made our way along Jubillee Terrace.

"We've got a game on Saturday," said Johnny, "And Tucker obviously won't be playing."

"Yes," agreed Billy, "And it's Beeston school that we're up against and they're lying second, aren't they?"

At the beginning of the week, a league table was displayed on the notice board in the hall depicting the positions of all the schools we were playing against during the season. We weren't quite halfway through yet but the one most recently published showed Armley at the top, having won all of their games, Beeston in second place and us firmly entrenched at the bottom having lost all of ours. Armley School provided the team that beat us so heavily in our first game. I think had we begun by playing someone else then, perhaps, we might not have been quite so demoralised and might have performed a little better in the subsequent ones.

"Well, we haven't played for a while, have we?" I said. "The last game was before Christmas so it'll be almost like starting again, won't it? Let's just imagine this is our first game."

"Is your mam all right about you playing, Nicky?" asked Billy. "I mean you haven't had the pot off your arm for very long, have you?"

"Well it felt all right while I've been practising. Anyway, I'm not forced to be picked, am I?"

"I don't think any of us can be sure of being selected," observed Johnny, "But I suppose we've more chance now that Tucker won't be there."

As we reached the Electra, Billy and I paused to study the poster on the wall which advertised the week's films while Nicky and Johnny walked on. It was rare for us to visit the cinema at the beginning of the week, and all the best pictures seemed to be on at the weekend, anyway, as well as the serial.

"Oh, that looks like a good film on Friday, Neil" said Billy, pointing at the futuristic painting on the poster with the caption 'Destination Moon' over-printed on it.

"It's about time they put a decent picture on, and it means we won't have to trail down to the Royal in Meanwood Road or the Astra. It's a 'U' as well, so we won't have to ask anybody to take us in."

Films were censored into three categories: one designated for adults only, one where children were admitted only with an adult and one where a child was allowed to enter unaccompanied. The letter used for this particular film denoted the latter category.

"My Cousin Raymond told me about this picture last week," I told him, "But I don't think he knew it was coming to the Electra. He gets a magazine called 'Picture Show', and it was mentioned in that along with another film about space called 'Rocketship XM', which I think was about a trip to Mars. Anyway, he said it looked really exciting."

"Right, we'll go see it on Friday night then. I'm sure my mam will let me go, especially with it being a 'U'."

When I arrived home it was to find the house empty with the exception of Nell who, so long as there was a fire in the grate with a fireguard around it, seemed totally unconcerned as to whether she had any human companions or not. She lay stretched out on the clip rug and only gave me a cursory glance as I entered. I couldn't see any note on the table to explain her absence but I barely had time to remove my coat before my Auntie Molly arrived from next door.

"Your mother's had to go out," she said, "But she wants you to call at Doughty's for half a pound of lard and a loaf of bread. She said you'll know which one to get, and she's left the tick book on the shelf over the fireplace."

As I made my way to the shop the subject of Valentine cards entered my mind. If it was not normal to sign a card to indicate who had sent it then why should I not send one to Susan Brown? There would be no embarrassing admition of my feelings as no one would know who it came from, even if Susan did have her suspicions. Nor, for the same reason, could I be laughed at by any of the other lads. However, deep down I knew that I would probably want her to know who the sender was, anyway. It was something that I needed to think over.

Just as I was about to enter the shop the subject of my thoughts, by a strange coincidence, was about to leave, the result of which was that we collided and the bag she was carrying fell to the floor. My face burned fiercely as I mumbled my profuse apologies and helped her to retrieve the various contents that had scattered all over the shop. Fortunately, there was no one else on the premises, but it seemed to me that every time I met her out of school I was destined to send her flying.

"You keep knocking me over, Neil," she admonished.

"I know," I said, rather sheepishly and being unable to think of anything to add to that statement.

When all her purchases were back in her shopping bag, I watched her turn around the corner into Melville Road and I realised that the prospect of a Valentine card coming my way from her direction was rapidly receding. I collected the loaf of bread and half a pound of lard and made my way home. Apart from my canine friend the house was still empty so I placed the loaf in the bread tin and the lard in a container on the cellar head. With the house to myself I took off my coat and reached under the seat of my father's armchair for a copy of the Knockout comic which I perused while waiting for her to come back. Nell announced my mother's arrival by barking a greeting before I became aware of her presence.

"Sorry I wasn't here when you got back," she said. "I went down to see your Auntie Nora in Back Craven Street. I heard she's been full of cold for several days and I wanted to see if she needed any shopping now that she's living on her own." I had heard that my Uncle Andrew didn't live there any more but nobody had ever told me why.

"Did your Auntie Molly tell you to go to the shop?" she went on.

"Yes mam, she said you wanted a loaf and half a pound of lard."

"Good, I can start to make us some tea now. Without the lard I couldn't have cooked any scallops to have with an egg."

"Mam, have you ever been sent a Valentine card?" I asked, though wondering whether she would tell me to mind my own business.

"Well, whatever prompted you to ask a question like that?" she said, with a puzzled expression on her face.

"Old Raw --- I mean Mr. Rawcliffe was telling us at school about certain dates being anniversaries and he said that February the fourteenth is St. Valentine's Day and that sweethearts send each other cards on that day."

"Well as a matter of fact I had more that one Valentine card when I was a lot younger."

"Was my dad very romantic then, mam?"

"Who said they were from your dad?"

She didn't add anything to that, but smiled and left me with a surprised expression on my face. I could tell that she didn't want me to question her further, so I didn't.

After my father had arrived and we had finished our tea, I decided to call round to see Billy.

"Are you coming out for a while?" I asked him as he met me at the door. "I thought we might walk down to the Royal in Meanwood Road and see what's on at the weekend, just to make sure that it's not better than the Electra."

"I don't see how it can be any better unless it's a Tarzan picture or Abbott and Costello."

I didn't expect it to be better than what was on offer at our local establishment either, but I just felt the need to exercise the new leeway I had been given with regard to a choice of Picture Houses. I think Billy must have agreed with that sentiment because he readily made himself available.

"Yes, let's go," he decided. "We might as well do this every week now that we've got three places to pick from."

It was a cold evening, but at least it was dry and it wasn't particularly slippery underfoot. We made our way down Speedwell Street and passed my Grandma Cawson's house before crossing over Buggy Park, which in no way resembled a recreation area which could be deemed suitable for the ladies and gentlemen of Woodhouse to take a casual walk in whatever finery they might possess. It was simply a piece of derelict ground behind Buslingthorpe School. From there we crossed over Meanwood Road close to the Junction Public House and walked along to the Royal Cinema just past the end of Cambridge Road.

When we arrived it was too early for a queue to be forming. Anyway, our only reason for being there was to consult the poster on the wall outside.

"John Wayne in Red River," read Billy. "Hey, that looks like a good film. Do you think it'll be better than the one at the Electra?"

I had no idea how to answer that. I was beginning to wish that we hadn't been given a choice. At least we knew that the picture that would be showing at the Astra in Woodhouse Street wouldn't be to our liking as we had seen the trailer on the previous Friday.

"I know we like John Wayne, Billy, but I think I fancy seeing 'Destination Moon', don't you?"

"I wonder if 'Red River' will be coming to the Electra, Neil."

"I don't see why not. It hasn't been there before, has it? Otherwise we'd have seen it."

After a few minutes more discussion the battle of the films was won by the one showing at our local picture house, and we decided to head for home via Cambridge Road. As we eventually entered Woodhouse Street, Billy decided to swing on the railings at the bus stop at the end of Craven Road. I watched the bus pull up to allow people to disembark just as Billy was coming to the end of his gymnastic display. Unfortunately, one of the passengers was unable to get out of the way in time and she caught the full force of his heavy boots on her shin. When I saw who the passenger was I knew immediately that Billy was going to have great difficulty in extracting himself from this predicament.

"I don't make any wonder that you two are always getting yourselves into bother," she admonished. "Why couldn't you look what you were doing? You must have known you were at a bus stop and that you'd be in the way of people getting off. No, I make no wonder at all. I bet you've broken the skin and I'll have to put some ointment on it. I know your mother, Billy Mathieson, and it would be no wonder to me if she gave you a good hiding if I told her what you'd done."

Billy looked crestfallen at this verbal abuse. Her name was Mrs. Chapman and she lived in the street almost opposite our own. She was known to us, however, and to many of the other lads who lived in our area, as Mrs. I-Make-No-Wonder. She was by no means as bad as she sounded though, and I had little doubt that her threat to inform Billy's mother would not materialise. I couldn't help remembering how she had intervened a few months ago and prevented me from being cheated by the Shoddy Man when I had taken some rags there from my mother

"I'm sorry, Mrs. Chapman," mumbled Billy. "I didn't see anyone getting off the bus."

"Well, I don't make any wonder at that what with you hanging upside-down from those railings. I make no wonder at all. I think it would be a good idea if you both got yourselves home before another busload of unsuspecting passengers arrived, don't you?"

He didn't need any more encouragement, suspecting that if he did as she asked then the incident might not be taken any further and the two of us made our way home.

When I went upstairs to bed later that evening and began to think about the happenings of the day prior to writing the usual entry in the chronicle I wondered whether I should mention the fact that my mother had received several Valentine cards when she was younger, but decided that it would probably be best if I did not.

CHAPTER TWELVE

"It wasn't too bad, really," declared Ken Stacey from the seat behind Billy and me. "I mean it was only 19 points to 12. I bet if Tucker had been playing we could have won."

I knew that Ken's surmise was probably correct. Despite his faults everyone was now well aware that Tucker Lane was an indispensable part of Woodhouse Junior School Rugby League team. We were all on the number 6 tram on its journey from Beeston to Meanwood, heading home with yet another defeat under our belts.

"I've still got to explain it all to my dad when I get home though, Ken. I don't think he'll accept anymore excuses, even one as important as this." I told him.

"Well, if he doesn't come back to school within the next few weeks," said Billy, "I can't see us winning even one game."

The season was now half way through and about the only achievement that we could strive for was to lift ourselves above the bottom spot. It would be two weeks before our next encounter which was designated as a home game and would therefore be played at Bedford's Field which was near the top of the ridge.

Mr. Barnes, the team coach, approached us, having evidently listened to our conversation and informed us not to be too despondent, claiming that we had played quite well. I knew that our losing week after week was as disappointing for him as it was for us, bearing in mind all the hard work he had put in, especially in trying to secure extra practice sessions for us.

Most of us disembarked from the tram at the Primrose Public House and began to make our way up the hill.

"It's a bit quiet at school without Tucker there," observed Phillip Thatcher," And I never thought I'd be saying that."

"I know what you mean, though," added Nicky Whitehead. "Nothing much seems to happen, does it?"

"You probably live nearest to him," he said, turning to face Ernie Peyton, "Don't you have any idea when he's likely to come back?"

"I haven't seen him since he had the accident," he replied "And anyway, I suppose he'll have to stay in the house for a while if he's not able to walk".

As some of the boys lived at the other side of Woodhouse Street and some nearer to Meanwood Road the group became fewer in number as we continued to walk up the hill.

"Did any of you go to the Electra last night?" asked Billy of those who remained. "The picture was called 'Destination Moon' and me and Neil thought it was great. Right near the end they found out that the rocket was too heavy to lift off from the moon and they started to throw tables, chairs and all sorts of things out of the airlock, but it was still too heavy. It meant that one of the four men would have to stay behind to lighten the load. They were about to draw lots for it when they noticed that one of them had already volunteered and stepped outside in his space suit."

"Crikey!" said Johnny Jackson. "I wouldn't have volunteered. So did the other three get back safely then?"

"All four of them got back," added Billy, "Because they found something else to get rid of."

"That's a picture I wish I'd have seen," said Johnny."

"Well, it's on again tonight. Why don't you see if your mam will let you go?"

"There was a Woody Woodpecker cartoon right in the middle of it as well," I added.

"Don't be daft. How can you have a cartoon in the middle of an ordinary picture?" asked Keith Battle, disbelievingly.

"I don't know," said Billy, "But it was there."

"I saw Tom and Jerry in a musical once," recollected Phillip Thatcher, "And they were dancing with Gene Kelly."

"I don't see how that's possible," said Keith Battle, not wanting to let go. "I mean, how can they put a cartoon character in the same scene as a real person? It doesn't make sense."

By the time we reached the end of Cross Speedwell Street only four of us remained and we said farewell to Johnny Jackson and Nicky Whitehead before Billy and I walked the few remaining yards home.

"Do you think we might have won if Tucker had been playing?" I asked just before opening the door to my house.

"I think we'd have had a good chance," he replied, "But we'll never know now, will we? Anyway, are you coming back out after dinner? It's not a bad day today, is it?"

Billy's observation was a little on the optimistic side. About all you could say about it was that it wasn't snowing, rainy or windy. It did, however, feel cold and damp. I looked up at the sky and could detect a break in the clouds, albeit a small one and I suppose, all things considered, maybe it wouldn't be too bad for a February afternoon.

"O.K! I'll call round for you as soon as we've finished eating," I told him, "Unless it's started raining."

As things turned out I was informed that we wouldn't be eating anything until I'd been to the fish and chip shop.

"I haven't had time to prepare anything this morning," said my mother. "When I got home from town I couldn't find my purse and I realised that I might have dropped it on the bus. I had to walk back to the bus stop and stand for the best part of an hour before the bus that I'd travelled on came back to the stop."

"And did someone find it on the bus and hand it in, mam?" I asked, worriedly, as I knew we would be in for a very difficult week if it wasn't found as I guessed it contained all my mother's housekeeping money that my father would have handed over after receiving his wage on the previous day.

"No, no one had, and I was very concerned about it until I got back home and your Auntie Molly popped round. She said that an elderly lady had seen it fall as I was getting off the bus, but couldn't catch me up to return it. I was a little later coming home than I had intended and I suppose I was hurrying to get the dinner ready. It's a good job I always keep our address in it, otherwise she wouldn't have known where to take it, would she? Realising we were out the lady decided it would be safe to leave it next door, especially after finding out that the person living there was my sister.

Your Auntie Molly asked what her name was and where she lived, but the lady said she didn't need any thanks and was just glad to be able to be of service. Now, that was very kind of her wasn't it? If everyone behaved in the same way it would be a much better world to live in. Anyway, that's the reason you'll have to go for some fish and chips. Now, here's the money for them. You know what to get and remember, don't go to the one --------"

"I know, mam. I know," I interrupted.

With my mother's faith in human nature restored I set off towards Jubilee Fisheries. As I walked past Billy's house I thought about asking him to accompany me, but I realised he would probably have already begun eating his dinner.

I detected the aroma of the fish and chips long before I reached the premises and I realised exactly how hungry I was. There was nothing like a game of rugby, whatever the result, to stimulate the appetite.

As I joined the queue which, fortunately on this occasion, was not a long one, two women in front of me were engaged in conversation.

"He's injured his foot," said one. "They were practicing in the schoolyard for the rugby team, just running and passing, that sort of thing, you know. Anyway, our Tommy slipped and his ankle swelled up to such a degree that he couldn't get a shoe anywhere near it."

As soon as I heard the name mentioned I listened more attentively.

"I don't know where that team would be without my Tommy," she went on.

It was immediately obvious to me to whom she was referring and, knowing his character, I thought it highly likely that he might not have told her that we hadn't actually won a game yet. However, I had to agree that he and Alan Bartle were definitely the best players and I had always believed that if either of them were missing the team would undoubtedly suffer. I decided to take a chance.

"Excuse me," I asked, rather timidly. "Are you Mrs. Lane?"

"That's right, lad. I'm Mrs. Lane."

"I was just wondering if you might know when Tucker, I mean Tommy, might be coming back to school."

"There you are; what did I tell you Barbara?" she said, addressing her companion. "They're missing him already."

She turned towards me. "I take it that you're in our Tommy's class then."

"That's right, Mrs. We've all been wondering when he'll be able to play in our rugby team again."

"Well, that's very nice of you to ask, and I think I can tell you that Tommy will probably be able to return to school in about two weeks time, though he might not be able to play rugby straight away. What's your name, boy? I'll tell him that you've all been asking about him."

"It's Neil Cawson. Mrs. Lane."

I went back home with the fish and chips, but I couldn't wait to tell Billy what I'd heard about Tucker. So I handed them to my mother and dashed outside again before she had the chance to notice I was missing.

"Tucker should be coming back in about a fortnight," I told him, surprising myself by the fact that I was looking forward to the return of someone who had so often in the past been one of my main antagonists.

Billy also seemed pleased by the news. The truth was that, regardless of the effect his absence may have had on the rugby team's performance, school activities had seemed much more boring during his absence.

As soon as dinner was over we were both outside and heading towards the ridge.

"Do you know what I think, Billy?" I said. "I think I might send Susan Brown a Valentine Card."

"Aw, Neil, that's so soppy. I think I'm going to be sick."

"Yes, but what if she sends me one and I haven't got one for her?"

"Think what'll happen at school if any of the other lads found out that you'd been sending out Valentine Cards. Life wouldn't be worth living. They probably wouldn't even want you in the rugby team and we might not be able to be friends anymore."

"It's only one card, Billy. I wasn't planning to send one to all the girls. Anyway, how would anyone find out? I mean I wouldn't even mention who it was from."

"Well I certainly wouldn't tell anybody, but if Susan Brown didn't know it was from you, there wouldn't be much point in sending one, would there?"

That was one thing that had also occurred to me and I was beginning to think it might not be such a good idea after all.

We approached the steps which led onto the ridge. This meant that we had probably already passed the house where she lived, but I still didn't know which one it was.

We had no particular activity planned but eventually found ourselves at the foot of the Monkey Tree, which I think just about every lad in Woodhouse must have climbed at some time during his juvenile years. Billy reached out and hauled himself onto the lowest branch. I watched him climb towards the top of the tree.

"Do you remember last September on the last day of the summer holidays?" I asked him. "You were just where you are now, counting chimneys, while I was down here. I'm not lying on the grass today, though. It's too damp. It was a lovely sunny day then. I remember thinking about the new rugby team starting, but I didn't think we'd be losing every game, did you?"

"Well, we never got enough practice, did we Neil? Nearly all the other schools already had a team and some of them had been playing during the previous year."

I decided to climb up and join him. After a couple of minutes, I was settled on a branch approximately parallel to the only other one that was occupied. For a while we both stared contentedly ahead of us across the Meanwood Valley, and even the sun made a brief appearance to lift our spirits as we continued to reminisce about all the things that had happened to us since the end of the previous summer.

"What do you think was the best thing we did since then, Neil?" he asked.

His question immediately projected an image into my mind of sheltering in the doorway of the Electra Picture House with Susan Brown after we had run from school in the wind and hail on the last day of term, having just won the Christmas quiz together instigated by the headmaster and the even stronger image of the hailstones shining in her hair. I suspected, however, that that wasn't the sort of answer that Billy was expecting, being more concerned with some event that both he and I had been involved in.

"Finishing the Long Sledge together," I announced, proudly.

"Yes, that's what I was thinking. It was great, wasn't it? And the lad on the finishing line told us that we were the youngest ones ever to do it."

The lad he was referring to turned out to be Susan's elder brother, and that fact did cause me some embarrassment for a day or two as I had fastened her red ribbon onto the sledge as a good luck token.

"Are you really going to send Susan Brown a Valentine Card, Neil?"

"I'm not sure now, Billy. I've been thinking about what you were saying and perhaps it wouldn't be such a good idea after all."

Billy seemed relieved by this statement. To his way of thinking this particular act would in some way diminish the close bond that had existed between us for as long as I could remember.

We remained on the uppermost branches before both of us noticed the gradual drop in temperature and decided to climb down.

"I think we might as well head back now," I said. "I'm starting to feel really cold."

"So am I. I don't think there's much chance of the sun coming back out, do you?"

I left the question unanswered as we began to retrace our steps along the concrete path. Billy's supposition proved to be correct, yet as we climbed the steps which led off the ridge and onto the road I remained in a cheerful, reflective mood as we slowly made our way back down the hill towards the comfort of home. I looked around me at the terrace houses which lined either side of the street and all the ones leading off it. By no means could they be called imposing abodes, being the habitats of simple, working class people, but to me they were soothing, warm, reassuring places for families possessing little more money than they needed for their everyday existence to retreat to.

"Do you know what, Billy" I said, pensively. "I think I'd rather live around here than in any place in the world."

"What, even places like America, Africa or Australia?"

"Well, I'd like to visit all of those places, but I'd still want to come back here after I'd seen them. We've got everything round here, right on the doorstep. We've got the ridge and Woodhouse Moor with the feast coming twice a year. We've got three picture houses we can go to. You can walk all the way to Adel Woods from here almost without having to cross a road. We've got Test Matches at Headingley as well as Rugby League and we can catch a tram to Meanwood woods or to Elland Road to watch Leeds United play. I think I'd always want to come back, Billy."

I could also have added 'And it's also got Susan Brown' as I was always on the lookout for her whenever I was in this area.

"I don't think I would," he said. "I'd just want to keep travelling around the world and visit all the different countries."

He thought for a moment. "I don't think I'd like to stay in Greenland long though," he added. "I don't think the Eskimos even have wirelesses in those igloos."

I laughed at the thought.

"I bet I know something you don't, Neil," he went on. "I bet you sixpence that you can't tell me how old Ken Stacey is."

"Well, that's fairly easy, Billy. He's in our class, isn't he? So he must be either ten or eleven. I'll guess that he's eleven, same as me. So my second guess is ten."

"That's wrong, Neil. He's two and three quarters."

"Don't be daft, Billy," I said, fixing him with a look of incredulity. "How can he be two and three quarters? Look at the size of him. He must be nearly as tall as Barnesy."

"Well, he is that age and I can prove it. He told me the other day that he was born on the 29th of February, and that means that he's only had two birthdays. So as there isn't another Leap Year until next year, that means that he must be two and three quarters and you owe me sixpence."

I thought about the paradox of the situation. "That doesn't stop him being ten or eleven, Billy. In fact if he was born in on the 29th of February he must have been born in 1940. So that makes him eleven."

"But if he's only had two birthdays he won't even be three until next year, will he?" he said, in an attempt to justify the sixpence he expected me to hand over. As a matter of fact I think he must have known that I didn't have sixpence on me.

"Look," I said with exasperation. "If he was only two and three quarters he wouldn't be able to play rugby with us, would he? The school wouldn't let him."

"How many actual birthdays has he had? asked Billy, unwilling to concede. "I mean birthdays that were on the 29th of February, the same day he was born."

"Two," I acknowledged, "But he's still lived for more than two and three quarter years, hasn't he? I mean he's not still talking baby-talk, is he? The way you're reckoning it, when he's sixty years old, he'll only be fifteen. That means he'll only be sixteen and a quarter when he retires and starts getting his pension."

The dispute continued as we approached home until my companion eventually relented. "All right," he said. "Let's forget about the bet, but I still say I'm right. I'm glad I wasn't born on the 29th of February, anyway."

When I went to bed that night and made the usual entry in the Chronicle I made a note about meeting Tucker Lane's mother and also Billy's revelation concerning Ken Stacey. I closed the book, settled down in bed and was asleep very quickly. It was not to be a peaceful sleep, however, as I dreamed that there was an enormous Valentine Card on my school desk from Susan Brown and as I walked over to thank her for it I could see that she was much smaller than she should have been. She looked at me and she said "Hello, my name's Susan and I'm two and three quarters."

CHAPTER THIRTEEN

All the pupils standing in Assembly were wondering who he was. He was certainly an impressive looking individual of about our age; tall, though not as tall as Ken Stacey. Yet his muscle tone was equal to, if not superior to, that of Tucker Lane. I couldn't help noticing that most of the girls were looking at him with admiration, especially as it was the second school gathering of the week, the day before St. Valentine's Day. I couldn't help wishing that I looked like that as we all eagerly awaited some explanation of his presence. It was not long in coming.

"Before the assembly gets underway, I'd like to introduce you our new pupil," began Mr. Rawcliffe. "His name is Brian Kershaw and he will, unfortunately, be with us for a few weeks only because of work commitments by his father, which has made it necessary for him and his family to temporarily move into the area. It was hoped that he would be with us at the beginning of the week, but unforeseen events prevented it."

I couldn't help noticing that the boy in question did not appear to be very pleased by his change of circumstances.

After the assembly disbanded and we made our way into our various classrooms I couldn't help but notice that the newcomer seated himself at the desk we were all used to seeing Tucker occupy. I suppose it was fitting in a way, bearing in mind the way things were to develop. We knew very little about him until the morning break when his character and demeanour became obvious to us all. He approached a small group of us consisting of Nicky Whitehead, Ernie Peyton and Alan Bartle, in addition to Billy and me.

"Who's the cock of this school?" were his only words of greeting, with no other expression on his face other than what could only be described as a sneer.

"Tucker Lane," said Billy and Nicky together.

"Where is he?" asked the new arrival.

"He's still at home," I informed him.

"He's not fit to come back to school yet," added Billy.

"He can't be much of a fighter then if he's lying at home poorly."

"He injured his foot while we were playing rigger," I informed him. "He hasn't been able to walk on it."

"Well if any of you see him you can tell him from me that there's a new school champion and it's me. It's a pity he's not here, all the same. Then I could have told him myself, and if anyone wants to challenge me you can do it now."

He looked really threatening and it did occur to me that when Tucker did come back to school he would probably have great difficulty in beating the confident and menacing creature that stood before us.

"Right then, no takers I see."

It was obvious that no one had any intention of challenging him. For my own part, if he wanted to regard himself as cock of the school, I was quite happy for him to do so. At least it would make for a very interesting situation when Tucker returned.

"There's another thing," stated the newcomer. "I don't want to hear anyone calling me 'Brian'. Most people know me as 'Krusher' and they all know why; and if you ever spell it, make sure you spell it with a 'K'. I think a 'K' looks much more threatening, don't you?"

During the remainder of the morning it seemed that everyone's opinion of the school's newest pupil was a negative one. Even the girls who earlier were appearing to admire his physique seemed to be revising their judgement. As Billy and I made our way home for dinner at twelve o'clock, he was the obvious topic of conversation.

"I don't like this new lad," said my companion. "I think I prefer Tucker Lane to him."

"So do I," I told him. "At least everyone's got used to Tucker and you know where you stand. I think this Kershaw kid could be a lot worse, don't you?" I was reluctant to use the name 'Krusher'.

Billy thought about this for a few seconds before replying. "I think you might be right, Neil. I wonder who'd win if they were both in a fight."

"I'm not sure Billy. This new lad looks a lot bigger to me, but I can't wait to see what happens when he comes back, can you?"

Before he had time to answer, just as we were approaching the ginnel opposite the Electra, Johnny Jackson caught us up.

"You missed it," he said. "Just after you left this new kid pushed Gerry Sutherland just as he was about to go through the door. Everybody could see that he'd done it on purpose. Gerry turned round to him and said 'Who do you think you're pushing?' The new kid then shoved him down the three steps leading into the school yard and his arm was all grazed where he had scraped it on the floor. He got up with an angry look on his face and some of the other lads started shouting 'Fight! Fight!' Before either of them had a chance to do anything about it though, Barnesy came outside and put a stop to it. I think it's a good job he did anyway, because I'm sure he'd have got the worst of it."

I found myself agreeing with Johnny's assessment. Gerry Sutherland would have been fair competition for anyone except Tucker Lane, but this Kershaw lad seemed to have muscles more in keeping with a fifteen year old.

"I hope he doesn't play in the rugby team," observed Billy. "He'd probably get sent off in the first ten minutes."

"There's no fear of that," said Johnny. "Barnesy said that he's not eligible to play for us because he still belongs to a different school."

"That's right," I added. "Old Rawcliffe told us he's only going to be here for a few weeks."

At least, that was one consolation. I couldn't picture him as being any other than a handicap if he were allowed to become a member of our team, and as we hadn't won a game all season that was the last thing we needed. That didn't prevent him from becoming a problem within the school premises, however, and when we returned for the afternoon session it became clear just how obnoxious he could be. The first incident occurred while the headmaster interrupted his English lesson to speak to Miss Hazlehirst who had just knocked on the door. As the two of them were in conversation, I watched the self-named Krusher Kershaw, seated a few positions to my left immediately behind Jenny Unsworth, raise the inkwell from its slot in the desk and proceed to dip several strands of her considerably long hair inside the offending liquid. Yet he managed to do it in such a way that she remained completely unaware of what had occurred. From the expression on his face it was obvious that he felt very pleased with himself. Several pupils had witnessed the event and one or two of them were even giggling about it but, shamefully, when Mr. Rawcliffe returned and asked what all the noise was about, no one said a thing.

The second incident took place in the schoolyard. Two of the lads were kicking a ball around. When the school's newest pupil arrived they assumed that he just wanted to join in but he obviously had other thoughts. He got hold of the ball and booted it as high as he could, taking it over the school wall to land in a builder's yard in Craven Road. There was no possibility of anyone climbing over the wall in order to retrieve it as there was a drop of about twenty feet on the other side. There was no way he should have got away with it but no one wanted to take him on, and two onto one was never an option as even if the pair were victorious they would still lose face in the eyes of the school.

It was the third incident which I, rather rashly, became involved in. During the final lesson before the end of school, Pauline Dixon began coughing really badly and the headmaster asked Susan Brown, who was sitting behind her, to bring a glass of water from the cloakroom. By the time she came back with it, the intended recipient had acquired a more calm demeanour but, just as she was walking past Krusher at the end of the row he gave her arm a nudge which resulted in the contents of the glass drenching three pupils on the opposite side of the aisle and the container itself shattering on the floor. Mr. Rawcliffe was not very pleased as he looked up from his desk to see what all the noise was about.

"You clumsy girl," he bellowed. "Have you seen the state of those exercise books on the desk? They're ruined. You can go get a sweeping brush and sweep up all those shards of glass."

It occurred to me that perhaps he should have been more concerned with the soaking that three members of his class had received, but he appeared not to notice.

"It wasn't my fault, sir," she attempted to say, while pointing to the perpetrator of the crime. "He deliberately knocked my arm."

Her antagonist looked aghast, while displaying a look of complete innocence.

"Never blame someone else for your own clumsiness, Miss Brown," admonished the headmaster. "That's a lesson I expect you to learn. Now go and get a sweeping brush."

I knew that several pupils had witnessed the incident, yet no one seemed willing to speak out. As Susan began to walk out of the room in an obvious state of distress and, before I could even think about it, I was on my feet.

"What Susan said is perfectly true sir," I found myself saying. "Brian Kershaw knocked her arm on purpose. It was definitely intentional. There was nothing she could do about it."

The new boy gave me a look of pure hatred and it suddenly occurred to me that I had placed myself in a perilous position, but I knew I just could not let him get away with it. Whether I would have done the same if was one of the other girls instead of Susan I have no idea. This, to me, wasn't just a case of telling tales about someone because of some prank, which is perhaps how some of the other lads might have been looking at it; it was a case of someone I cared about having to take the blame for his pure vindictiveness.

Now that I had committed myself, Billy decided to back me up. "I saw it as well," he said, while trying to avoid Krusher's gaze. "He definitely knocked her arm."

Susan had paused before reaching the door as she realised that her version of events might just be about to be accepted.

"I see," said the headmaster. "Do you have anything to say about this, Master Kershaw?"

"It's all a pack of lies," he angrily stated. "I never touched her."

I was hoping that someone else might say something, but the room was eerily silent as our head teacher pondered this latest development. At least I was grateful for Billy's show of loyalty.

Mr. Rawcliffe looked across at Susan, who was still standing by the doorway, unsure what to do. "Why are you still standing there, girl?" he said. "Didn't I ask you to fetch a sweeping brush?"

"Yes, sir," she replied, and I could see that she was bravely attempting to hold back the tears as she thought about the injustice of the situation.

The headmaster continued to speak. "This is one person's word against another," he decided. "So as soon as the area has been cleaned up we can get back down to some schoolwork."

I regarded his statement as totally unfair as it was obviously the word of one person against three. The whole incident had left me with a bitter taste in my mouth. When all the commotion had subsided and Susan had returned to her seat, looking visibly shaken by the fact that her explanation of events had not been accepted in its entirety, Mr. Rawcliffe continued with his lesson, but not before Krusher gave me a threatening look and, drawing his finger across his throat, he mouthed the words 'You're dead'. Billy looked anxious too as it seemed extremely likely that the same sentiments were probably addressed to him. As the lesson came to an end and we were about to leave the classroom I could see that Billy looked as worried as I was. I knew that Susan's tormentor would almost certainly confront me the moment I stepped out of the building. However, as I rose from my desk the headmaster had something to say.

"Brian Kershaw, I want you to stay behind for a few minutes."

I immediately had a glimmer of hope. Had he known who was responsible all the time and was going to do something about it? It would, of course, probably only delay the inevitable until the following morning. However, it did allow Billy and me to leave the school without being disturbed, though the subject of Mr. Rawcliffe's demand looked even more menacing. Neither of us spoke to Susan and we both made our way home as quickly as possible, each of us dreading the thought of what we might have let ourselves in for.

After we had all finished our tea I decided to call at Auntie Molly's next door. I recalled how my cousin Raymond had provided a solution to the Scottish Dancing problem we had during Mrs. McIntyre's reign as head teacher and I hoped he might find a way out for me from my current predicament. I knocked on the door and pushed it open.

"Is Raymond in, Auntie Molly?" I asked, being unable to see him.

"He was here a minute ago," she replied. "He must have popped into the other room. You can go through if you like."

I did as she suggested and found him reclining on the couch with his head buried in a football magazine.

"Leeds United has been drawn against Chelsea in the F.A. Cup," he announced as he noticed my arrival. "That's good news, isn't it?"

It was Raymond who had got me interested in football, with his superb knowledge of the Football League set up. It was through him that I had come to know the names of most of the grounds and where they were located. "Do you think they've got a chance of winning?" I asked him.

"I don't see why not. They reached the quarter finals for the first time ever last season and only lost 1-0 to Arsenal, and that was on their own ground at Highbury."

We spoke about football for a few minutes before I got around to the purpose of my visit. I gave him a full account of what had occurred at school during the afternoon and of my worry about the likely consequences of my intervention. I asked him if anything similar had ever happened to him and. If so, what he had done about it.

"Well, nothing exactly like you've explained to me, but there were fights going on at school all the time. Every school has its bullies. The thing you must not do is let them know you're frightened of them."

"But I am scared," I told him. "You should see this kid. He's probably got more muscles than Bruce Woodcock."

My cousin laughed at my imagined comparison to the famous British heavyweight boxer. "I'm sure it can't be as bad as that," he suggested.

"Well, he's the biggest school kid I've ever seen," I countered.

"Did you say he's threatened Billy Mathieson as well?"

"Yes, because he backed me up when nobody else did."

"Well, there you are, then. All I can suggest is that the two of you stick together until he eventually forgets all about it. After all, he's hardly likely to take two of you on, is he?"

I knew that what he suggested was not really a plausible solution. He'd just pick on one of us and while the remainder of the lads probably looked on, the tradition among the pupils regarding schoolyard scraps would not allow a situation that involved two against one no matter who the instigator of the fight happened to be. I realised that my problem was not going to be resolved to my satisfaction and returned home. I had so many anxious thoughts in my mind when I went to bed that I decided not to make an entry in the chronicle and to leave it until the following day, but I was still wide awake in the early hours of the morning.

CHAPTER FOURTEEN

"I don't suppose you fancy bunking off school, do you Billy?" I asked as we apprehensively made our way towards the schoolyard on the morning after my encounter with Krusher. I already knew what his answer would be, just as I knew that mine would have been the same if he had asked. If we failed to attend every boy in the school would know the reason and we both knew that we couldn't allow that to happen.

"I don't think we can do that, Neil," he answered, just as I expected he would.

Because of the circumstances I found myself in I had abandoned all thoughts of sending Susan a Valentine card. I doubt if I could have done it anyway as I just couldn't face the embarrassment of anyone finding out as I felt sure that none of the other boys in the class would have even considered placing themselves in that position. However, just as we entered the classroom she came over to me.

"Thanks for standing up for me yesterday, Neil," she said.

There was no way I could stop my face from burning on this occasion and I just mumbled something in acknowledgement, but it did occur to me later that perhaps a card might have been welcomed after all.

Both Billy and I tried not to look at our antagonist, but his eyes seemed to be burning into us as we took up our seats. It wasn't only Krusher's unwelcome attention that we were receiving. It was painfully obvious that every pupil in the room was fully aware that we were in the firing line.

It was during the morning break, however, that he was able to approach us and put his perceived threat into words. Billy and I had already agreed to stay together and therefore share the brunt of his wrath.

"I want a word with you two," he snarled as he walked menacingly towards us. I could see that some of the other pupils, especially the lads, were watching the proceedings with great interest. "That old geezer in charge made me stay behind last night. He half believed what you told him and he said he'd be keeping on eye on me, but I can promise you, you're both going to pay for it."

We stared at him, trying our utmost not to show any trace of fear, even though we felt it. He stared menacingly at us and continued speaking.

"It'll be you first," he snarled, pointing at me, "And then you're next," he went on, indicating Billy. "Four o'clock in the schoolyard on Monday, straight after school. I want you to have plenty of time to think about what's in store for you, and you'd better be there, both of you."

So that was it. The gauntlet had been thrown and there was no way that either of us could refuse to pick it up and still retain any degree of respect among our fellow pupils. He didn't elaborate any further but, if his intention was to inject fear and apprehension into our veins, then he didn't need to as they were already there.

When we got back to the classroom, each time he got the opportunity he would hurl threatening glances in our direction, which of course did nothing whatsoever to restore our spirits. As the morning wore on, however, I began to appreciate the fact that Billy and I were now the centre of attention among the other pupils as news of what we were about to endure on the following Monday began to circulate around the room. I realised that, from their point of view, it was something for them to look forward to. By the time the final lesson of the morning ended I was beginning to feel much less apprehensive about the situation as it seemed to me that my place in the school pecking order had been enhanced. I didn't know whether Billy felt the same so I decided to put the question to him as we walked home for our midday meal.

"I don't think I feel quite as bad about things, Billy. What about you?"

"Well, we do seem to be the centre of attention, don't we? But I'm still not looking forward to Monday, though."

His comments reminded me that that was something we would still have to face.

"We've no chance of beating him, have we?" I asked him, hoping that he might provide me with some reason to be optimistic about the outcome."

"None whatsoever, Neil. I mean look at the size of him. I'm not even sure that Tucker Lane could beat him. Anyway, he's dealing with you first before he gets round to me. So if you're still my best friend I think what you ought to do is to keep getting up again every time he thumps you to the ground and make it last as long as you can. It would make him tire more easily and it might give me a better chance."

"Thanks a lot, Billy. That's just what I needed to hear."
I had not found his latter statement very helpful as it put
things into perspective and diminished considerably the
improved peace of mind that I had experienced earlier.

"I hope Tucker comes back before this new kid
leaves." he said. "I can't wait to see what happens."

I couldn't hold back my reply. "I don't think you'll see
it anyway, Billy. We'll probably both be in hospital."

When we arrived back at school for the afternoon
session, I realised that the dramatic events of the morning
had erased from my mind the fact that the day was
St. Valentine's Day. I had not seen any cards passing
around the room and to the best of my knowledge no
pupil had received one. It would seem, therefore, that the
headmaster's reference to the significance of the date
had not resulted in any great surge of interest. I hadn't
expected it to among the boys, but I wasn't too sure
about the girls. Anyway, it did appear that I wouldn't
be receiving one from Susan Brown. What I wasn't too
sure of, however, was whether I was relieved or not.
Krusher Kershaw did not appear to involve himself
in any unpleasant activities during the remainder of the
afternoon, so I could only assume that he was lying low
for a while until Mr. Rawcliffe ceased to be quite so
vigilant regarding his conduct.

In the schoolyard during the afternoon break Alan
Bartle walked over to me. "How are you going to get out
of fighting Krusher on Monday?" he asked.

"I can't, can I?" I replied. "If you've got any suggestions
let me know, because I can't think of any, and there's no
way I'll be able to beat him, is there? And that goes for
Billy as well. Why didn't the rest of you say something
when he knocked Susan's arm? I mean, he couldn't have
fought all of us, could he?"

"I think they were thinking the same as I was, that it was like telling tales. But I suppose, looking back, he needs taking down a peg or two, doesn't he? It's a pity Tucker's not here. I can't wait for him to get back; there should be some real fireworks when he does."

"I don't think me and Billy will be in any fit state to see them," I told him.

He laughed and, for the first time, I found myself being able to see the funny side of the situation. It was just a pity that I was personally involved.

As I returned to the classroom I found myself walking alongside Susan Brown who had obviously chosen that moment to express a view.

"I'm sorry that you have to fight Krusher on my account, Neil," she whispered.

"That's all right, Susan," I said, with a bravado that seemed to have been summoned from nowhere in particular. "I just couldn't let him get away with it."

Her words gave me a warm, contented feeling and, surprisingly, a new-found confidence that I knew, unfortunately, would all too soon disappear.

The remainder of the afternoon was uneventful and I saw no evidence whatsoever of anyone receiving a Valentine card. In fact, the subject, among the pupils, seemed to have been totally ignored. I found this, in a way, to be rather disappointing as, after Susan's words as we were about to enter the classroom, I was secretly hoping that one might have been heading in my direction. At least, Krusher didn't make any further comments regarding his intentions towards Billy and me.

As the two of us left school the sun was shining, which was in contrast to the previous few days.

"The days are starting to get longer," I said. "It'll be spring soon and we'll be able to go out a lot more."

"I think I'll be more interested once Monday's out of the way," responded my companion. "I can't get all that enthusiastic at the moment."

"It's a pity we can't just go to sleep at night and wake up with a body like Johnny Weissmuller," I suggested, naming the actor who had appeared in all the Tarzan films that had thrilled us at the Electra.

"That'd be great," Billy agreed. "Just imagine Krusher's face when he saw us. The trouble is though, it's not going to happen, is it?"

"Look, Billy," I said. "There's nothing we can do to stop Monday coming round, is there? But it's a few days away yet; so don't let it stop us from enjoying the rest of the week."

I decided to change the subject. "I expected to see a few Valentine card going round today, from the girls I mean. I couldn't really imagine any of the boys sending one, but there weren't any, were there?"

"Are you sure about that, Neil?"

"Why? Did you see any going round?"

"No, but that doesn't mean that they didn't, does it?"

"How do you mean?"

"Well, how do you explain this, then?"

From inside his jacket he miraculously produced a hand-made Valentine card. On the front cover it had the shape of a heart with the words BE MY VALENTINE written inside it, followed by four crosses which I assumed represented kisses.

"Where did you get that from?" I asked, astounded.

"I don't know. It was inside my desk when we came back into the classroom after the afternoon break."

"Well, who sent it?" I persisted, beginning to feel a little envious.

"Well, how can I know that, Neil? Nobody's signed it, have they?"

"Haven't you any idea at all? I mean which girls at school do you like best?"

"I suppose if I had to like any of them in the way that you mean it would probably have to be Sally Cheesedale, but she doesn't know that, does she? So she's hardly likely to be sending me a Valentine card, is she?"

"What about Sophie Morton?" I suggested.

"That's not funny, Neil. No, the only person I can think of that might send me one is Susan Brown, because I backed you up yesterday."

"No way, Billy; if she hasn't sent me one, then she isn't going to send you one, is she?"

"Why not? Maybe it's me she's fancied all the time. Yes, I bet that's who it is. It's from Susan Brown."

Billy's statement, though it didn't really sound logical, got me worried all the same. Could it have been Billy she liked all the time? Had I read the signs wrongly? I really didn't want to believe it, but I just couldn't extract the possibility from my mind.

"I think you'd better try to find out who sent it to you, Billy? Can't you ask if anyone saw who put it into your desk? Someone must have seen her, whoever it was."

I was desperate to discover that the card had not been sent by the only girl in the entire school to whom I felt any measure of affection.

"Don't be daft Neil, scolded my companion. "How can I do that? I don't want any of the other lads in the class to know that I've been sent a Valentine card, do

I? They'd think it was all soppy and I'd never live it down."

So that was that; and I was left with a nagging question that would just not go away no matter how hard I tried. Had Billy received the card that should rightly have been mine? We hung around for a short while outside the Electra gazing at the posters, but my mind, for once, wasn't really focused on what picture we might be going to see at the weekend.

"Have we to come straight back out again, Neil, after we get home?" asked Billy.

This is something we usually did providing the weather at this time of year was not too inclement, but I think on this occasion my answer surprised him.

"No, I don't think so, Billy. I think I'll stay in tonight." I needed to think things over.

When I entered the house, in a state of melancholy, and took off my coat I couldn't help noticing Nell's look of disapproval from her place on the clip rug in front of the fireplace, the expression on her face seeming to say 'What are you looking so miserable about?'. Before I could do anything else there was a knock on the door accompanied by a familiar voice as it was opened.

"Are you there, May?"

Come on in Mr. Senior," beckoned my mother, which seemed a little unnecessary as he was already inside. "How are you today?"

"Oh! Just fair to middling, lass: just fair to middling, but we mustn't grumble, must we?"

"Is there anything I can do for you?" she responded.

"Well there is as a matter of fact," he said, "If it's not being too much of a nuisance. No, what it is, do you see, I was wondering if the next time you go to that cobbler's at the bottom of Marian Road, whether you wouldn't mind taking a pair of boots for me to be soled and heeled. I've got so used to them over the years, do you see, and they've been so comfortable, that I'm reluctant to part with them."

It occurred to me that, when he got them back with new soles and new heels, then they wouldn't really be the same boots any more, but I didn't say anything. Nell, who had become so used to Mr. Senior making an entrance in this fashion, decided to ignore the proceedings. However, as I had just made up my mind to settle for a few minutes on the arm chair before my father arrived to claim it I was totally unprepared for my mother's next statement.

"There's no need to wait until the next time we have anything to take. Neil can go now for you. Then they should be ready to pick up by tomorrow afternoon. He's only just taken his coat off. He hasn't got settled down yet.

"Well, that's very good of you, May. It's much appreciated."

I couldn't help wondering why his words of appreciation were addressed to my mother rather than to me. Nell decided to take an interest at last and gave me a look that seemed to me to say 'It's your own fault for being so miserable'.

Mr. Senior went back home and returned a couple of minutes later with his worn-out boots wrapped in a piece of newspaper.

"You've plenty of time to take these to the cobbler's and be back before your dad gets home from work," stated my mother.

The establishment in question was at the bottom end of Marian Road, which ran into Melville Road. It was beginning to get dark when I arrived, and it was also very cold. I had been to the shop, if that is what it could be called, on many occasions. The owner, who I would have suspected was nearer seventy than sixty, didn't really sell anything other than a few boot laces and the odd belt or two. His entire trade was in the repair of worn-out footwear. The smell of leather was everywhere, but I didn't really mind it. When I left the premises I was starting to shiver and I couldn't think of any reason to hang about. I set off walking along Melville Road, but was approached by Ken Stacey, who I knew lived in the area. After the initial greeting he asked me if I knew who Billy had sent a Valentine card to.

"He hasn't sent one to anybody," I told him. "He doesn't believe in doing anything so soppy." I decided not to mention the fact that he had actually received one.

"Well, I saw him writing a card," replied my companion. "So he must have sent it to somebody. It was during the afternoon while old Rawcliffe was looking through his books and we were supposed to be writing a composition. As soon as he thought I might be watching he shoved it inside his desk."

I couldn't understand how he'd managed to do that without my noticing, especially as I was sitting at the side of him. Then I realised that, while he was doing that, I was deeply involved in trying to do justice to a composition we had been asked to write entitled "The Countryside In Winter" and, by doing so, attempt to dislodge for a while the prospect of my forthcoming encounter with Krusher Kershaw.

"So, do you know who he sent to?" persisted Ken.

"No, I've no idea," I replied, but then a suspicion began to nag at me. "Did you see what this card looked like?"

"Yes! It had a heart drawn on the front and he was writing the words BE MY VALENTINE inside it."

I told him that I still had no idea who he had sent it to and that I was surprised that he could be so soppy. I was pleased however that my suspicions regarding the card had been confirmed. After arriving home and informing my mother that Mr. Senior's repaired boots would probably be ready for him on the following afternoon, I announced that I was just popping round to see Billy.

"Well, make sure you're back in time for tea," was my mother's only comment to my announcement.

"Is Billy coming out, Mrs. Mathieson?" I asked after the door was opened.

"I thought you didn't want to come out," said Billy, as he peered from behind the door.

"I didn't, but I've changed my mind."

After Billy's mother had issued the same conditions as mine, he put on his coat and stepped outside.

"Have we to see if Nicky's coming out?! He asked.

"Not yet; I've got something to tell you first. I know who sent you the Valentine card."

A puzzled expression appeared on his face. "How can you know that, Neil? Like I said I think it must have been Susan Brown."

"No, it wasn't, Billy. I met Ken Stacey when I walked over to the cobbler's with Mr. Senior's old boots and he told me that he had seen Eva Bentley writing one and he asked her who it was for. He said he hadn't expected her to tell him, but she actually seemed eager and she said it was for you. So there you are Billy. The problem's solved. It wasn't from Susan Brown. It was from Eva Bentley."

"That's not possible, Neil," he spluttered. I was enjoying watching him squirm. I had wanted to tell him that it was from Sophie Morton, but I knew that if I had, he would realise immediately that I was joking. This way I could see that he was desperately searching for a way out of his predicament.

"Why not?" I persisted. "Why couldn't it have been Eva Bentley? I bet she's fancied you all along, but never said anything."

"It can't be her, because---because, I wrote it out myself," he finally admitted.

"I know that, Billy. Ken Stacey saw you writing it."

"I just wanted to see your reaction if you thought I'd received a card from Susan Brown instead of you. It backfired on me, though, didn't it?"

At that point we both started laughing as I realised that what he had done was just the sort of jape that I might have played on him.

So I didn't receive a Valentine card and, as far as I was aware, no one else at school received one either, but I found out that I didn't really mind. Maybe it was all a little soppy after all.

After writing the usual entry in the chronicle I decided that it had been a very interesting day, but I was still very concerned about the threat that was hanging over me on the following Monday.

CHAPTER FIFTEEN

"I hate going for a pee when my hands are frozen," announced Billy as he squeezed out the last few drops, left the tree and made his way back up the grassy bank to join me on the concrete path at the top of the ridge. The temperature was, indeed, well below freezing and I knew exactly what he meant.

"Why didn't you wear those gloves that you have in your pocket, then?" I suggested.

"Because it's no good with knitted gloves, is it?" To begin with it takes you ages just to pull your willy out, especially with it shrinking in the cold weather, and then you can't direct the flow as high as you want to. Anyway, apart from that, if there's any wind about it blows back on you and it wets your gloves."

It was probably the coldest day since we'd explored the frozen pond at the bottom of the ridge. It was Saturday morning, just two days before we were due to meet Krusher Kershaw in the gladiatorial ring known as Woodhouse Junior School playground. Over the week Krusher had gradually drifted back to his bullying ways whenever he thought that the headmaster was not being quite so vigilant. Several of our classmates had been his victims, but so ingrained in them was the pupils' code about not telling tales that he invariably got away with everything.

Despite the temperature both Billy and I had preferred to go out rather than stay in and be bored silly. It had been that way ever since Dick Barton, Special Agent had stopped being broadcast on the wireless.

"What shall we do, Neil?" asked Billy. "Do you want to see if that pond that we went to last month has frozen over again?"

I thought about my ghostly encounter on the previous occasion that I had visited the site and I realised that I would prefer not to tempt providence.

"No, I don't think so, Billy. Why don't we go have a look at Death Valley? All the vegetation will be frozen over and we can pretend that it's the end of the world and that the sun has stopped shining forever."

He seemed keen and when we approached the area it did resemble the sort of landscape that any ten or eleven-year old might think belonged to some alien planet. Death Valley and Table Top, the small plateau about twenty feet above it, which could be reached via a steep, but narrow, path was a favourite haunt of most of the children who lived in the vicinity of Woodhouse Ridge, especially the boys. The terrain was perfect for all manner of adventurous games. On this occasion, however, we seemed to have the place to ourselves.

"I'm not surprised nobody's here," observed Billy. "I think it's getting even colder, don't you?"

"I think you're right," I said, my earlier enthusiasm for the venture rapidly fading. "I'm freezing."

"What if we both got a cold, Neil? We wouldn't be able to go to school on Monday then, would we? And we wouldn't have to fight Krusher. Why don't we keep opening our mouths and breathe cold air in. That should do it, shouldn't it?"

I thought about his suggestion which, at first, appeared to have some merit, but I could see there were drawbacks.

"I don't think that would do any good," I informed him. "There's no guarantee that we'd both get a cold, is there? And pretending wouldn't do any good because my mother can always tell if I'm trying to skive off school. Anyway, none of the lads would believe it and they'd say we had chickened out, and we'd still have to fight him some time. I mean, I can't see him forgetting about it, can you? No it'd have to be something a lot more serious than a cold so that we didn't get back to school before he left."

Billy seemed to accept my view of the situation and he went quiet for a while as if he were trying to think of another way out.

When it began to snow, just a few minutes later, it didn't take us long to decide to return home. Thoughts of a glowing fire followed by a warm dinner had been growing in our minds for quite a while.

"Are you having fish and chips for dinner, Neil?" asked Billy.

"I don't think so," I replied. "My mother always tells me to make sure I'm home early if I've to go to the fish and chip shop, but she didn't say anything like that this morning."

The snow was beginning to settle on the already frozen ground as we made our way back along the topmost path. As we approached the old man's shelter, which my father had told me had been there for as long as he could remember, we considered taking refuge for a while. We decided against it though, as we had no idea how much longer it would continue to snow and we were both, by now, in a hurry to reach the comfort of home.

We had traversed no more than a hundred yards, however, before Billy stepped off the path, lost his footing and slid down the steep banking before coming to rest against a tree. I clambered down to join him while being as careful as possible to avoid the same mishap. Could he have done it on purpose in order to obtain the sort of injury that would enable him to avoid going back to school on Monday? I knew, however, that I couldn't really believe that. Surely an action of that nature would be much too drastic and could easily result in a really serious injury.

When I arrived at the scene of the accident I asked him if he was all right.

"I think so, Neil, but I think I've hurt my back a bit."

"Well, at least there's one consolation. It's not the same tree that you peed on earlier."

He laughed at that comment.

"Do you think you can walk back up to the path?" I asked him.

"I think so." He winced as he stood up and proceeded to rub his back. "I'll get my mam to look at it when I get home. Anyway, there's another consolation. I might be able to stay off school for a few days."

"Aw, that's not fair Billy. You'd be leaving me to face Krusher on my own."

"I can't help that, Neil." He rubbed his back again. "It hurts something rotten."

We managed to climb the banking without further mishap, and I had to admit that he did seem to be in considerable pain. By the time we entered Cross Speedwell Street the snow had stopped falling, but it remained extremely cold. I left Billy to his mother's nursing skills with the remote hope that he would be feeling sufficiently better to go to school on Monday.

When I entered my house my father had still not returned from work, but my mother was already in the process of making some stew and dumplings. I would much rather have had fish and chips, but I wouldn't have fancied going for them in the freezing conditions anyway, as I knew there would be no possibility of being asked to go to the nearest one which was just around the corner opposite Doughty's. So I decided to make the best of what would be on offer and immediately walked over to the pan on the gas ring and examined the contents that were merrily bubbling away. Even Nell, from her usual place in front of the warm coal fire kept raising her head to take a sniff, knowing that she would soon be getting a share.

"I've got some news for you," said my mother as I took off my coat. "You're Auntie Minnie's coming next weekend. She'll be staying with your Auntie Brenda for a few days. Now that's good news, isn't it?"

I was fortunate or, as it seemed on some occasions, unfortunate, to have three aunts living in the same street as us. Auntie Molly, who lived next door, and Auntie Eileen, a few doors away, were my mother's sisters. Auntie Brenda, who lived near the far end of the street, was the widow of my mother's brother. Her sister, Minnie, wasn't actually a real aunt of mine, but my brother and I had always called her that, anyway.

She lived with my Uncle Mark, who was also not a real uncle in the strict sense of the word, in a small village near the town of Saltburn on the Yorkshire coast and we had enjoyed their hospitality on several wonderful holidays over the past few years.

"Isn't Uncle Mark coming as well, mam?" I asked.

"I'm afraid not. Your Uncle Mark will be working I'm afraid. He works in a quarry you know, and he can't get much time off at this time of year. So your Auntie Minnie is coming by herself."

From what I remembered from my visits to her house my aunt was a very pleasant and jolly woman and also very fussy. She was also quite portly and anyone under the age of about eighteen was invariably greeted with the sort of hug that left the recipient gasping for breath. Once the greeting was out of the way, however, I always enjoyed my visits there, despite her having two daughters who were slightly older than I, and who used to torment me mercilessly. If I complained, however, my protestations were always answered with a laugh and a comment that they were only teasing. I had no recollection, though, of her visiting our house in the past. If she did so it must have been when I was very small.

After my father had arrived home and we had devoured my mother's stew and dumplings I decided to call round to see how Billy was doing.

"Billy's lying on the settee in the other room for a while," said his mother. "His back is quite painful you know." She said it in such a way that it looked like she was blaming me for his mishap. "You can go through and see him if you like," she added.

I did as she suggested and found him lying on his side with his back towards me.

"Look at this, Neil," he said, pulling up his shirt as he saw me enter the room.

There was indeed quite a substantial amount of bruising.

"Crikey, Billy," I said, "It looks like you might be leaving me to face Krusher on my own after all."

"Well, I can't help it Neil. It really hurts." The trouble is though it means everyone at school is going to think I was too scared to come to school. You'll tell them what really happened, won't you? I mean I'd have done the same for you if it was the other way round."

I was disappointed that he probably wouldn't be there, which made me even more fearful of Monday's encounter with the school's self-elected new champion, but I knew there was no way I could let the other pupils think that he was deliberately missing school with a fake injury.

"My Auntie Minnie's coming next weekend," I told him, deciding to change the subject. "She's going to stay for a few days at my Auntie Brenda's."

"Is your Auntie Minnie the one that lives at the seaside somewhere; the one that you've told me about?"

"That's right, Billy, she lives near Saltburn, but this will be the first time I've ever seen her here."

Billy looked thoughtful for a moment. "I wonder where people who live at the seaside go for their holidays," he said. "I mean coming to Leeds wouldn't be very exciting would it? I suppose they'd just go to another seaside place, a bit further away. Maybe they'd go outside Yorkshire altogether."

"I think they might go to Blackpool or Morecambe or somewhere like that. My dad says that people in Lancashire aren't very much different from us, just less fortunate, that's all: but if you go below Sheffield people get stranger the further south you go."

"Did you know Neil that you're not allowed to play cricket for Yorkshire unless you were actually born in the county?"

"Yes Billy; my Cousin Raymond told me. He said that he'd heard of one lady who was going to have a baby while they were travelling back to Leeds after staying in Blackpool. The train had got as far as a place called Clitheroe, which meant it was still in Lancashire, when the baby started to arrive. They managed to find a doctor on the train, but the husband kept telling her to hang on as long as she could so that it could be born on the right side of the Pennines just in case it was a boy. He wanted to make sure that he would be eligible to play for Yorkshire if he proved to be good at cricket. The doctor came from Huddersfield so he could understand how important it was and he did everything he could to encourage her to try to wait a little longer."

"Did she manage to wait until the train had crossed the border?"

"Yes, she did, and the baby was born in Skipton. Everyone in the carriage cheered and they had a big celebration on the train. It was a boy and they decided to call him Lenoard after Len Hutton."

"I think I'd rather play cricket for Yorkshire than I would for England," announced Billy.

"Me too, but it's not likely to happen, is it?"

I stayed with him for the best part of an hour before going home. I was upset by the fact that it was most unlikely that he would be able to accompany me to school on Monday to give me moral support. I realised, however, that it wasn't his fault and tried not to be too despondent. I was extremely apprehensive about what I was going to face, however, and I couldn't help wondering whether it was all really worth it just to enable Susan to think favourably of me.

When I left his house it had just started to snow again and the temperature seemed to have dropped even further. I stayed at home for the remainder of the day and, for the most part, competed with Neil for occupation of the comfort zone in front of the fire. Unfortunately, this did not prevent the necessity of my having to brave the elements by visiting the lavatory yard on several occasions. At least in these conditions it was extremely unlikely that Mary Pearson would be lurking around hoping to pay a surprise visit.

As I wrote in the chronicle about Billy's accident before retiring for the night, I couldn't help wondering if I would be in a far worse state than he was when I returned home after school on Monday. Whatever fate had in store for me I could think of no way whatsoever of avoiding the planned encounter with Krusher Kershaw and its inevitable conclusion.

CHAPTER SIXTEEN

When the morning I had been dreading finally arrived I found myself, surprisingly, feeling not too despondent as I had slept fairly well. That, however, could probably be explained by the fact that I had dreamed that I had knocked out my adversary with a single punch making it unnecessary for Billy to engage him. I was just appreciating my newly-acquired hero status in the eyes of Susan when I awoke, and within seconds my mind latched on to the reality of the situation.

"What's wrong with you?" asked my mother at breakfast time as she watched me eating my Weetabix with a forlorn expression on my face.

"Nothing, mam," I said.

"I know you don't like Mondays," she went on, misunderstanding the reason for my disconsolate mood, "But if you had to do what I have to do this morning you'd probably have a valid excuse for feeling miserable."

Nell barked her agreement. I knew she hated washday just as much as I did and couldn't understand why she had to be ejected once a week from the comfort of the clip rug in front of the fireplace, which she considered to be her natural habitat, and be replaced by those cold, wet, dangly things that my mother insisted on draping over a clothes horse, and no doubt wondered whether this was something that was afflicted on the whole canine world or simply for her benefit alone.

As I set off on the short journey to school the bitterly cold weather only served to lower my spirits and as I passed Billy's house I didn't bother to knock as I realised that the chances that he would be able to join me were almost negligible. I had spoken to him on the previous day but the bruises on his back had not in any way healed. As I passed the ginnel opposite the Electra Picture house, however, I heard a voice call out.

"Hang on, Neil," it shouted. "You never called round."

As I turned around I felt like hugging him. "What about your back, Billy?" Have the bruises all gone?" I asked him.

"Not all of them, Neil, but I'm a lot better than yesterday. I had to come, didn't I? Otherwise all the other lads would think I was scared."

"I am scared, Billy, but I bet all the other lads would be as well if it was one of them that was expected to fight Krusher as soon as school finished." I knew, however, that my mood had lightened considerably now that my closest friend was there for support and my admiration for him increased.

Every so often during morning lessons Krusher would look in our direction and smirk to himself. Some of the other lads were conveying sympathetic looks while others were giving us looks of eager anticipation. In their eyes a schoolyard fight was always something to look forward to, even if this particular one did promise to be a little one-sided. I couldn't help wondering whether Susan Brown would stay around to watch it or whether she would decide to go straight home. What I was totally unprepared for, however, was the unforeseen circumstances that would occur when we returned to school after the dinner-time break.

I called round for Billy after I had finished eating and we made our way back along the street. "Do you know what I think?" he said. "I think nearly all the lads in the school will be watching the fight and they're all going to be cheering for you, aren't they? It might put him off and it might just give you a chance of winning."

I wanted to believe that but I knew that there was little prospect that the outcome that he was suggesting would materialise. My only concern was that I did not disgrace myself by showing signs of fear.

"No way, Billy. I can't see any point in kidding myself, and don't forget it'll be your turn when he's finished with me."

We entered the classroom and took up our seats. What occurred next, however, took everyone by surprise. There was a knock at the door. The headmaster opened it to see Mr. Barnes standing there. I watched them huddled together in close conversation but was unable to hear any part of it. After a couple of minutes Mr. Rawcliffe re-entered the room, but he wasn't alone.

"I am pleased to announce," he said, "That Tommy Lane is able to resume his lessons, beginning this afternoon. He was hoping to attend this morning but he had to get the doctor to examine his foot to ensure that it had properly healed."

Everyone seemed to brighten up at this unexpected announcement, as they realised that things could start to get interesting.

"Now then, Tommy," said the headmaster, "If you'd like to go to your seat we can continue with our lesson."

"There's someone sitting in it," he said.

"That is Brian Kershaw, and he'll be with us for a few weeks only while his father is working in the area. Now, there's a seat at the back of the class, Tommy. You can sit there today."

I couldn't help noticing the glare he directed towards Krusher as he walked past him and I could hardly wait to see how things might develop during the remainder of the day. As things turned out I had to wait until the afternoon break to find out.

"Welcome back, Tucker," I said as Billy and I followed him out of the classroom. "Is your foot okay now?"

"Doctor Dunlop said so this morning. I was dying to come back to school anyway as soon as I heard about this new kid."

"Nobody likes him," said Billy, and went on to inform him of all the mean things he had done since he arrived. I was glad that he had not mentioned, at that stage, our own involvement, as I wanted to see his reaction to the other things he had mentioned.

"He's told everybody he's the new cock of the school," I added for good measure.

"Well, we'll soon get that sorted out," he said, with one of the most menacing looks I had ever seen, even from him. I couldn't help thinking though that, despite his muscular appearance, his intended adversary was just as well-endowed in that respect, but was also considerably taller. Before long Tucker was surrounded by several of the other lads and Billy and I wandered over to the low school wall and sat down on it.

"Somehow," I said to him, "I feel a lot better about things now that Tucker's back."

"I think I know what you mean, Neil. Anyway, Krusher might change his mind and decide to fight him instead."

Our hopes were immediately dashed when the subject of our conversation walked over to us. "Don't forget you two," he said, "Make sure you're out here waiting when school finishes, and I'll tell you now, it could be the last time you'll be able to sit on the school wall for a long time."

After he had left we remained seated there for the few minutes before the bell sounded for the remainder of the afternoon's lessons, while contemplating what fate had in store for us. What we didn't know until we re-entered the school, was that the situation had changed dramatically. Our informant was Phillip Thatcher.

"It looks like you two might be off the hook," he announced as we walked slowly along the corridor to the classroom. "Tucker confronted this new kid and told him that he wants his seat back by tomorrow morning, but he was told that there was no way he was going to get it. So Tucker told him he was going to beat him up straight after school. He told him that he was the cock of the school and that now that he was back he was going to make sure that he knew it."

Krusher told him that he'd have to wait until tomorrow because he was dealing with you two for grassing on him. Tucker wasn't having any of it though, and if the bell hadn't have rung at that particular moment the fight would have started there and then. "It's you and me straight after school," he demanded. "I'm not bothered about anybody else."

I felt that a huge weight had been lifted from my mind. Had Billy and I actually found a way out without having to suffer any disrespect from the remainder of the class? I could now hardly wait for the afternoon session to come to an end and I had the distinct impression that hardly anyone would be hurrying home at four o'clock. Mr. Rawcliffe struggled valiantly to make his lesson sufficiently interesting enough to take the minds of the pupils away from the contest that would be taking place immediately after the school bell sounded, though he, of course, was blissfully unaware of it. I knew what the reaction of the teachers usually was to schoolyard fights, as I had witnessed it many times before. To them it was an accepted part of child development and providing it was an even contest that was taking place and there was no sign of bullying, then they usually let the participants just get on with it. It would be monitored to a certain degree, however, to make sure that it didn't get out of hand. Eager eyes surveyed the classroom clock and eventually, when the bell sounded for the end of the afternoon's activities, no one needed ushering from the room. Tucker and Krusher glared at each other as at least half of the pupils in the top three classes made their way towards the back of the school where the old air raid shelter and the toilet blocks were, this being the accepted venue for disputes to be settled.

It was probably the biggest gathering ever seen at Woodhouse Junior School for a dispute between pupils being settled in the traditional manner, and as I sized up the two contestants for this particular bout I could see instantly that this was certainly the toughest challenge that Tucker had ever faced. I immediately felt intrigued by the possible outcome of this encounter, while at the same time being very relieved that I was no longer a part of it. I found it inconceivable that Tucker could be disposed of so quickly that his antagonist would then be able to fulfil his promise and make a start on me.

There were to be no preliminaries and the newest kid in the school barged straight into his opponent and knocked him to the floor. Mr. Barnes chose that precise moment to appear from around the corner. He observed the action that was taking place, shook his head, tut-tutted and immediately retraced his steps. Tucker got up and grabbed Krusher around the waist. Within seconds both of them were rolling around on the ground. The noise from the spectators was deafening, and nearly all of them were shouting for the boy they had known the longest, despite any antagonism they might have felt for him in the past. It seemed to me though that, because of his extra few inches in height, the new kid appeared to be in control. If I was proved right, then there was a strong possibility that I might be in for a beating after all. As the bout wore on, however, I could see that Krusher was beginning to tire, whereas his opponent seemed as fresh as when the fight began, for whenever he was knocked down he just bounced back to his feet again.

"Tucker's going to win this," whispered Billy in my ear, obviously coming to the same conclusion. "I'm sure of it."

Within a few minutes this observation became clear to everyone else. The excited shouts became more intense as the battle neared its climax. I couldn't help noticing that there were several female voices among them. I looked around to see if I could see Susan, but it appeared that she wasn't there. Eventually Tucker Lane had his opponent face down on the concrete playground and his muscles bulged as he twisted his arm behind his back and put as much ptessure on it as he could muster.

"Say 'chicken'," he snarled at the prostrate figure.

"Chicken," said Krusher.

"Say it louder."

"Chicken," he shouted.

Cheers emanated from the watching crowd as the winner of the contest released his opponent, who, much to my relief, did not appear to be in any fit state to engage Billy or me. He had been soundly beaten and he knew it, his bloody nose and dishevelled appearance providing sufficient evidence for any observer.

"It's worked out all right," I said to Billy. "We won't have to fight him after all."

This was to go down in school history as Tucker Lane's finest hour and as the undisputed champion of Woodhouse Junior School was being congratulated by his supporters, which was just about everybody as the newcomer had alienated virtually the entire school, we decided to make our way home, very much relieved that we would be arriving on the doorstep in a much better condition than had seemed likely when we left.

"I thought Susan might have stayed behind to watch," I said, as we walked along the street, "Especially as I might have been involved."

"She doesn't like watching fights, Neil. She told me once."

I was disappointed all the same, as I knew I would have looked for a little sympathy coming from that direction if I had suffered a beating on her behalf.

Although I didn't know it at the time that afternoon, as far as I was aware, was the last time that any of the pupils saw Brian Kershaw, whose nickname of Krusher no longer seemed appropriate. I can only assume that he was too demoralised to see out the remainder of his short period at our school and had decided to feign illness rather than face up to the humiliating consequences of his defeat. It proved to be very difficult for anyone to feel any sympathy for him in view of the number of boys and girls he had offended in such a short time.

With the way things had turned out it had been quite a joyous day for me, and I made quite a long entry in the chronicle that night, and as I lay in bed I realised that it was the only time that I can remember when everyone in the school had been rooting for Tucker Lane.

CHAPTER SEVENTEEN

I couldn't help laughing as the would-be tackler lost his grip on Billy's waist, though it didn't prevent his victim from going down anyway and sliding about ten or twelve yards in the thick mud, eventually coming to an undignified halt beyond the touchline. It was a sense of mystery how anyone could identify where the touchline was supposed to be as the white line which depicted it had long since been obliterated. However, the referee unhesitatingly indicated a scrum down. This particular Saturday was the beginning of several days away from school because of the mid-term break, and every member of our team was hoping to herald the beginning of the holiday with a long overdue win. The weather, however, was not in any mood to assist the efforts of either team. The previous day had seen torrential rain and Bedford's Field near the top of Woodhouse Ridge had taken the full force of it.

Everyone on the team had begun the game in high spirits, knowing that none of us would have to return to school until the following Wednesday. The extremely muddy conditions were proving to be a great leveller and with only a few minutes remaining we found ourselves only two points down and we knew that one try would settle it. Unfortunately for us it was scored at the wrong end of the pitch. As the two teams attempted to form a scrum with everyone slipping and sliding about the whole thing collapsed, but not before the ball had been thrown in. It eventually found its way to the wing-threequarter of Lower Wortley Junior School who, I couldn't help noticing, looked remarkably dry compared to everyone else on the pitch. He managed to avoid two attempted tackles before placing the ball beyond the line. The try wasn't converted and that proved to be the end of the scoring with the result that we lost the game by thirteen points to eight. It was, however, probably our best performance to date and if we kept on playing with the same spirit then surely it couldn't be long before we actually won a game.

"Well done, lads," said Mr. Barnes as we trudged over to the wooden shed to get changed. "That was a good performance today. We'll win next time out. You mark my words."

There were no washing facilities and most of the lads decided to walk home in their playing strip rather than risk the wrath of their mothers by putting on clean clothes over the grime and mud that covered their bodies. Tucker Lane was almost unrecognisable as he had, as usual, been right in the thick of the action and everyone was really pleased to see him back in the team.

"Are we going back via the ridge?" asked Billy.

"I think I'd rather go the shortest way," I told him.

We didn't bother to get changed and stuffed our street clothes into our duffle bags. Within a few minutes the two of us, plus Nicky Whitehead and Johnny Jackson were making our way down Woodhouse Street. We must have been a sorry sight, with each of us caked in mud and I was beginning to feel cold with only my rugby strip to keep me warm. I immediately started to look forward to the hot bath that my mother would insist upon my having before I could sit down to eat.

"We could have won that game," observed Johnny as we turned onto Johnston Street.

"I think you're right," said Billy. "It was good to have Tucker back in the side."

"I don't think we should have started the game," said Nicky. "It was obvious that the ground was going to get churned up like that. Alan Bartle passed the ball to me once when we were only a few yards from the try line, but it was so slippery I just couldn't hold on to it. I mean, it's all right for Barnesy to go on about how well we played but the only way either team could have won this morning would have been by luck."

Johnny Jackson said farewell as he continued walking to the end of Johnston Street as the three of us clambered down the steps leading to the street below and continued our way down the hill towards home.

"Are you coming out with us this afternoon?" asked Billy, turning towards Nicky and obviously assuming that I would be outside with him.

"I can't," said our companion. "My mam's taking me to see my Auntie Alice at Cross Gates. I wish I didn't have to go though."

Never mind, Nicky," I said. "At least we've got a long weekend ahead of us."

"Don't take your coat off," said my mother after we had split up and I had entered the house. "I want you to go to the fish and chip shop. You're grandad's coming and he should be here soon."

Nell looked up, knowing that her comfort zone in front of the fire would not be under threat until I came back. The hot bath that I had been eagerly looking forward to had now been relegated down my mother's list of priorities. I was made to have a quick scrub down and change into my street clothes.

"Before you go, you can call round to see Mr. Senior," she informed me. "He might fancy some fish and chips himself. He can't go out. He's only just getting over his cold you know."

When he opened his door to me I could see that he was wrapped up a lot more than was usual, and the pipe that usually resided between his lips was noticeably missing.

"Come on in. lad. Come on in," he said, though the weakness of his voice was another indication that my mother's assessment of the state of his health was correct. There was no way that he could be described as fair to middling on this occasion.

I followed him inside. The usual aroma of tobacco smoke was totally absent.

"Have you stopped smoking your pipe, Mr. Senior?" I asked him.

"Nay, lad, not altogether. No, I don't think I could be without it indefinitely. No, what it is, do you see, since I got this here cold I reckoned I was coughing enough without doing anything else to encourage it. So I thought I'd put it away for a day or two. Still, I think I'm starting to get over it now, so fingers crossed, eh. Now, what is it you want to see me about? I reckon it's not just a social call."

"No, my mam's sending me to the fish and chip shop and she asked me to call round to see if you wanted any bringing." As an afterthought, I added: "I'll be going to Jubilee Fisheries rather than the one round the corner opposite Doughty's."

"Well, that's very thoughtful of your mother I must say. As a matter of fact, there's nothing I'd like better at the moment. I daren't go out for them myself, do you see; not until my cold's better."

He handed me a two-shilling piece from the shelf over the fireplace and I told him I'd call back with them later, and left.

As I approached the designated establishment I was pleased to notice that no one was queuing outside which was rather surprising for a Saturday dinnertime. I soon discovered the reason for it, however. A sign in the window boldly announced 'CLOSED FOR DECORATING PURPOSES - REOPENING NEXT SATURDAY'.

Now this situation left me with a dilemma. What I really wanted to do was to visit the one opposite Doughty's. I was curious to know why my mother and others never wanted me to go there. Could I get away with it without them knowing? After much thought I decided not to risk the consequences that would probably arise if my mother found out. With this in my mind I set off towards Craven Road. I was not surprised on my arrival that the queue was a fairly large one and just spilled out into the street. What I hadn't expected, however, was the fact that the two bringing up the rear would be known to me.

The smaller of the two ladies was the first to speak. "Is that the one, Edna?" she asked, pointing down the street. "Is that the shop?"

"Yes, that's the one all right, Phyllis, that's the off-licence I was telling you about and his fancy-piece lives right next door to it."

"Ee, it's a real shame is that, Edna. How long has it been going on for then?"

"Well, for the best part of a year, to my reckoning, and I'll tell you one thing, Phyllis. She's no better than she ought to be isn't that little madam. I'll tell you something else as well. If that so-called blonde hair on top of her head is real then I'm the Queen of Sheba."

"Oh, who's she then Edna?"

"I don't really know, Phyllis. I think she's someone in the bible, isn't she?"

"Oh, fancy! I didn't know that. So where is this here Sheba then? I suppose it must be thousands of miles away from here because I've never heard of it."

"No, you don't understand, Phyllis. It's just a figure of speech you see."

"What's a figure of speech then, Edna?"

"Well, it's quite simple, really. It's when you say something but it means something else."

"Well, it doesn't sound simple to me. Why would you say something if it meant something else? I mean, how would anybody know what you were trying to say? It would be like telling someone that you're going to the Town Hall when you're really going to the railway station."

"No, that's not the same thing at all, Phyllis. When I said that if her hair was real then I'm the Queen of Sheba, I could just have easily have said Florence Nightingale and it would have meant the same thing.

"Oh, now I have heard of her. She was a nurse wasn't she? But I can't understand why you'd want to be her. It's a wonder she didn't catch all sorts of diseases from all those soldiers she used to look after. No, I can't understand why you'd have liked to be her."

"I don't want to be like her," answered Edna, exasperatedly. "Like I said it's just a figure of speech. Oh, it doesn't matter. Look the queue's moving up."

Edna's companion hadn't quite finished, however. "Look, now that you know where she lives," she said, "Why don't you just go and knock on her door and confront her?"

"Because I wouldn't lower myself, Phyllis. I wouldn't lower myself."

"But you're letting her get away with it, Edna."

"I don't care, Phyllis. She's too far beneath me. I'm not going to give her the satisfaction of thinking that she's hurt me, but I'll tell you this Phyllis, and I don't care who hears me, I'll make sure that everyone knows just what a proper little madam she is."

The conversation dried up as we approached the front of the queue and I couldn't help wondering whether Edna's husband was really as bad as she made him out to be.

When I got home my mother told me to call round with Mr. Senior's fish and chips. When I got back Grandad Miller had just arrived and was taking off his coat.

"By heck, lass, they smell right grand," he announced, as the aroma of the fish and chips drifted towards him. "Are they from Jubilee Fisheries, then?"

"That's right," said my mother. "We always get them from there."

"Jubilee was closed," I got in quickly. "They're decorating and won't be open again until next Saturday. I had to go somewhere else for them."

Nell walked across and gave me a questioning look. The look on my mother's face, however, was almost bordering on panic. "You didn't go to---" she said.

"No, mam," I interrupted. "I went to the one in Craven Road. There was a very big queue, though." I detected expressions of relief all around.

As my father appeared from the other room after changing out of his work clothes, my mother began unwrapping the fish and chips and placing them onto the plates that had for several minutes been residing on the dining table ready to receive them. Nell, as always, took a great interest in the proceedings and immediately took up her accustomed mealtime position at the side of my father's chair while hoping that no one noticed.

"Minnie's coming over this weekend," announced my mother, addressing her remarks to my grandfather.

"You mean Minnie from Saltburn?" he responded.

"That's right. Well, just outside Saltburn. She'll be staying for a few days with Brenda."

"By heck, it's quite a while since I've seen her. It must be about six or seven years. She doesn't come over to Leeds much though, does she?"

"Well, it's certainly been quite a while, I know that."

I listened to the conversation with interest. I certainly didn't remember seeing my Auntie Minnie anywhere but at her own cottage on the coast.

"I don't suppose Mark will be coming over with her," observed my grandfather. "I can't see him being able to get much time off from the quarry at this time of year. What about those two young lasses of hers though, will they be coming?"

"You mean Janet and Barbara? As far as I know she'll be coming alone. They'll surely have to go to school, won't they?"

It occurred to me that it could be half term in the schools in the Saltburn area just like it was at ours, but my mother obviously hadn't thought of this possibility.

"How old are they now, then?" asked Grandad Miller. "They must be nearly grown-up."

"Well, not exactly. I think Janet's probably fifteen and Barbara thirteen, but I'm not too sure. Anyway, she's not likely to get to Brenda's before teatime and I reckon she'll be tired as well as hungry, so we're not likely to see her before tomorrow."

The conversation continued while everybody ate, including Nell from the hand of my father whenever my mother wasn't looking. As the meal drew to a close I glanced through the window and noticed that the sky had become very dark.

"I think you'd better put the light on, Neil," suggested my mother. It looks like we're in for a downpour."

A few minutes later her prediction proved to be correct. The rainfall was so heavy that I knew that any prospect of my going outside with Billy was looking remote. I also knew that if the conditions outside did not improve then my grandfather would be due for a severe soaking when he decided to return home, which would normally be in mid afternoon, as I knew he always liked to be back in time for the football scores on Sports Report on the wireless. Whether he walked to the tram stop in Meanwood Road or to the bus stop in Woodhouse Street the result would undoubtedly be the same. As the afternoon wore on, and the weather grew worse, my mother reached the same conclusion.

"You can't be going home in this weather, dad," she decided, "Especially after you've not been out of hospital for more than a few months. You'll catch your death if I let you go home in these conditions."

"Aye, lass, I suppose there's something in what you say. I can always listen to the football scores here. I'll stay the night then if it's not too much trouble."

I was pleased that he was staying over. Grandad Miller's conversation was never boring. It was the next best thing if I was unable to go outside with Billy. With my brother Tim being at army camp my grandfather would be occupying the other single bed in my bedroom. As my mother had expected we saw no sign of my Auntie Minnie during the remainder of the day so we just had to assume that she had arrived safely. I was also unaware of whether her two troublesome daughters had arrived with her.

It was rather crowded around the fireplace for the remainder of that dismal afternoon. Grandad Miller, much to my disappointment, decided to take a nap in the chair usually occupied by my father who, unable to repose on his favourite piece of furniture, pulled one of the dining table chairs nearer to the fire and began to read the Daily Herald while Nell and I competed for possession of the clip rug, and eventually, after I had opened my current copy of the Knockout comic, decided to share it between us. She then put her head on her paws and immediately fell asleep. Things did not liven up until later that evening after we had all finished our tea. The rain had stopped falling but it was obviously very cold and I did not really fancy venturing outside, at least not before my stomach would inevitably compel me to make a trip to the lavatory yard. I decided to pop upstairs and make the evening's entry in the chronicle while Grandad Miller and my father were listening to 'Henry Hall's Guest Night' on the wireless and my mother was doing the washing-up. After about ten minutes I heard the signature tune that always signified the end of the programme and it was followed by the sound of footsteps coming up the stairs. My grandfather entered the room as I was perusing some earlier entries in the book.

"Thought I'd just pop up and make sure I've still got a pair of pyjamas here," he volunteered. "I must say you seem very interested in yon book."

"It's a chronicle," I informed him. "I've been recording all the things I've been doing during this year."

"A chronicle, eh; that seems a rather fancy title to me. Why not just call it a diary?"

"Well, Mr, Rawcliffe took us for a history lesson at the back end of last year and it was all about the Anglo-Saxons and how some of the monks in the monastery started this book called the Anglo-Saxon Chronicle. They recorded all the events that had happened in Britain ever since the Romans left. I wanted to do something similar though there are no battles in it of course or anything like that. I decided not to mention Tucker Lane's epic conflict with Krusher Kershaw. Anyway, I think it's a bit more important than an ordinary diary."

"Aye lad, I suppose you might be right at that. So what's that red thing sticking out of the page then? Is it supposed to be a bookmark, or what?"

I blushed and hoped my grandfather hadn't noticed.

"You've just brought something back to me lad," he said, saving me from making an embarrassing answer to his question, "A childhood memory so to speak." He sat down on the bed. "Did I ever tell you about a mate of mine called Harry Crabtree?"

"Yes, grandad."

"Well he was my best friend around the turn of the century and we were both about the same age as you are now."

I put the book down and gave him my full attention.

"Well, one day," he began, "Harry told me that he'd just started to do something similar, although he didn't give it a fancy name or anything, he just called it his notebook. Anyway, he started to record all the various escapades we'd been up to and I think it's fair to say that we could never be described as angels, though we never did anything that was really nasty. We did, however, stray a bit at times from what my parents would have described as acceptable behaviour. Our main victim was a woman who lived in our street who was known to all the local kids as Old Ma Tubshaw. She was a worthy recipient for any prank we chose to play as she must have been the meanest woman in our locality. It wasn't just the kids who she was mean to, for she seemed to offend most of the adults in the area as well with her vindictive spite."

My grandfather had mentioned this woman before when he told me how he and his mate had shoved frogs through her letterbox on Mischievous Night. This had provided Billy and me with the idea to engage in a similar escapade just before Bonfire Night, though it had not provided the kind of result we had been hoping for.

"Anyway," he went on, "Every so often Harry used to show me the entries he'd made and I told him that, because of some of the things he'd written in it, if his parents or any of the neighbours saw it he'd be in real trouble. He didn't take any notice, however, and one day he took it to school with him as he thought it would be amusing to show it to some of the lads and lasses in our class. Unfortunately, it was spotted by the teacher who made him come to the front of the class and hand it over for him to scrutinise. As some of the remarks he'd made were about this same teacher, you don't have to be very clever to work out what the result was. The book was confiscated and Harry was given several strokes of the cane. The embarrassment he felt at having his trousers round his ankles in full view of the entire class was worse than any pain he might have felt for his misdemeanours. That was the end of Harry's notebook and, as far as I know, he never attempted to do anything like it again. So, I don't know what you've been putting in this chronicle of yours, but whatever it is if it contains anything that you might not want others to see you'd best guard it with your life. By the way, that thing you're using as a bookmark looks suspiciously like a girl's ribbon to me. Is that why you were blushing earlier?"

I didn't answer him despite feeling rather uncomfortable and Grandad Miller, having satisfied himself that he had something suitable to sleep in, didn't pursue the question but made his way back downstairs while leaving me to stare at the book. The thought of anyone else getting their hands on it and what the consequences might be if they did had never occurred to me. I contemplated the various entries I had made and I knew that, with the possible exception of Billy, I would much prefer it if the contents of the Woodhouse Chronicle remained secret.

CHAPTER EIGHTEEN

We could both see immediately that Nicky wasn't very happy. Billy and I had called on him to see if he fancied joining us on Woodhouse Ridge as, surprisingly, the weather on this Sunday morning, was a big improvement on the previous day's heavy rain. Grandad Miller would be staying for dinner before catching the tram to take him to the corn Exchange, followed by another to take him home to Harehills. My mother had insisted that if I went out I had to promise to be back by twelve o'clock.

"You know how I told you that I had to go with my mother to see my Auntie Alice at Crossgates," said Nicky, "Well, because of the heavy rain we didn't go. I was glad at first, but then she told me that we would have to go today instead, before saying something that made it even worse."

We both listened intently, wondering what he was going to tell us that could make it any worse than having to visit a relative instead of playing with your friends out on the ridge.

"She told me that it was my cousin Wendy's birthday and that she was having a party. I was made to go last year and there were about seven or eight girls and only one boy. That was my cousin Jack, who was only four years old."

"Errgh!" said Billy. "That's awful. It'll be all girly games that you'll be playing."

"I know, but it's worse still because when I give her her birthday present my mam says that I have to kiss her on the cheek at the same time."

"I think I'm going to be sick," said Billy, his face a picture of disgust. "Isn't there any way you can get out of it?"

"Nothing that I can think of. The trouble is my mam keeps telling me that I'll enjoy it, but I think the only reason she didn't mention yesterday that it was Wendy's birthday was because deep down she knew that I'd hate it. Why couldn't she have had the party yesterday like she was supposed to, instead of cancelling it because of the weather? The only difference is that we'll be going this morning instead of this afternoon, so I should be back by teatime."

"How old is Wendy?" I asked him.

"She's nine, just a year younger than me."

"Crikey, that makes it worse. It wouldn't be so bad if she was a few years younger."

"I could ask my mam if you could come with me," he suggested, hopefully.

"Don't be daft," answered Billy on behalf of both of us. "There's no way you'd get us going to a birthday party for girls."

Nicky looked a picture of despair. His face couldn't have portrayed a more miserable expression if he had been found guilty of murder in a court of law and the judge had just donned his black cap to indicate a hanging sentence. I would have liked to have found some way to get him out of the intolerable situation he found himself in but I knew there wasn't one that would work.

"We'll see you tomorrow then Nicky," said Billy "And you can tell us all about it."

Before letting us go on our way he made us promise that we would not mention anything of his plight to any of the lads at school.

We had decided to spend some time by the beck at the bottom of the ridge. When we got down there the water was very high from the previous day's rain, though it had not yet burst its banks. This particular morning though was quite sunny and the fast-flowing water was crystal clear. We took off our shoes and socks and began to wade through it, searching the bottom for anything that looked interesting while paying particular attention to the avoidance of any sharp objects that might cause an injury. The beck was teeming with life that morning and we were beginning to wish that we had brought our fishing nets. It wasn't long, however, before my feet were sufficiently cold for me to suggest to Billy that we climb back onto the bank.

"I wish we had a towel with us," I said. "It's going to take ages for my feet to dry out enough for me to put my socks back on."

"I know what you mean," he replied, "But there's nothing round here to dry them on, is there? Even the grass is soaking wet."

All we could do was to stand with our backs to the tree and hope the sun shining on them might do the trick, but it held very little power. As we were contemplating how long we might have to stand there before we were able to put on the remainder of our clothing our peace was suddenly disturbed when a huge, shaggy dog came charging down the hill and jumped straight into the beck, sending spurts of water in every direction. It was no longer our feet that were wet it was virtually every part of our body. Not satisfied with the carnage that it had already caused it clambered back onto the bank and vigorously shook itself immediately in front of us. Our protestations at this treatment were to no avail as the dog sat down and stared at us in a playful manner as if to say 'Didn't you like that?'. We looked up the hill in an attempt to find its owner but there was no one in sight.

Deciding that we were the perfect recipients for its sense of fun, it suddenly took a fancy to one of Billy's shoes and ran off with it. Pausing after a few yards, it dropped its newly-acquired toy on the grass, sat down and looked at us expectantly. Billy had immediately charged after it, but just as he bent down to retrieve his footwear, the dog picked it up again and ran towards me. I was soaking wet and in no mood to encourage its playful behaviour. Before it had a chance to involve me in its mischievous activities I hurriedly picked up my own shoes and socks and held them close to my chest as I huddled closer to the tree. Billy came racing over. The dog suddenly dropped its prized possession and Billy retrieved it. As he was examining it for signs of damage, our newly-found, but on this particular occasion unwelcome, friend decided to attack one of his socks instead, shaking it vigorously and inviting him to join in the fun. He grabbed hold of the other end and the two of them began, what to me, was a hilarious tug-of-war. Billy won the contest but only because his opponent deliberately let go of its trophy and in so doing sent my closest friend hurtling backwards until he lay prostrate on his back in the mud close to the bank of the stream. I just couldn't stop laughing although Billy, at first, refused to see the funny side. Eventually, however, the two of us were having a fit of hysterics.

At that moment a middle-aged lady hurried down the slope, calling after the dog. It came over to her still wagging its tail and, with a little perseverance, she managed to get it onto a lead.

"I'm really very sorry," she said, as she walked over to us as Billy was just getting back onto his feet. "She seems so boisterous this morning. I hope she hasn't done any damage."

"No, I don't think so, Mrs.," I said as soon as we had stopped laughing, hopefully on Billy's behalf as well as my own.

"You're both soaking wet," she observed. "Look, my house is only five minutes away. Why don't you come with me? The least I can do is to let you dry yourselves in front of a warm fire before you go on your way."

I looked at Billy. I don't think either of us wanted to go home in the dishevelled state we were in so we agreed to accompany her.

As we moved up the slope, the dog became less fussy as if it too was conscious of the cold water that was seeping into its skin and was looking forward to the warmth of its home. When we entered the lady's house she quickly disappeared into what I assumed was a bedroom and returned with a couple of fleecy blankets.

"What time is it, please?" I asked, being very much aware that I had promised to be back by twelve o'clock.

"It's just ten minute to eleven," she answered, "Look there's a clock on the mantelpiece."

"Right then, lads," she said. "If you take off your outer clothing I'll pop it all into the other room to dry. I've got a fire in there as well today. While you're getting ready I'll go into the kitchen and bring you a hot mug of cocoa. That should warm you up in no time."

Billy and I looked across at one another. Neither of us fancied sitting around in our underwear, but neither did we relish the thought of returning home in the state we were in. We quickly divested ourselves of our jacket, pullover and shirt and wrapped the blanket around us as we removed our trousers. No sooner had we finished than our hostess returned with two steaming mugs of cocoa.

"There you are boys," she exclaimed, before gathering up our discarded clothing, "Get yourselves stuck into those. You'll be warmed through in no time. I've put Lassie, that's the dog, in the spare room at the back of the house. I'll rub her down in a minute. She gets so overexcited sometimes. I'm really sorry that she got you into such a state, but in her mind she was only trying to be friendly. I'm Mrs. Bradshaw by the way."

"Do you live here all by yourself?" asked Billy"

"Well, just me and Lassie, but my niece usually calls on a Sunday morning. She's usually here by this time so I guess she's unable to make it today."

We both had to admit that the cocoa was delicious and I was beginning to feel much more comfortable. I think it took Billy a while longer as he was in a worse state than I was. My only concern was that I knew I would have to leave the house by quarter to twelve in order to fulfil the promise I made to my mother. I just hoped that I would look a little more presentable when I left.

"Well, I guess I spoke too soon," announced Mrs. Bradshaw. My niece is just walking along the street now."

Billy and I looked nervously at each other, aware that each of us was wearing very little beneath the blanket.

"Come on in, love," said our hostess.

"Thanks, Auntie Kath," offered Mrs. Bradshaw's niece. "I'm sorry I'm a bit late this morning."

Our nervous expressions turned to ones of horror as we gazed at the newcomer, while the expression on her face couldn't have been more different.

"What are you two doing at my auntie's?" asked Mary Pearson.

Neither of us could manage to say anything and it was left to the lady of the house to provide the explanation.

"Their clothes are drying in front of the fire in the other room. I'll just go and put the kettle on for you love."

"There's no real hurry, Auntie Kath," she said, beaming, "I'll just sit and talk to these two lads for a while."

Our situation could not have been worse. There we were sitting in our underwear with nothing but a blanket to cover us with Mary Pearson sitting opposite providing an effective barrier between us and our trousers.

"It's very warm in front of this fire," she observed. "Why don't you take those blankets off for a while? I bet you'd be a lot more comfortable."

"Not likely," responded Billy, wrapping the blanket more tightly around him.

I looked at the clock on the mantelpiece. It was showing twenty-five minutes past eleven. I knew that I ought to be heading home very shortly.

"There's nothing wrong with sitting in your underpants," said our tormentor, not wanting to give up. "Anyway, I've seen both of you in them before, so I don't know what you're so embarrassed about. I've seen more than that anyway."

This was getting really intolerable but fortunately Mrs. Bradshaw chose that moment to re-enter the room, bearing a cup of cocoa for her niece.

"I'll have to be going soon," I said, knowing that my face was burning, though not from the close proximity of the fire. "I have to be home for dinner by twelve o'clock."

"Well, I think you're clothes are probably dry enough now, though I'm afraid yours are still very dirty from when Lassie knocked you onto the muddy bank," she said, addressing the latter remarks to Billy. "You can both go into the other room and put them back on, if you like."

We needed no further prompting. Clutching the blankets tightly we headed towards the door to the adjoining room.

"I'll show you where they are," said Mary Pearson, grasping the opportunity to try to inflict further embarrassment on us.

"No, you stay where you are, Mary and finish your cocoa, I'll show them."

She pointed out the clothes drying on a clothes horse. "You can put them on while I go into the kitchen."

Relieved that we hadn't been followed into the room we hurriedly divested ourselves of the blankets and put on our trousers.

"It's a good job she made her stay in the other room," observed Billy. "I thought she was never going to leave us."

However, as we finished dressing by putting our jackets back on the sound of giggling could be heard from the open doorway.

"I'm never going to tell anybody about this, Billy," I said, "And you'd better not say anything about it either."

"You've no need to worry, I'm not telling anybody."

We thanked Mrs. Bradshaw when she came back downstairs, ignored Mary Pearson, who was still giggling, and almost ran out of the house.

"We were really unlucky there, Billy," I said, as we hurried home. "Why did it have to be her who was the woman's niece?"

I managed to get back with five minutes to spare, and was keen to put the events of the morning to the back of my mind.

After we had all finished eating Grandad Miller left for home and my mother told me that Auntie Minnie had arrived from Saltburn but she had left her two daughters behind. This was a relief to me as they could both be quite mischievous at times. I spent most of the afternoon listening to the wireless as two of my favourite programmes were on. One was a comedy called 'Much Binding In The Marsh' and the other was a western adventure called 'Riders Of The Range' which featured a cowboy called Jeff Arnold. I went round to see Billy again though after they had finished.

"Do you want to come out again?" I asked him after he had answered my knock.

"I wonder if Nicky's back yet," he replied. "I want to know how he got on at the party with all those girls. I don't think I can wait until tomorrow."

"Right, then, let's go see."

As we walked along the road we made a pact not to mention our unfortunate ordeal at Mrs. Bradshaw's while at the same time hoping that Nicky could be persuaded to reveal the happenings at the girly party to which he had been invited. He answered the knock himself and stepped outside.

"How did you get on at the party?" asked Billy, eagerly.

"I don't want to talk about it," said Nicky, looking very unhappy.

"Why was it that bad?" I asked him.

Nicky's reluctance to speak gave way, as he began to unburden himself with the despair he was obviously feeling. "It was much worse than I expected," he began. "To begin with my Cousin Jack, the only other boy that was supposed to be there, couldn't go because he had a cold and there weren't eight girls there this year there were nine and I had to sit with them while all the adults had there meals first. It was all girly talk and there was nowhere I could go to get away from it. When it was our turn to eat it was exactly the same. After dinner we played 'Pass the Parcel' and I won a sewing bag."

Both Billy and I burst into unsympathetic laughter at this humiliating experience.

"You'd better not tell anybody about this or I'll never speak to you again," he said indignantly.

We both promised and, as much as we would have enjoyed allowing the other kids at school to join in the merriment, we decided to keep that promise as we knew it would be so easy for him to get his own back.

"What happened then?" I urged him.

"Well, the girls decided they would play skipping games where you had to skip in rhythm while they were chanting. My mother suggested that I should show willing and join in and they all laughed because I couldn't do any of them. When someone got the doll's house out

I decided I'd had enough and I went outside and sat on the doorstep in the yard. My mother must have realised how miserable I was as shortly after she made her excuses for leaving and we came home."

I began to feel really sorry for him and I realised that the humiliation that Billy and I had suffered during our encounter with Mary Pearson was as nothing compared to what Nicky had been subjected to. All in all, however, not one of us could possibly have said that it had been a dull day.

CHAPTER NINETEEN

The following morning, shortly after I had finished breakfast, there was a knock on the door. I opened it to find Nicky standing there.

"Hi," he greeted, "Are you coming out? I want to do something interesting so that I can forget all about yesterday. Anyway, it's not a bad day today. The sun's out."

"Is it all right if I go out with Nicky, mam?" I shouted as I knew she was upstairs making the beds.

"Yes, but make sure you're back home in time for dinner," she responded.

"Let's call and see if Billy's coming," I said, while I was putting on my jacket.

"I was just going to say that," replied my companion.

Billy needed no prompting whatsoever and we decided to go back onto the ridge as I think all three of us were anxious to wipe out our memories of the previous day, though neither Billy or I had any intention of telling Nicky of our own humiliating experience and as we set off for our intended destination it was clear from the conversation between us that the events of the previous day were a taboo subject.

"Has your Auntie Minnie arrived then?" asked Billy.

"Yes, but I haven't seen her yet."

"What's she like?" inquired Nicky. "I've never heard you mention her before."

"Yes, you have. I've told you that she comes from near Saltburn and we sometimes go there for a holiday. I've never known her to come to Leeds before, but my mam said that the last time she came was when I was very small."

"Oh, is that her? I didn't know that was her name, though."

"Anyway, she's very fussy and she says daft things like 'Ee, I feel right grand' or 'we'll be righty just nowie' and sometimes she talks back to the wireless when the news is on."

"What about those two girls you told me about?" asked Billy. "You said you didn't like them very much. Have they come as well?"

"You mean Janet and Barbara. No, they've both stayed at home with my Uncle Mark. I didn't say I didn't like them. Most of the time they're all right to say they're girls, but they keep doing mischievous things and it gets me embarrassed sometimes."

We left the road at the entrance to the ridge, walked down the steps and began to make our way along the top path.

"We've got a game on Saturday," I said. "I want to be on the winning side this time. We haven't got all that many games left, have we?"

"No," said Nicky, "And I think it's against a school in Headingley. So that would be a good one to win, what with Leeds playing there."

"The problem is," announced Billy, "That we always seem to go behind in the first few minutes and it puts everybody off. If we could be the first to score for once then we might have a better chance."

The fact that the sun was shining and that the temperature was about as warm as you could expect in late February lightened our mood and we eagerly left the top path and made our way onto what the local lads had always referred to as the Indian War Path. It was really nothing more than a narrow track cutting across the steep bank of the ridge while meandering in a less boring fashion than the more formal paths above and below it. We suddenly broke into a run in a carefree fashion, content to sample the freedom to do just the sort of things that appealed to ten and eleven year old boys in such an enchanting location with which they were most familiar.

We eventually found ourselves at the old bandstand. The seats on the banking from the time long ago when brass bands had performed on the site had long since disappeared, but there was a ghostly atmosphere to the place which I feel we all experienced as we clambered onto it. We just stood for a while enjoying the stillness and contemplating the Destructor chimney which rose majestically from its base on the far side of Meanwood Road. It belonged to the Council Refuse Department and was said to be the tallest structure in Leeds.

"I wonder what it used to be like," observed Billy. "I mean, I bet you'd be able to hear the band playing from the top of Sugarwell Hill."

"My dad says that they only used to play on a Sunday," I volunteered, "But that was when he was a lad. It was always well attended though as nearly everyone used to go either to the ridge or onto the moor after church."

"Not everybody goes to church these days," said Nicky. "I haven't been for ages." He paused for a while.

"Do you think that'll stop me going to Heaven?" he added.

"I think it's more about doing good things," I said, hopefully, as I didn't go to church either.

Billy continued to stare at the Destructor.

"What are you thinking, Billy?" I asked him as he looked so intense.

"I was just thinking how much I could see if I was sitting on top of it."

"It's not something I'd like to do," I said.

"Me, neither," added Nicky. "Even if you somehow managed to get up there, you'd never get back down again."

"I think I'd be all right if there was a helicopter with a rope ladder waiting to pick me up," said Billy, enthusiastically.

We left the bandstand and wandered down towards the beck, secure in the knowledge that yesterday's unfortunate turn of events was not likely to be repeated. There were a couple of other lads of about our age who were playing there. We didn't know either of them but we hung around together for about half an hour before going deeper into Batty's Wood, which was located at the far end of the ridge. The sun was still shining and I was thoroughly enjoying the morning's activities. We climbed up the banking and decided to see who could climb highest in the Monkey Tree. On this occasion, Billy proved to be the winner. Eventually, after spending a short while playing in Death Valley and on Table Top we began to feel the first pangs of hunger and, deciding that it was time to make our way home, headed back along the topmost path.

"Did you notice anything peculiar about the Old Man's Shelter?" asked Billy as we had just hurried past the construction in question.

"No," I said.

"Why, what's odd about it?" asked Nicky.

"There was an old man in it, that's what."

"But that's why it's called an old man's shelter, Billy," I said. It's for old men to go shelter in."

Billy persisted. "Tell me, when was the last time you saw an old man in it."

I thought about what he said and the numerous occasions that I'd walked past but I had to admit that I couldn't recall ever seeing an old man in there before. It was nearly always empty, but occasionally there might be some kids playing inside and on a couple of occasions I remembered witnessing a young couple kissing each other.

"Come to think of it, Billy, you're right. I don't think I have ever seen an old man in the shelter. What about you, Nicky?"

"No, I don't think I have either, but I don't usually bother looking. I just walk straight past."

"Anyway," continued Billy, "The thing about this old man is that he looked really upset. Perhaps he might be poorly. Maybe we should walk back and find out."

"I've got to get back home for dinner soon," I told him, but it shouldn't take more than a few minutes, should it?"

"Yes, let's go find out what's the matter with him," agreed Nicky.

We turned around and walked back to the shelter and I realised immediately that my assessment of the situation was the same as Billy's. I guessed that the man was probably in his sixties and his countenance suggested a look of despair.

"Are you all right, mister?" asked Billy.

"Not really son," he replied, "I'm suffering inside you see. I have been for a long time, but I reckon I'm just about at the end of my tether now. I don't think I can take much more of it."

"Why, what's the matter?" I asked him.

"Well, you see, I'm Walter Zimmerman."

My face, and those of my companions, showed the same blank look.

"You don't get it, do you," said the old man, "Walter Zimmerman?"

Our faces continued to show the same emotion.

"Well it's all my mother's fault really and she even admitted to me that she was responsible. Anyway, she's passed on now."

He was obviously very distressed, but none of us had a clue what was making him that way.

"You see," he went on, "Back in Victorian times when my mother was nineteen years old, and a very handsome woman she was too by all accounts, she was engaged to a fine young chap called John Anderson. Everything was going along fine as both his parents and my mother's parents were in favour of the match. The date for the wedding had been fixed and the banns were about to be read in church when one day, about two weeks before the big occasion they had an almighty row. My mother, you see, was beginning to have second thoughts as she had been seeing another suitor. Before she could properly make up her mind, however, she discovered that someone had seen them together and had passed on the information to the man who was about to be her husband. The result was that the wedding was called off. The prospective bride ran off with his rival and they were secretly married. His name was Sam Zimmerman. So there you are you see. That's why I've been so miserable for most of my life."

"But why should all that make you feel so miserable?" asked Nicky, a question that also puzzled both Billy and me.

"Do you still not see?" he gasped. "I'm a victim of alphabeticalorderism. I have been all my life and it's totally unfair, If my mother hadn't changed her mind I'd have been called Walter Anderson instead of Walter Zimmerman. I first became aware of my unfortunate circumstances when I went to school. I used to listen to the teacher calling out the register and, despite concentrating really hard, by the time she got to my name right at the end I'd usually got bored and begun to fidget. One day a boy arrived at my school with the same surname as me. I knew that his first name was William and I had worked out that, alphabetically, Walter came before William. So I listened intently when the register was called out and when she came to the second last name on the list I was just ready to shout out 'Here, Miss' when she suddenly called out Bill Zimmerman, so I had lost out again. Sometimes I missed hearing my name altogether which always made her angry. Even after I joined the army I had to wait until the end of Roll Call before my name was called out and the sergeant that we had was really strict. It also meant that I had to stand to attention longer than anyone else before being dismissed. Yet if anyone was made to volunteer for a particularly nasty job, he always seemed to select the person whose name was at the bottom. It's been like this for as long as I can remember. Did you know that Pension Books and Ration Books were handed out in alphabetical order? I had to wait ages to get mine.

"Haven't you got used to it now, though?" enquired Billy.

"You never get used to it. You'd feel the same way if your name was Zimmerman. Just recently my local Working Men's Club organised a free trip to Bridlington by bus, as they had quite a bit of money left over from the yearly subscriptions. Twenty-seven people put their names down for the trip, but the coach had only twenty-six seats so the club steward decided to take the first twenty-six names in alphabetical order. Now, I was really looking forward to going to Bridlington as I hadn't been there for quite a few years, and all he said to me was that it was the only fair way of doing it as it was oversubscribed. Fair? What on earth was fair about it? That's what I wanted to know. It didn't escape my notice though that the steward's surname was Bartlett, so he wouldn't have had a clue what was fair and what wasn't, would he?"

"Can't you change your name to something else?" I suggested. "I've heard of people doing that."

"I wish I could, but it has to be done officially, you see, through the proper channels, otherwise nobody would take any notice of it. Unfortunately, it's quite an expensive procedure and all I have to live on is my pension. I wrote to Winston Churchill once when he was Prime Minister to ask if he could arrange it so that everything was in alphabetical order when the year ended in an odd number and reverse alphabetical order when the year ended in an even number. That way everyone would get a chance and those people whose surnames were in the middle would stay in the middle, so they wouldn't be affected. I waited until just after the war had finished though, because I knew he'd be too busy to do anything about it otherwise."

"What did he say?" enquired Billy. Did you get a letter from him?"

"No lad I never did. At first I thought it was because there had been an election and that he had probably passed it on to the new occupant of 10 Downing Street, but then the penny dropped."

"What do you mean?" asked Nicky.

"Well, the new Prime Minister was called Mr. Atlee, so changing things wouldn't have been in his best interests would it? It was at that point that the injustice of it all really started to get to me. You see even Mr. Churchill's name began with a 'C'. I started to check on all the previous Prime Ministers and it's fair to say that I wasn't in the least surprised at what I discovered. Before Churchill it was Chamberlain and before him, Baldwin. When I looked up the one before him I thought I'd made a breakthrough as his name was McDonald, but when I ran through the alphabet I found out that the letter 'M' is the thirteenth in the alphabet and therefore just makes it into the first half. Before that there was Lloyd-George, Asquith and Campbell-Bannerman and if you go back into late Victorian times they seemed to be dominated by Gladstone and Disraeli. So, as you can see, anyone with a surname beginning with a letter from the second half of the alphabet barely got a look in.

Having failed to cheer up our adopted patient I realised that if we didn't get a move on I would be in trouble when I got home for being late.

"We'll have to be going now, Mr. Zimmerman," I told him.

"Well then lads, best be off with you then. I know there's really nothing you can do to help me, but thank you for being good listeners, anyway. I'll have to try to sort it out by myself."

We left him sitting there and went on our way.

"It's a pity he can't change his name." I said, as we headed along the path towards home. "He said it was too expensive, didn't he? I wonder how much it costs."

"I don't see why he should have to pay, anyway," decided Billy. "It's his name, isn't it? Why can't he just announce to everybody that he's decided to change it to something else? I don't think it's anything to do with any other person, what he wants to be called."

"Well, let's say he went ahead and did it," I said. "It would take ages for him to get round everybody he knows and tell them that he wants to be called by another name. I mean, it's no good going into the pub one night and just telling everybody that he isn't Walter Zimmermman any more. They'd all probably think he was joking and not take any notice."

"I know what," said Billy, excitedly, "He could make an announcement in the Yorkshire Evening Post or the Yorkshire Evening News. That way a lot more would find about it. Think how many people read the newspapers."

"Yes, but I would imagine that would probably be too expensive as well," I said, hoping I hadn't dented his enthusiasm.

As the three of us climbed the steps that led off the ridge and onto the road I couldn't help noticing that Nicky had gone very quiet and his expression suggested that his mind was somewhere else.

"What's the matter, Nicky?" I asked him. "You haven't spoken for ages."

"I was just thinking," he said. "My name's Whitehead, isn't it? And that's nearly as bad as Zimmerman. Am I going to be like him when I get old? I never thought much about it before, but now that I have I realise that I always have to wait ages at school when they're calling out the register just like he did. The only name called after mine is Cathy Williams, so that means that I'm the last boy. It's all right for you. You're name starts with a 'C' so you're one of the first. I wish we'd never gone past the Old Man's Shelter now."

We both did our best to console him. Don't worry, Nicky," said Billy. "I bet you'll have forgotten all about it by tomorrow."

"If you weren't bothered about it before," I added, "Then why worry about it now?"

As he entered his house Billy and I continued along the street.

"He still looks like he needs cheering up," I said to my remaining companion.

Before he had time to make any comment a plump lady with a very pleasing smile on her face chose that moment to step out of my Auntie Brenda's house. Walking over to him she put her arms around him, while lifting him off his feet at the same time, and buried his face in her ample bosom.

"You've grown a lot, young Neil," she said as she attempted to squeeze the life out of him. "I almost didn't recognise you."

"Hello, Auntie Minnie," I managed to stumble out while laughing uncontrollably.

A look of surprise covered my aunt's face as she realised her mistake. "Who's this then?" She asked as she allowed my best friend to slip from her grasp onto the floor.

"That's Billy Mathieson," I informed her. "He lives two doors away."

I could see that Billy was gasping for breath.

"Oh, well," she said, "You've got to bear in mind that it's a long time since I saw you. You were much smaller then. Anyway, we'll be righty just nowie, eh."

She then proceeded to give me the same treatment that my closest friend had just endured.

"I was just calling round to have a word with your mother," she said, and as she entered the house Nell began to bark furiously, being unable to identify the intruder. I took it for granted that my canine friend would be spared the indignity that Billy and I had just suffered.

"I could hardly breathe in there," he complained, "And my feet weren't even touching the ground. If that's your Auntie Minnie I think I'll stay away from her. She's so strong I bet she could have been an all-in wrestler."

"She took me by surprise as well. I think she's even bigger than she was the last time I saw her."

I found out later that day that my aunt had invited us all to her cottage on the coast sometime during the summer. I wasn't told exactly when, but I assumed, if it was for a full week, then it would almost certainly have to be the first week in August when my father, as well as most of the manual workers in the area, had their paid holiday. I noted the fact when I made my daily entry in the Chronicle, but most of what I wrote concerned our rather odd encounter with Mr. Walter Zimmerman.

CHAPTER TWENTY

"You lads, down there, you'll have to do something to help me." We both recognised the voice, but it seemed to be coming from above us. We looked up just in time for a wet cloth to land neatly onto Billy's upturned face. I just couldn't stop myself from laughing at his misfortune as he removed the offending article that had assaulted him amid a lot of coughing and spluttering. The sight that met our eyes was Mrs Wormley's ample posterior which, bring directly above us, was large enough to hide all her other endearing features.

"I didn't intend to drop the cloth lads," she declared, "But at least it got your attention."

It was obvious that she was attempting to wash her bedroom window by perching on the outside ledge with the window pressed firmly down onto her thighs to prevent her from falling.

"What's wrong, Mrs. Wormley?" I managed to say after battling hard to control my laughter. "Are you stuck?"

"You can say that again, lad. I've been up here for about half an hour and I can't shove the window back up. Will you push the door open and come up and give me a hand?"

What our neighbour had been doing was nothing more than the acceptable way in our locality for the lady of the house to clean the outsides of her windows. The official window cleaner was Mr. Morris, but he only came round once a fortnight and sometimes he failed to turn up altogether. It is fair to say that almost every housewife was very house-proud. Despite the working-class nature of our local community it was a sense of pride for each one to ensure that the house was spotlessly clean. Failure to perform this household chore would inevitably lead to being labelled as 'No better than she ought to be' by her contemporaries.

This was the final day of the short break from school and Billy and I had been wondering what we could do to make it an exciting one. We hadn't realised that all that was needed was to walk a few yards down the street.

I attempted to open her door. Three attempts produced three failures before I abandoned the task.

"I can't open it," I shouted up. "It must be locked."

"It can't be," she said. "Oh, just a minute, I did lock it. I was going to go back to bed for an hour after I'd finished doing the windows."

As the only part of Mrs. Wormley that was visible to us was incapable of showing any noticeable sign of emotion, we could only wonder at the distress she must be feeling.

Mr. Senior chose that moment to step outside and walk towards us. "What's going on?" he said. "I was just listening to the wireless, do you see, but I could hear all that shouting over the sound of it."

He suddenly realised what the problem was before we could answer him.

"By heck, lass," he said in astonishment, "Are you stuck then?" It occurred to me that Mrs. Wormley was probably the one person in the street who could probably be identified from the only part of her body that was in view.

"Of course I'm stuck," she shouted down. "I've been like this for more than half an hour. I can't push the window back up and the door's locked so nobody's able to get in"

"Well, I reckon you've landed yourself in a right pickle there and no mistake. I don't think I'd like to find myself in that predicament," said her neighbour sympathetically. "I bet you're feeling really cold as well. It's to be hoped it doesn't start raining or you're liable to freeze to death. It reminds me of the time when I was in the merchant navy. We were cruising off the coast of Newfoundland up near the Arctic ocean."

He went on to describe the freezing conditions that existed aboard his ship and how things got extremely worse when a blizzard came up.

"You'll have to get a ladder," shouted Mrs. Wormley, having decided that Mr. Senior's comforting words were not having the desired effect. "There's no other way, is there?"

"I haven't got a ladder, admitted Mr. Senior. Never had a need for one, do you see?"

"My legs are starting to go numb now," she complained. "Somebody will have to do something soon or I'll never be able to walk on 'em again. Don't you know anybody who's got a ladder?"

By this time most of the inhabitants of Cross Speedwell Street were witnessing the drama. For the housewives in particular it was proving to be a welcome break from the routine of their household chores. My mother, though, was absent as she had gone to visit my Grandma Cawson who lived next to the nursery near the Old Carr Sunday School. She called there sometimes to make sure that she was feeling well and to see if she needed any shopping bringing in. I could hear Nell, however, barking furiously. I knew that she hated being left out of anything exciting that might be going on, though it was difficult to understand what useful input she might be able to make to this particular incident.

"What about that builder's yard in Craven Road?" suggested Billy's mother. They should have a ladder."

"Good idea," said Billy. "Come on, Neil; let's go see if we can borrow one."

"Just a minute," said Mr. Senior, "I've been thinking, do you see? They're not likely to hand over a ladder to two young lads just like that, are they? They'd probably think you were joking. Anyway, if they did lend you one I don't think you'd be able to carry it back, would you?"

"Well, we might as well go to find out. We might be able to persuade one of the men there to come back with us."

"Wow!" said Nicky Whitehead, who had just raced along the street to join us. "I could hear all the commotion. I just had to find out what was going on. How long has she been stuck up there?"

"Well over half an hour," I informed him. "She can't push the window back up and the door's locked."

"We need a ladder then," suggested Nicky.

"We know that," said Billy. "We were just talking about getting one when you arrived. We're going to the builder's yard in Craven Road to see if we can get someone to come round with one. You can come with us if you like."

"You'd better hurry then," shouted Mrs. Wormley, because my bladder's beginning to complain."

At this revelation the scene could be described as being very similar to the parting of the Red Sea during the Israelites' escape from Egypt as everyone in the vantage point immediately below the lady in distress took two paces to the side.

The three of us ran down the ginnel opposite the Electra and onto Craven Road. However, when we arrived at the yard which we had hoped might provide a solution to the problem we faced it was to find the gate securely locked with no sign of anyone inside. We stood there for a few minutes, shouting to make sure the place was entirely empty, before realising that there was nothing more to do but to retrace our steps. When we returned to the scene of our neighbour's misfortune there seemed to be even more people gathered there than before, but it soon became obvious that no one had come up with any other plan to bring the unfortunate occurrence to a successful conclusion. It did nothing at all to improve the situation when we announced that the yard was regrettably closed.

"Can't somebody do something about that dog?" said one voice. "I can't hear myself think."

Nell continued to bark frantically at the injustice of being shut away from all the excitement.

"Either lock her in the cellar or bring her outside," suggested my Auntie Molly, rather forcefully.

I preferred the latter option as I knew that it would also best suit my canine friend. As I led her out of the house though I knew that her feelings at this treatment were mixed for, although she would much prefer to be outside rather than locked in the cellar, she wasn't too happy about suffering the indignity of being led out on a lead rather than being allowed to walk out freely with her head held high in order to take command. She immediately sized up the situation by looking up at

Mrs. Wormley's extended posterior and announcing in her own language to anyone who was prepared to listen that someone was stuck in the window.

My mother also chose that moment to make an appearance. There was no need to offer her any kind of explanation as to what was going on as she could see for herself. That didn't prevent Nell, however, from rushing towards her while dragging me along on the other end of the lead, and filling her in with the details. I suppose in terms of doggy worlds this was something tremendously exciting that didn't occur very often. She probably suspected though that humans must be pretty stupid to allow it to happen in the first place.

"As I was walking back up the hill from your grandma's," said my mother, "I met Mrs. Behind and she told me that there was an awful racket coming from our street. Her unfortunate name for the lady to whom she was referring puzzled me at first before I realised that she must reside in the street behind ours. She would usually say Mrs. Round-The-Back so I assumed that the person she had been in conversation with was a different lady altogether. I suppose if she got to chat with anyone else from that street then she would have to come up with yet another name.

"The door's locked and nobody knows where they can get a ladder." I informed her.

"Oh, dear, that happened to me once, but fortunately I was able to shout down to your Auntie Molly as she walked back from the lavatory yard, and she came in and got me free. It was quite a nerve-racking experience though, being trapped like that and not being able to get back inside." She looked upwards. "Are you all right Mrs. Wormley?" she shouted.

The person to whom her words were directed did not bother to reply.

"Well, if we can't get hold of a ladder," said Mr. Senior, "Does anyone else have any bright ideas?"

"We could ring the Fire Brigade," suggested Nicky enthusiastically. "I don't remember seeing a fire engine in our street before."

Both Billy and I greeted that idea with the same enthusiasm. Our trapped neighbour, however, had other ideas.

"You've no need to bother," she shouted down. "There's no way I'm coming down in one of those fireman's lift things."

"Well we've run out of ideas, do you see?" explained Mr. Senior. "Nobody knows what else to do."

"Our Lily's Jessie," said Mrs. Wormley, "Our Lily's Jessie; she's got a spare key. I gave her one in case of emergency, you understand, and if this isn't an emergency I don't know what is."

"Why didn't you tell us before?" asked my Auntie Molly.

"Because I've only just remembered, that's why. You can get the key from her."

"Where does she live, then?"

"She lives in Institution Street, number fourteen. She should be in at this time of day."

"Me, Billy and Nicky can go," I volunteered, on behalf of the three of us. "We'll be able to run faster."

The plan was decided upon and the three of us ran off, turning up the road at the side of the Electra and then left onto Melville Road.

"What are we going to say?" asked Billy, which caused Nicky and me to slow down to walking pace.

"What do you mean, Billy?" I asked.

"Well, we can't just knock on the door and ask her if she's our Lily's Jessie, can we? I mean what's her last name? Is it the same as Mrs. Wormley, or not?"

"I never thought of that," I said.

We paused outside the newsagent's at the end of the road. "Let's think it over," announced Billy. "Let's just wait here for a while until we know what we're going to say."

"Baggy that Captain Marvel comic," said Nicky as we stared into the shop window deep in thought."

"I don't," said Billy. "I bags that Tarzan comic."

"You always told me that you liked Captain Marvel, Billy," I said.

"I do, but I like Tarzan better. If there hadn't have been a Tarzan comic there, then I might have baggied Captain Marvel"

"In the comic he doesn't look a bit like Johnny Weismuller, does he?" Observed Nicky.

"That doesn't make any difference to me," insisted Billy. "Anyway, my dad told me that there used to be a different actor playing Tarzan before Johnny Weismuller."

"I didn't know that," I said. "But I did hear that he won an Olympic medal for swimming before he started in films."

"I like Cheetah best," declared Nicky. "I wish I had a pet chimpanzee at home."

I couldn't help laughing at his statement. "I don't think that would work, Nicky. I mean it would probably spend a lot of time climbing up the front of the cupboard. Your mam would go bonkers."

"I can't see it walking to the lavatory yard to go for a pee either," added Billy.

"I wonder if Mary Pearson would add it to her willy-spotting collection if it did," I said.

Each of us couldn't help laughing out loud at the thought.

"I dreamt about Jane once," I uttered, after the laughter had eventually died down. "She'd been tied to a pole by cannibals and I was going to rescue her because Tarzan had been knocked unconscious, but when I got nearer I discovered that it was Susan Brown that was tied up."

"I like Jane as well," said Billy. "I think the actress that plays her is called Maureen O'Sullivan. She never seems to have many clothes on either, does she?"

"That's because Tarzan doesn't either," I suggested. "I mean it must be really hot in the jungle, mustn't it? It wouldn't look right to see people walking about in suits."

"Some of the big game hunters seem to wear ordinary clothes though," said Nicky.

"Yes," I replied, "But they won't have been living in the jungle as long as Tarzan, would they?"

"Anyway," said Billy, "I'd rather see Jane just the way she is in the pictures."

I suddenly realised that we were supposed to be making our way to see Mrs. Wormley's niece in Institution Street and I immediately reminded my companions of the fact.

"I bet she's got herself free by now," suggested Nicky. "Can't we just go back and say that she wasn't in."

"What if she's still stuck though?" I said. "I think we'd better go through with it and knock on the door. We could just ask her if she knows someone called

Mrs. Wormley and ask if she's got a spare key for her door."

We reluctantly left the delights of the newsagent's window and crossed the road to enter Institution Street, still undecided as to how to approach the task we had been given. We could tell by the low numbers on the houses that greeted us that number fourteen would not be far away.

"What if she doesn't believe us and won't give us the key?" said Billy.

"Well, we won't be able to do anything about it, will we? We'd just have to go back and tell everybody."

"I hope she doesn't give us the key," said Nicky, mischievously. Then we'd have to get the Fire Brigade, wouldn't we?"

We arrived outside number fourteen and Billy, tentatively, knocked on the door. There was no answer.

"I don't think there's anyone there," I said. "I can't hear a wireless or anything."

We tried again, but still got no response. Just as we were about to give up and head back down the street a youngish woman, probably in her mid twenties, came round the corner carrying a shopping bag. "Why are you lads knocking on my door?" she asked, greeting us with a look of suspicion."

"Are you Our Lily's J-----?" began Billy. "I mean, do you know Mrs. Wormley in Cross Speedwell Street?"

"Yes," she acknowledged, as she fumbled for her door key while struggling with the shopping bag. "She's my aunt. "Why, what's the matter with her?"

We started to explain, but she seemed to be struggling to open the door. "Damn thing's jammed again," she complained, exasperatedly. "It's always doing that. If

I can't get it open I'm going to have to go for the spare key."

"Where do you keep it?" I asked, expecting it to be under the flap of the cellar grate or hidden somewhere else near her door.

"My aunt in Cross Speedwell Street has it and it looks like I'll have to pay her a visit if I can't get this door open. Did you say she's poorly or something?"

We explained to her in full the story of her aunt's misfortune, though it was obvious to me that if she couldn't get her own front door open and obtain the required key then there wasn't much chance of her being able to render any assistance.

"How long did you say she's been stuck?" she asked.

"It must be over an hour now," said Billy, "Unless she's managed to get herself free."

"We were going to get the Fire Brigade," added Nicky, "But she wouldn't let us."

"I'm going to have to get over there," said Our Lily's Jessie, "But it won't do any good unless I can get this blasted door unlocked."

She tried turning the key again and I could see her face getting redder as she struggled to deal with the frustration she was feeling as the door still refused to budge. Eventually, she tried to dislodge it altogether but it was firmly stuck in the keyhole.

"You boys stay here," she commanded, designating us as guardians of her key, not realising for a moment that no one could probably pull it out anyway. "I shan't be a minute. I'll go see if Mr. Garnett, my neighbour's in. He always manages to get it open for me."

She walked up the street a short way, leaving us standing as sentries, before crossing to the other side of the road and knocking on a door. Someone must have opened it for she soon disappeared inside. Within a couple of minutes she reappeared accompanied by a man who I would guess to be in his fifties and they started to walk back towards us.

"I can't believe you've got it stuck again, Jessie," said her companion as they arrived at her door. "I keep telling you, you need to be gentle with it and not try to force it open. Look I'll show you again. Seize hold of the doorknob and pull the door towards you as far as it will go, then just give the key a gentle twist."

There was an audible click as the door opened first time.

Our Lily's Jessie immediately realised the urgency of the situation, even if I and my companions had been rather lax in that department. She thanked Mr. Garnett, found Mrs. Wormley's front door key and decided to accompany us back to the scene of all the excitement

When we arrived nothing much had changed but we were admonished for having taken much longer than had been expected. The newcomer, however, leapt to our defence and explained to everyone that it wasn't our fault as the delay had been caused by her having difficulties with her own house key. This, of course, did nothing whatsoever to relieve my own feelings of guilt concerning the time we had spent staring into the newsagent's window. As soon as the door was opened everybody rushed forward in an attempt to be the first to dash inside in order to stake a claim to be called the hero of the hour. Eventually, with a lot of pushing from the inside of the window, the prisoner was mercifully released. Billy, Nicky and I, along with Nell, who wanted to do her bit and was obviously very frustrated at being held back, remained outside and watched the proceedings from there, so I never knew who eventually dislodged the window, though I suspect it was several hands working together that did the trick.

Mrs. Wormley seemed none the worse after her ordeal and was probably very relieved that it had proved unnecessary for her to be brought down in one of those firemen's lift things and I suspect that she was already contemplating what a fine topic of conversation it would all prove to be for her in the months ahead.

Realising that whatever we might decide to do in the afternoon could in no way be as entertaining as what we had already witnessed during the morning, I didn't bother going out after dinner and spent most of the time either reading comics or listening to the wireless.

Later, when I was making my entry in the chronicle, there was only one possible topic to write about, but it did prove to be rather a long one.

CHAPTER TWENTY ONE

"Someone's put some blotting paper in my inkwell," complained Billy as he walked over to me after the bell had sounded for the end of the final lesson of the week, "And it's soaked nearly all the ink up."

This wasn't an unusual occurrence in the classroom. Things were always being shoved into inkwells.

"Haven't you any idea who it was?" I asked him, as I placed the exercise book, pen and ruler that I had been using, inside my desk.

"No, but I know it wasn't like that this morning."

"I found a piece of chewing gum in my mine a few weeks ago," I told him. "It took me ages to get it out of there, and when I did I couldn't get it off my fingers."

Before we had time to leave the classroom and retrieve our coats prior to heading for home Mr. Rawcliffe decided to make an announcement.

"The girls may go, but I would like all the boys to stay behind for a while as Mr. Barnes has something to say to you all. He shouldn't keep you for more than five or ten minutes."

After waiting for the girls to leave our rugby coach entered the room. He had a serious expression on his face.

"I know you won't all be playing in the rugby team tomorrow, but I hope you will just be patient while I address those who are. It would also be appreciated, however, if you could turn up to support the team even if you aren't personally involved."

Tucker Lane gave a menacing glare at those who he knew would not be taking part, demonstrating that he was in full agreement with his mentor. Mr. Barnes continued his speech.

"I know you have all been tremendously disappointed with the results that the team has obtained during our inaugural season in the Leeds schools league, as indeed have I, but the fact remains that it is our first season and I knew at the outset that it was going to be difficult due to our lack of experience. However, I have been suitably encouraged by our performances of late and I feel that we are now on the verge of winning our first game. It has not escaped my notice that our next game is against a school from Headingley. Now Headingley is the home of rugby league football and this fact alone should provide all the encouragement you need to put in a winning performance."

I remembered that Nicky had more or less told us the same thing a few days previously. I could also see that Tucker had a look of sheer determination on his face. I knew that no one wanted a victory more than he did.

Mr. Barnes continued speaking for a further five minutes as he attempted to instil into us that feeling of confidence that had been noticeably absent since the beginning of the season. I think, to a certain degree, he succeeded. Whether that would be carried forward to the following morning was another matter.

"If only we could score first," said Billy, as we left the school behind.

We paused outside the Electra, which we often did on a Friday on our way home, and glanced at the notice board which depicted what entertainment would be on offer on that particular night. We already knew that the film would be 'Red River', starring John Wayne and Montgomery Clift, the one that we had contemplated seeing at the Royal Picture House a week or two earlier, but just staring at the images on the poster seemed to heighten our enthusiasm.

"I really like John Wayne," admitted Billy. "I think it should be great.

"I'll call round for you at ten to seven," I told him. I had very little doubt that both of us would be able to go, providing that the film was something that my mother regarded as being suitable.

"I suppose you'll be going to the pictures again," she said, after I had taken off my coat.

"Yes, please mam," I answered. "It's a John Wayne film tonight."

"You see too many of those cowboy films, all guns and shooting."

I didn't make any comment. It always seemed to me that the only kind of film that my mother might deem as suitable for a child to watch would be one where there was very little action at all, like those sloppy romantic films that she adored, though she was quite partial to the occasional musical or comedy. My father, fortunately, took an entirely different view, realising that schoolboys needed adventure. Sometimes I was a little suspicious that she might even regard 'Tom and Jerry' or 'The Three Stooges' as too violent.

I called round for Billy five minutes before the appointed time, but he was ready to leave all the same. He was just as keen to see the film as I was. As we took up our seats we felt fortunate to find two together as the place was packed. It was always busy on a Friday night, but John Wayne was always a big draw. It would be the best part of an hour, however, before the main film started, or the big picture as it was always referred to by all the filmgoers in the area. Prior to that would be the usual assortment of short films, advertisements and trailers followed by the weekly cliff-hanger serial and a very short interlude which always heralded the stampede down the aisles to sample the delights that were on display on the ice cream girl's tray. On some occasions, especially at the weekend, there would be two feature length films showing, though I knew that wasn't the case on this particular evening, which suggested to me that the main film would be quite lengthy in duration, a situation which suited me admirably. Everything went along splendidly, at least for the first part of the evening. There was an interesting film, though a very short one, about the link between The Great Exhibition of 1851 and the Festival Of Britain which was taking place in the summer. This was followed by a Tweety and Sylvester cartoon. Then there was the latest episode of 'The Scarlet Horseman' and a couple of trailers of films which would be shown at the cinema in the near future. After that things began to happen.

At the start of the brief interval the ice cream girl made her entrance at the bottom of the aisle close to the screen. This, as always, was accompanied by a series of wolf whistles as she stood in the spotlight in her short skirt. There then proceeded a mad rush to form a queue. While this was by no means an unusual occurrence, this particular occasion proved to be quite different. The poor girl was knocked off her feet causing all the contents of her tray to be displayed on the floor. As some of the containers lost their lids in the process, dollops of ice cream covered the immediate area. Billy and I, who always seemed to succeed in being near the front of the queue, looked on in dismay as we realised that the treat that we had been looking forward to would not now be forthcoming. The victim of the crush did not appear to have suffered any injury but the look on her face indicated her extreme displeasure as she disappeared behind a curtain. As we made our way back to our seats we were greeted by a massive cheer as an elderly lady with a mop and bucket emerged into the spotlight which was still shining on the scene of the mishap. There then followed an announcement over the loud speaker.

"WE APOLOGISE FOR THE INCONVENIENCE. NORMAL SERVICE WILL BE RESUMED AS SOON AS POSSIBLE"

"I suppose we'll have to wait until she's mopped it all up now," observed Billy after we were re-seated.

Billy's statement proved to be correct and the short interlude was extended by a further ten minutes. When the lady with the mop had completed her task to her satisfaction she picked up the mop and bucket and made her way to the same exit that had swallowed up the ice cream girl, but not before she received another huge cheer, which prompted her to pause and curtsey, for which she was generously applauded. She then stepped behind the curtain, no doubt feeling very pleased with herself that her efforts in the service of the British cinema industry had been suitably rewarded. The audience by this time was good humoured and shouts of approval rang around the auditorium as the lights went out and the big picture began.

John Wayne played the part of a cattle baron named Tom Dunstan who was attempting to drive his cattle to market. He portrayed a much deeper and darker character than the cowboy hero he usually depicted in the less complicated films that we had seen him in. Nevertheless, both Billy and I were thoroughly enjoying the story that was on offer.

The second incident of the evening occurred at the point where Mathew Garth, played by Montgomery Clift was assisting a wagon train that was being attacked by Indians, perhaps the most exciting part in the whole film. Everyone had settled down after the ice cream fiasco and all eyes were fixed on the action in front of them. Suddenly, as the Indians circled the wagons, they began to move in slow motion and their high pitched yells and howls turned into deep groans. The picture disappeared, being replaced by a series of flashing numbers, before it darkened altogether. The members of the audience stared at the blank screen for several seconds before comprehension hit them. This was followed by boos and the stamping of feet as they realised that the film had broken in the projector. It is true to say that this sort of breakdown to the service on offer happened on several occasions throughout the year and the reaction was always the same. Usually the projectionist managed to splice the reel and continue with the picture but occasionally the manager was left with no option but to refund the evening's takings.

"WE APOLOGISE FOR THE INCONVENIENCE. NORMAL SERVICE WILL BE RESUMED AS SOON AS POSSIBLE," emanated from the loud speaker.

"Oh, no," said Billy. "I was getting really interested in that."

"I think that's the third time it's happened this year," I acknowledged. "Do you remember when it happened in the Superman serial?"

"Yes, and we never saw the end of it, did we?"

"I hope we see the end of this though. I reckon there's about half an hour to go, don't you?"

After a further ten minutes a round of cheering heralded the resumption of the film, though all the movement in the opening sequence was speeded up and all the men's voices were high-pitched, before everything settled back down to normality.

As the picture neared its end and the cattle had been driven to market Tom Dunstan was marching towards Matthew Garth for the final showdown when the third incident occurred. Sounds were heard on the roof as if it was being bombarded with missiles and sounds of thunder could be heard outside. Suddenly there were shrieks of consternation coming from the circle above. It soon became obvious to all that the hailstones had penetrated the roof and were targeting the audience. All interest in the film was abandoned and there was a mad rush to the exit. Other leaks suddenly appeared and there was no announcement on this occasion about normal service being resumed.

Billy and I became separated in the frenzied rush to get to the door. The situation became worse, however, as those at the front suddenly ceased there insane flight when they saw that the conditions outside were much worse than those from which they were attempting to escape.

The hailstones were much larger than the ones that Susan and I had sheltered from just before Christmas, being almost the size of golf balls. I could just make them out through a gap in the crowd as the surface of Cross Speedwell Street was turned white in a matter of minutes. However, the deluge halted as quickly as it had begun and the crowd, realising that all they now had to fear was the occasional clap of thunder accompanied by a flash of lightning, dashed outside and hurried home in the best way they could over the strange alien landscape that confronted them.

I hung back for a while in an alcove near the ticket office until I was joined by my closest friend.

"Crikey!" said Billy as we watched the throng disperse, "I've never seen anything like that before."

"I bet all the seats in the picture house are soaking wet," I added. "It's a pity we didn't see the end of the film though."

"I think it had nearly finished anyway, Neil."

"You know what this means, though, don't you Billy? They're going to have to repair the roof before it can open again and that could take ages."

Billy looked pensive for a moment. "What if it never opens again? What if they have to pull it down?"

That supposition was one I didn't want to dwell on. "Come on, we might as well go home. I want to tell my mam all about it."

"You haven't got wet, have you?" were my mother's opening remarks before I had time to take my coat off.

"No mam, but did you see it? I've never seen hailstones as big as those before."

"No, as a matter of fact, I don't think I have, but you'd better stand in front of the fire for a while and get warm."

The first thing I noticed was Nell's absence from her favourite place on the clip rug. I looked round and noticed that she was cowering under the sideboard. In her mind I suppose thunder was similar to all the firework noises she had grown to hate on Bonfire Night and she couldn't resist casting an accusing glance in my direction as if she held me responsible for the severity of the weather.

I explained to my mother about the roof leaking in the Electra. She seemed surprised.

"Well, I've never known that happen before and me and your dad have been in all sorts of weather. It's an old building, though. It used to be a chapel, you know."

My father walked in from the adjoining room, choosing not to make any comment regarding the thunder storm. "Are you playing in the rugby team tomorrow?" he asked.

"Yes, dad. We're playing at Bedford's Field against a school from Headingley."

"Well then, I've got some good news for you. I'll be able to come and watch you play for the first time. The factory doesn't have enough work at the moment to open on a Saturday. Now that's good news, isn't it?"

I greeted his statement with mixed feelings. I had always been keen for my father to be a spectator, providing I managed to do something to make him feel proud of me. However, as we had lost every game so far I remained apprehensive as to what he might think of the performance. I think my mother was uncertain too. She usually paid a visit into town on a Saturday morning and perhaps she considered that her husband should have been accompanying her on one of the rare occasions that he had a morning free. She did not complain however.

The Chronicle entry that I made before retiring was concerned mostly with the happenings at the Electra, but

I thought long and hard about the film we had been watching. It occurred to me that the only reason that the cattle drive reached a successful conclusion was due to the sheer determination of John Wayne's character Tom Dunstan, and I realised that if our team could display the same tenacity on the following morning then there was no reason whatsoever that we should fail to win our first game.

CHAPTER TWENTY TWO

"So who are you playing this morning?" asked my father after we had finished our breakfast

"It's a school from Headingley, dad."

"Headingley, you say. Well, that would be a good one for you to get your first win, I should think. What time does the match begin?"

"We kick off at ten o'clock, dad, but all the members of the team have to arrive by half past nine."

"And what time does it finish then?"

"Well, we play half an hour each way and have a break in the middle, so we should finish at about quarter past eleven."

"Well, I suggest that you walk up there with your mates like you usually do, and we'll get there just before ten."

A feeling of dismay engulfed me at his use of the word 'we'. The fathers of some of the lads had often been seen standing around the edge of the pitch, but I felt I would never live it down if my mother was there as well. It was invariably a males only environment. She glanced at him as if he had taken leave of his senses.

"I'm going into town, Tom," she firmly announced. "I've already arranged it with Mrs Who's-Got-A-New-Hat. There's no way I'm standing all morning in a muddy field, especially as it looks like it might rain."

I couldn't help wondering what name she had given her travelling companion before she acquired a new hat.

"I know, love," he explained. "I was just thinking of taking Nell for a walk on the ridge and ending up by watching the match."

Nell walked across to who was probably her favourite member of the family, sat by his feet and stared at my mother as if to say 'And what do you think about that, then?'.

"Right, well make sure you're all back by twelve o'clock because it'll have to be fish and chips today and you know how busy they get on a Saturday sometimes."

Nell barked her approval. She didn't like to miss out on her favourite food, even if she did receive it by devious means when my mother wasn't looking.

As Billy, Nicky and I walked along Melville Road towards Woodhouse Street the topic of discussion, rather than the forthcoming rugby match, was the disaster that had struck the Electra on the previous night. There was no sign in the streets of the brief but violent storm, but we all knew that considerable damage had been done to the picture house. Billy raised the question first.

"When do you think it'll re-open again?" he asked.

"It might open on Monday after the weekend," suggested Nicky, hopefully. In fact they might even be able to do something today and open tonight as usual."

"There's no chance of that, Nicky. There were holes all over the roof."

As we turned the corner into Woodhouse Street I considered the context of the film we had been watching when the disaster had struck. I decided to share my thoughts with them.

"I was thinking about the film in bed last night. I know you didn't see it, Nicky, but John Wayne played the part of a rancher who was driving his cattle hundreds of miles to market. Anyway, the only way he managed to do it with all the odds stacked against him was by sheer determination and by becoming mean and nasty. He didn't let anything stand in his way. I was thinking that if we became as determined as he was we could get our first ever win this morning. What do you think?"

"What do you mean?" inquired Nicky. "Do you think we should start tripping everybody up or nudging them with our elbows?"

Billy started laughing.

"No, of course not," I explained, looking at Nicky in disbelief. "There'd be no point in doing that, would there. We'd all get sent off and then we'd have to forfeit the game."

"Well, what do you mean then?" he asked, rather puzzled.

I suddenly realised that I wasn't quite sure what I meant either. I couldn't get out of my mind that my father would be on the touch line observing my every move and I was desperate to impress him.

"I mean that we should fix it in our mind that we are going to win. My dad's going to be watching today and I just can't bear the thought of us losing again."

"If we could score first it might make a big difference," said a voice immediately behind us as we neared Johnston Street. "We haven't scored first in any of the games we've played so far."

We all turned around to greet Ken Stacey.

"That's it," I said. "It all depends on how we start. Let's just make sure that we score first. It might make the other team feel disheartened."

We arrived at the venue half an hour before the game was due to begin just in time for a team talk by our coach. After he had finished I had to admit that there did seem to be a lot more determination rather than the usual despondency among the players.

"If we don't win today," announced Alan Bartle, the team captain, quite forcefully, then I don't think we'll ever have a better chance to start pulling away from the bottom of the league table.

"We'll definitely win," snarled Tucker Lane, "If I've anything to do with it. I can promise you that. You'll all just have to raise your game a bit nearer to my standard."

It was with this new found fortitude that we watched the arrival of our opponents. As I assessed each one there certainly seemed nothing special about them. It definitely wasn't a team of giants like the one we had encountered in our first game at Armley the previous October, and I began to feel reasonably confident. As we took up our positions on the field of play I searched among the sparse spectators for my father and his companion but couldn't see either of them. The whistle sounded and the game began.

Despite the severe weather of the previous evening I realised that we had played in far muddier conditions than those which existed on this particular morning, yet it was still very slippery underfoot. We began well enough and got close to the opposing try line in the first five minutes, yet the Headingley boys rallied and soon pushed us back. However, after fifteen minutes play it was obvious to me that the game was probably the most even one we had yet played. This was the time when my father decided to make an appearance with Nell at his side, though kept firmly on a lead. I spotted them just as

Ernie Peyton passed the ball to me. In my distracted state I fumbled with it and a scrum down was called for a knock-on. On witnessing this Nell immediately turned round and sat with her back towards me as if to indicate her disgust. I was more concerned, though, with the stern glare that Tucker Lane was directing towards me. I decided not to dwell on my error, however, and was even more determined to play well. The halfway point arrived with no points on the board and we were congratulated by Mr. Barnes who reminded us, as if we didn't already know it, that this was the first occasion of the season that the opposing team had failed to score in the first half of a game. I walked over to my father during the fifteen minute interval and Nell decided to give me another chance to make amends by greeting me in the typical canine fashion.

"You've probably got the best chance of winning that you've had since you first started playing," he said. "As you know I've played quite a bit of rugby in my time and I mean it when I say that there's very little between the two teams. The one which is the most determined will win. So you've got to make sure that that's you."

Nell barked her agreement.

The second half began in splendid fashion for our side. From the kick-off we managed to hang on to the ball through a long series of tackles before Alan Bartle touched over in the far right hand corner. It was the first time that we had been the first to score and our ecstatic celebrations bore testimony to that fact. It would have been a difficult conversion attempt even for Bert Cook, the famous Leeds player, so it was no surprise that Tucker Lane failed with his goal-kicking attempt. Nevertheless, Woodhouse Junior School led by three points to nil. There then followed a period of stalemate where first one side would come close and then the other before, following a pass from Nicky, I found myself with the ball. Holding it close to my chest I think I ran faster than I had ever run before, though I was a little puzzled that I seemed to have left all would-be tacklers so far behind me. I ran directly behind the posts and planted the ball firmly on the ground. I immediately turned around to receive the expected appreciation of my efforts and was a little taken aback to see everyone standing there laughing. The referee signalled a scrum somewhere near the centre circle and I realised that I had been running outside the touch line for almost the entire distance. I grudgingly walked back down the field.

"Never mind, lad," said my father as I walked past him. "At least you showed you can run a bit."

With ten minutes to go and with us desperately trying to hang on to our lead, one of the Headingley lads intercepted a pass from Johnny Jackson and raced over the line. Despite the try having been scored behind the posts, the boy who took the goal kick failed miserably and the score remained at three points each.

As we kicked off I could hear my father's encouraging shout.

"Come on, Woodhouse. A draw's no good." What Nell thought of the situation I had no idea as she was just contentedly sniffing the ground.

The Headingley boys started to come forward again and tackle after tackle only resulted in a play-the-ball situation. As they approached the twenty-five yard line the man in charge blew his whistle for an infringement by Tucker Lane. Admittedly, he had been a little over-zealous in his desire to prevent them from scoring as he picked up the lad with the ball and hurled him to the floor. I looked to the touchline as I could hear Nell barking furiously at the referee. Our opponents chose to go for goal. It was a difficult kick to attempt and fortune smiled on us as it just skimmed the outside of the post. Within minutes of the game restarting the ball found its way into touch. I don't know what mischief Tucker might have got up to in the thick of the scrum but the ball came out on our side. Alan Bartle passed it to me and I began to run up the field. I only covered a few yards before being heavily tackled. After playing the ball it eventually found its way to Ken Stacey and we all began to run up the field again. I glanced across at my father who was almost running up the touchline alongside us. Nell had been let off the lead now but she sensibly stayed away from the field of play. She seemed just as excited as my father, however. I found myself with the ball again as we neared the try line. I could see there was an overlap with Tucker now running on the wing. Just before I was about to be tackled I passed the ball to him. He caught it cleanly and dived over for a try. I knew there could only be minutes remaining. The tension we had endured during all those defeats since the start of the season evaporated immediately and we went berserk in celebration. Nell could contain herself no longer and ran onto the pitch to join in. We knew there would only be time to take the resulting goal kick before the game would come to an end. After my father had recaptured the only four-legged supporter of the Woodhouse Junior School rugby league team, the difficult conversion attempt was a failure, but nobody really cared. We had won by six points to three, our very first win. We all stood in a group on the pitch with no one really wanting to leave.

Mr. Barnes walked on to congratulate us and, after a couple of minutes, we all walked off together.

After receiving the long sought-after praise from my father he decided to return home the same way that he had arrived, rightly believing that I would prefer to celebrate the event with my team-mates. Nell did not appear to be very happy with this decision, however, as I detected from the way she struggled against the lead that she would much prefer to join the team's triumphal march down Woodhouse Street as I feel sure that, in her mind, she thought she had done more than enough to deserve it. Nevertheless, I watched them both exit Bedford's Field onto the ridge. I slung the shirts and shorts that I had been playing in into my duffle bag which, when I presented it to my mother, would provide a suitable trophy for washday.

"That was fantastic," said Billy, excitedly as the team began to walk towards Woodhouse Street. "Why can't we play like that every week?"

The short journey home was one of the most joyous that I can remember. We were still bottom of the league table but no one seemed to mind. We were all so elated that we had won our first game and I felt sure that things could only get better now.

I was the first to enter the house, my mother arriving shortly afterwards. I explained to her that my father was taking the longer route home in order to give Nell a run free of the lead. I also explained to her the manner in which we had secured our first victory. She gave a polite acknowledgement of our achievement but the enthusiasm was decidedly lukewarm.

"Jubilee Fisheries should have re-opened today, so you can go for some fish and chips. Better get three times," she said.

It was only recently that I had been promoted to adult level with regard to food portions.

"Oh, and you'd better call on Mr. Senior to see if he wants any bringing back. I know he likes his fish and chips on a Saturday."

He answered the door immediately and the aroma of tobacco smoke engulfed me.

"That's very kind of you, lad," he answered in response to my question. "Yes, I'd like you to bring me some if you don't mind."

"Is it just fish and chips then, Mr. Senior?"

"Aye, that's right lad, but can you ask them not to put any vinegar on, please? I much prefer brown sauce on mine, do you see? Oh, and I'll have a few scraps on them as well if that's all right with you."

After leaving my neighbour's house my nose detected the smell of them cooking before I had reached the schoolyard and it made me hurry. When I arrived there were a lot of people in the shop and the smell of paint was just detectable alongside the aroma of fish and chips. No one was looking very happy, however, and I could hear Mrs. I-Make-No-Wonder's voice in full flow.

"I didn't expect that I'd be helping to pay for your decorating," she said, scowling. "I don't make any wonder you're looking red-faced. Yon notice on the wall says it all."

I looked at the notice she was referring to. 'THERE HAS BEEN A PRICE INCREASE TO FISH AND CHIPS DUE TO UNFORSEEN CIRCUMSTANCES', it boldly stated.

Mrs. I-Make-No-Wonder hadn't finished her verbal assault. "I haven't forgotten how you put your prices up last summer. The notice then said it was because you were having to use new potatoes. Now I didn't make any wonder at it at the time because I know new potatoes are more expensive, but did you put the prices down again when you went back to using old potatoes? No, you did not."

"That's right," said another voice from the queue. "I thought myself that that was a bit unfair."

"Yes. I remember that as well," said another.

"I think we'd better have a word with your husband," demanded the undisputed leader of the rebels. He's the one who makes the decisions, isn't he? Mind you, I wouldn't make any wonder if he was in hiding somewhere."

The queue was no longer moving. I had no idea whether the ones who had been in earlier had accepted the new price without complaining or not. I was conscious of the fact, though, that my mother had only given me the amount of money that she usually paid.

"Eddie's in the back making chips," announced the harassed proprietor.

In the back of my mind I just knew that she was going to say that.

"Well then, he might just be wasting his time," said her chief tormentor, "Because I wouldn't make any wonder if everybody decided to walk out of here."

There were a few murmurs of assent, though none quite as forceful as that of the previous speaker.

"I'd better go have a word with him then, I suppose," said the lady behind the counter.

A couple of minutes later she returned. "Eddie says he's decided to keep the prices at the same level for the time being, but he may have to revue the prices in the near future." I noticed that she didn't immediately take the notice down, however.

After taking Mr. Senior his vinegar-free fish and chips I told my mother what had happened and that there might be a price increase very soon.

"Well, if that happens," she said, "Then we might just have to start going somewhere else, might we?"

"I could find out how much they are at the one round the corner opposite Doughty's if you like," I suggested, helpfully.

"No, there won't be any need to do that. They'll probably be dearer there anyway. No, we can always get them from Craven Road."

So that was that. I spent the afternoon with Billy and Nicky, most of the time playing with the rugby ball I had been given at Christmas as, in view of our victory during the morning it seemed to all three of us to be the only worthwhile activity to be engaged in at that particular moment.

The entry I made in the chronicle at bedtime was quite a cheerful one.

CHAPTER TWENTY THREE

Sunday morning was a little cloudy, but there was the faint suggestion that the sun might make an appearance later in the day. For the time of year, however, it wasn't particularly cold. Billy and I had decided to make our way up to Woodhouse Moor for a change and call at the Astra Picture House in Woodhouse Street on the way. We were anxious to see what film was on offer the following weekend as my father had confirmed what I had suspected, that the Electra would be likely to close for several days at least, if not for several weeks. Repairing a roof as big as that one, he had said, would take some doing and he believed that it would also be very costly. If the management didn't have sufficient funds there was no telling when it might reopen, if at all. I did not dwell on this particular thought and Billy did not seem too despondent either. Both of us had been given a huge psychological lift after the previous day's sporting achievement and as we walked along it would appear to any bystander that we did not have a care in the world.

After reaching our first destination we scrutinised the poster on the cinema wall. 'KING SOLOMON'S MINES' it screamed, urging us to pay a visit.

"It looks like a jungle film," observed Billy, if that picture's anything to go by."

"Should be all right, then" I said. "It probably won't be as good as Tarzan, but at least it looks as if it's in Technicolor. I think we might as well go, don't you?"

"Yes," agreed Billy. "I don't think we need to bother trailing down to Meanwood Road to see what's on at the Royal."

So, with Friday night's entertainment decided upon, we made our way towards the moor. Woodhouse Moor was a very popular location for the local inhabitants especially on a Sunday. It was a wide, open space where they could walk the dog, or mothers could push a pram and show off their offspring to anyone who passed by. Courting couples could be spotted walking arm in arm while old folk would sit quietly on benches to watch the world go by. On one corner of the moor was a children's playground which was always lively. The centre point, however, was the old bandstand and, just like the one that stood on Woodhouse Ridge, it had not heard the sound of music for many a year. It was to this point that we found ourselves being drawn. What had attracted our attention was the fact that a crowd seemed to be gathering, though it seemed to consist almost entirely of the male variety. We could only spot two or three women. Their focus seemed to be fixed on a middle-aged man who was standing on a box in the middle of it.

"I wonder what he's going to do, Neil," said Billy.

"I've no idea," I replied. "Maybe, he's going to start singing."

"I don't think so," said a rough looking man who was standing beside us while blowing huge puffs of smoke from his clay pipe. "That's Albert Dobbs, that is. He's a Trade Union man and he's always stirring the crowd up about something. You'll find him here on most Sundays. He can be very entertaining sometimes. I wonder what's driving him today."

The man who was the centre of attention began to speak. He had a very powerful voice though he himself was quite small in stature. It was obvious that he was used to making himself heard. "Gather round, lads and lasses," he said. "Gather round."

"It won't be union talk today, boys," said the man with the pipe. "If it's union business he always addresses the crowd as brothers and sisters. No, something else must have got him all riled up today."

"I've just got back from a little place on the Yorkshire coast called Skipsea," he began, "And I feel sure, as the true Yorkshire folk that you are, that your senses will be as outraged as mine when you hear what I am about to relate."

I was as intrigued as much as the rest of the onlookers. "Have you ever heard of Skipsea?" I asked Billy.

"No, I've heard of Skipton but that's not on the coast, is it? I went through there on a bus once on the way to Blackpool."

The speaker in the bandstand continued his address. "Now, when I was in this tiny seaside resort I was told that the cliffs kept crumbling and falling into the sea. I decided that I wanted to hear more about this phenomenon, so I called at the local post office to see if anyone there could tell me any more about it. The postmaster did more than that. He showed me a small booklet called 'CLIFF EROSION ON THE YORKSHIRE COAST' and what I read filled me with horror, and I'm sure that what I'm about to tell you now will do the same for you."

Everybody in his captive audience was eagerly waiting to hear the next part of his story.

"I told you it'd have nothing to do with union business," said the man with the pipe. "He does this sometimes."

The orator continued.

"Bits of Yorkshire have been dropping into the sea at a rate of three yards a year. So that is thirty yards over a decade and about two hundred yards over a Yorkshire man's lifetime. Villages that existed at the time of the Norman Conquest are now in the middle of the North Sea, and it can't be long before Spurn Point at the mouth of the Humber disappears for ever. Now, in case there's anyone thinking that thirty yards is not very much to get excited about then I would like to remind you that it is eight yards longer than a cricket pitch. Now, I ask you this, friends. How many cricket pitches can Yorkshire afford to lose?"

He paused for effect as gaps of horror were heard from the crowd at the mention of their favourite sport and the implications that threatened it.

"And there's more," the speaker continued. "What do you think is happening on the other side of the Pennines? Is the same thing occurring there, you might ask? Well I'll tell you friends. I'll tell you. You only have to visit places like Southport or Morecambe to see for yourself what's happening there. While we're losing thirty yards every ten years Lancashire is expanding by the same amount. Bits of land are being constantly recovered from the Irish Sea, bits of land that are rightfully ours. Before you know it it'll be possible to walk from Southport to Ireland without getting your feet wet."

"This is outrageous," shouted one voice.

"How long has this been going on?" said another?

The protests continued.

"We can't let them get away with it."

"They're pinching all our cricket pitches."

"Why weren't we told?"

"We've got to do something before it's too late." This latter statement came from the man with the pipe."

The members of the crowd were beginning to get really agitated as their birthright seemed to be under threat.

"We'll march, that's what," shouted another. "Those Lancastrians need to know that we're just not having it. That's right, we'll march. That'll show 'em."

"Those are my sentiments exactly," declared the speaker. "Yes, we will certainly march. That's the only way and, as a matter of fact I've already got the banners printed. Look I've brought one here with me."

He held it aloft and we could all see that it proudly proclaimed 'GIVE US BACK OUR THIRTY YARDS'.

While still holding the banner aloft he continued his speech.

"I'll tell you what we're going to do, lads and lasses. We are going to hire a series of buses to take us to Todmorden and then proceed to march through the town demanding that the boundary between Yorkshire and Lancashire be pushed back by a distance of thirty yards, and that's not all, we shall insist that it be pushed back by a further thirty yards every ten years. We shall rightly reclaim what is ours, never fear."

Voices in the crowd could be heard expressing their agreement in a forceful manner.

"That's the spirit. We can't let them get away with it."

"We're all behind you mister."

"They'll soon find out who they're dealing with."

It was obvious that Albert Dobbs was very pleased with the reaction that he was getting.

"Don't forget though, lads and lasses, that Todmorden is only a beginning. This coastal erosion is everywhere in Yorkshire, not just at Skipsea, so we'll have to push back the boundary in other places as well. Anyway, if you look at what we're planning to do in a different way then we're really doing a lot of Lancashire folk a favour. I mean anyone living within those thirty yards is really being liberated, you see. They will become bona fide members of God's own county without having to qualify for the privilege and if there are any decent cricketers amongst them they will be eligible to play for Yorkshire immediately. Now, who's with me?"

"We're all with you," shouted several voices at once,"

"Right then," said the voice from the bandstand, "That's the spirit. We'll all gather here at nine o'clock on Easter Monday and I'll make sure there's a fleet of buses waiting for you. We'll give those Lancashire folk on the wrong side of Todmorden something to think about."

The enthusiastic shouting suddenly quietened down.

"Easter Monday, you say," said a voice near the front. "My Annie always makes Jam Roly Poly on Easter Monday."

"Woodhouse Feast is on over Easter," said another.

Whereas the views of the crowd had hitherto been overwhelmingly in favour of marching across the Pennines to protest against what they considered to be a grave injustice, individual voices of dissent could now be heard from the assembled throng.

"We're supposed to be going to Bridlington on Easter Monday."

"I need to work in my allotment, especially now that spring's coming along."

"Our Alice is coming over from Pontefract during the Easter holidays."

"I don't think my wife will let me go."

"Mine neither."

Albert Dobbs looked on crestfallen as his hitherto enthusiastic marching army began to disintegrate. Eventually, Billy and I were the only ones left.

"Oh dear," he said, breathing out a huge sigh, "I suppose you two might as well go back home as well. I don't know. Some people have got no backbone. It was never like this in the old days."

"Never mind, mister," sympathised Billy. "They only said that they wouldn't go on Easter Monday."

"No lad, I'm sorry, but that won't wash. I've seen it all before many times. They'll have forgotten all about it by tomorrow, and it was such a worthy cause."

"If you're not going ahead with it, mister," said Billy, "Do you think we could have your banner?"

"Aye, lads. You might as well. It's no use to me now, is it?"

I looked across at him, wondering what he wanted it for. Then I realised that the idea of marching back home behind it did have some appeal. We decided to leave him, re-crossed the moor and set off down Woodhouse Street with Billy and me proudly holding the banner between us. We got plenty of questioning stares, yet only three people stopped us to ask about it. We attempted to explain in the best way we could, but we evidently did not possess the oratory skills of Albert Dobbs as our listeners remained unmoved by the story of the threat to our Yorkshire heritage.

I was happy for Billy to take the banner indoors with him and as I entered my house the aroma of roast beef reminded me that it was almost dinner time. What I hadn't expected was to see Grandad Miller sitting in the arm chair at the side of the fire. This was usually occupied by my father but whenever my grandfather or Grandma Cawson visited he always vacated it. Nell, however, did not believe that this rule applied to her and could not think of any reason to leave her place on the clip rug as, in her eyes, she was a fully-fledged part of the family, whereas they were only fringe members who only put in the occasional appearance.

Grandad Miller made his usual opening remark. "So, what have you been doing today then, lad?"

I told him about our encounter on Woodhouse Moor.

"Good Heavens," he gasped, "Is he still standing on his soap box every Sunday morning?"

"I don't think he's there every Sunday, grandad, but I think he goes there quite a lot. This is the first time that me and Billy have seen him though. I didn't know who he was until a man at the side of me told us all about him."

My mother walked in from the other room and looked inside the oven, which caused the heightened beefy aroma to travel further into my nostrils and made Nell decide to walk over to her side and take a big sniff, a sure sign that, in her view, it was taking far too long to cook.

"So what was he shouting the odds about today, then?" asked my grandfather. "Was it a load of stuff about the union?"

I let him have all the details about how Yorkshire was in grave danger of falling into the sea.

"Well, I think you can take all that with a pinch of salt, lad. I mean it's true that cliffs are crumbling all along the coast, but it's been going on for centuries and it's a very slow process. There's nothing much going to happen in your lifetime."

I felt relieved at his words. I knew that the situation was nowhere near as serious as Albert Dobbs had made it out to be but I was fully aware that I had been carried away by his oration just as much as the remainder of his audience.

"Yorkshire will carry on, whatever threats it might face," he continued. "You can be sure of that. God wouldn't have it any other way."

"Do you think they play cricket in Heaven?" I asked him.

"Well, I should imagine so. They'll have to have some way to pass the time, won't they? Anyway, it's supposed to be all about happiness isn't it? So what can be happier than playing cricket? There's another thing. Think how many Yorkshire men must be up there by now? If there was anybody who didn't understand the game, then they certainly will now, won't they? So you can forget about Yorkshire losing all those cricket pitches because God isn't going to let it happen. Besides, I'll probably be up there myself before too long, so I'll be able to find out, won't I?"

My mother wasn't too happy with those last remarks, and admonished him about talking about dying again, so soon after he'd almost done so. She walked over to the oven again, this time to check on the Yorkshire Puddings. Satisfied that they were ready she walked across to the door to the adjoining room, where I knew my father would be reading his copy of the 'Empire News'.

"The puddings will be on the table in five minutes, Tom," she shouted. "Don't let them go cold."

On hearing this, Nell immediately walked across to that part of the dining table where she knew he would be sitting and plonked herself down at the side of his chair to await his arrival.

The Yorkshire Puddings, as always, were eaten as a separate course. Each one was covered in rich, onion gravy and was only a fraction smaller than the dinner plate on which it had been placed. After we had eagerly devoured them and the roast beef was set before us my grandfather made an unexpected announcement.

"I've been offered a chance of going into a convalescent home for a while and I've decided to take it. I thought it might do me good especially after that bad do I had at the end of last year. What do you think?"

"Where is this convalescent home?" asked my mother.

"It's in Ilkley and I'll be there for four weeks. The Postman's Retirement Association has organised it for me. The place where I'll be staying is right on the edge of the moor and they say that the air there is much better for people with my sort of illness. There isn't all the smoke that you get with these modern cities like Leeds."

"It seems like a good idea to me," said my father." A good rest in peaceful surroundings is probably just what you need to get better."

"Well, I haven't had a really bad attack during these last few months and I'd like to keep it that way and it might increase my chances of living a few more years before they call me away."

"Will we be able to come and visit you, grandad?" I asked him.

"Of course you can, lad, every weekend if you want to."

The discussion continued throughout the remainder of the meal with my mother asking the most questions, mostly about the type of place he was going to, but I think Grandad Miller had already made his decision before he left home and was simply looking for moral support.

"It does mean that I'll be there all over Easter, though," he said.

By the time the meal was over everyone around the table had re-assured him that he was doing the best thing, with the exception of Nell, who did not appear to express any concern whatsoever regarding the prolonged absence of someone who was only a fringe member, especially as she was pre-occupied in devouring the piece of roast beef that she had just gratefully accepted from the hand of my father.

I, personally, was glad that Grandad Miller would be having a period of convalescence. I felt it was exactly what he needed as I had no wish to see him get another serious attack of asthma like the one that almost killed him just three months previously. I also thought hard about his comments regarding the events we had witnessed on Woodhouse Moor and willingly accepted his assurances that a second Wars Of The Roses was not about to break out.

CHAPTER TWENTY FOUR

The huge grin on Tucker Lane's face had said it all. It was the first day back at school after our victory over the Headingley boys, and he and Alan Bartle had been singled out by the headmaster as the two who had made the greatest contribution to what he regarded as a great achievement for the school. The fact that we had lost all the previous games did not seem to matter and I knew that there was a feeling among everyone concerned that at last the tide had turned. It was, in my view, quite fitting that Alan and Tucker were the ones to receive this accolade as they had undoubtedly been the most effective players, though the head had also been keen to offer praise to the entire team.

"I know we haven't got many games left, Billy," I said as we walked home for the mid-day break, "But I feel a lot more confident about us winning now, don't you?"

"I know what you mean. It was getting to the point where I wasn't too bothered about playing anymore, but now I can't wait for the next game."

As we walked past the ginnel opposite the Electra our attention was drawn to the huge poster on the wall. It read 'CLOSED UNTIL FURTHER NOTICE', and the other posters supposedly advertising the films that should have been shown that week had a large, red cross drawn across them.

"It looks like it's going to be closed for a long time, Billy," I told him.

"Yes, it's a good job we've got two other picture houses we can go to now, isn't it? If it had happened a few weeks ago we wouldn't have been able to go to the pictures at all."

My mother had made some onion gravy with dumplings to go with what had been left from the previous day's joint of beef, plus some mashed potatoes and carrots. It was the dumplings that made all the difference and I devoured everything that was set before me but not without her usual instruction to gently ease them apart with a fork and not to cut them with a knife or they would go sad, though I never fully understood what she meant. After the meal was over my mother decided to make an announcement.

"If you need to go to the lavatory before you go back to school there's something I need to tell you."

The lavatory yard consisted of six cubicles to accommodate twelve houses. Therefore, each one had to be shared between two families. As far back as I could remember we had always shared with my Auntie Molly who lived next door. The occupant of each house took it in turn to clean the lavatory on alternate weeks.

"Mr. Senior's getting on a bit as you know and he can't bend down so much these days which means that washing the lavatory out every two weeks is really too much for him, so recently the person he's been sharing with has been doing his week as well as her own.. However, she's started working in the factory again so she hasn't really the time to do it anymore. Your Auntie Molly, therefore, has decided to share with him, which means that we've swapped places."

"So who are we sharing with then, mam?"

"We'll be sharing with Mrs. Pearson. I'll be doing the cleaning most of the time, but she might be able to get her daughter, Mary, to help out on occasions. What's the matter? What are you looking so worried about?"

She couldn't have helped but notice the look of horror on my face that her words had produced.

"Nothing, mam, nothing," I managed to stumble out.

"Anyway," she went on," That means that we'll be using the fourth lavatory in the yard from now on instead of the second one. So there's a different key now hanging up on the cellar head."

After we had returned to school for the afternoon session I hadn't said anything to Billy regarding my mother's revelation, but as we walked home at the end of lessons I could hold back no longer, and told him everything.

"Crikey!" he said, "You'll never know whether she's hiding behind the door every time you go in now that she's got a key."

"I know, Billy, I know, but there isn't much I can do about it, is there? Can't you get your mother to swap with Mrs. Pearson instead?" I suggested, hopefully, though already knowing the answer.

"Not likely, Neil. I bet sometimes she'll wait until she sees you enter the lavatory and then walk in with a bucket of soapy water to start cleaning it."

As we neared home I decided to drop the subject as Billy's remarks were far from being helpful. In fact he seemed to be amused by the whole situation.

"Don't take your coat off," said my mother as soon as I entered the house. "I want you to go to that pork shop near the bus stop in Woodhouse Street. We need some polony for tonight's tea."

"They sell polony at Doughty's," I said, helpfully."

"Yes, I know, but it always tastes better if you get it from a proper pork shop. Anyway, I want you to get a roll of black pudding as well and I know they don't sell that at Doughty's."

I waited for her to ask me to call on Mr. Senior to ask if he needed something bringing as well, but on this occasion she didn't.

"I'll see if Billy will go with me, mam."

He'd hardly had sufficient time to take his coat off as well, but he agreed to walk round with me.

"They sell polony at Doughty's now, Neil," he said, as we walked along Cross Speedwell Street together.

I know, Billy, but my mam says it always tastes better from a proper pork shop."

We walked down the ginnel opposite the Electra and on towards the end of Craven Road. The pork shop was located by the bus stop just around the corner. As we left, after acquiring my mother's polony and black pudding we spotted two familiar figures alighting from the bus.

"It's Edna and Phyllis," I said, in a voice low enough for only him to hear. I'd already told him about the conversation I'd overheard on the tram going into town and the one they'd had in the fish and chip shop queue in Craven Road.

"Are you sure you're doing the right thing, Edna?" said Phyllis as they began to walk up Woodhouse Street. "I mean, what if it wasn't her that they were talking about?"

Billy and I made an instant decision to follow them.

"Oh, it was her all right, Phyllis. I'm convinced of it. I could tell by the way they were talking about her and they did say, don't forget, that she lived in Craven Road."

"Well, I'm not so sure, Edna."

"And what did they call her, a little trollop? I think that's putting it mildly. Well, they also said that she works at the laundrette at the end of Jubilee Terrace, so I'm going there right now to get it sorted once and for all."

"What's a trollop?" whispered Billy.

"I've no idea, Billy, but it can't be anything pleasant, can it?"

"Why didn't you confront her at her own house then, Edna, while you had the chance?" asked her companion.

"Because it's a house of sin, Phyllis, that's why, and there's no way that I'm ever going to set foot inside it."

"Well, I hope you're sure it's the right person, Edna, for your sake as well as for hers."

"I wish you'd stop going on about it being the right person, Phyllis. Of course she's the right one, I just know it."

We watched them halt outside the door of the laundrette.

"Look, it's closed, Edna," said the smaller of the two ladies.

"I can see that with my own eyes, Phyllis. You know what's happened, don't you? She's somehow got wind of the fact that I was coming to have it out with her."

"Oh, I don't think so, Edna. Look there's a notice on the door. It gives all the opening times and it says that they're closed on Mondays."

They remained standing in the doorway for a couple of minutes before continuing to walk up Woodhouse Street.

"I bet she knew it was closed on Mondays," said Billy, "And never intended to go in."

"So do I, Billy," I said. "So do I."

We watched them turn right into Melville Road before we set off along Jubilee Terrace in the direction of home. We were just passing the end of the cul-de-sac in which the building for the Jubilee Working Men's Club was situated, when we heard a door slam, followed by a muffled curse. We both looked to see who had emitted the sound.

"Look, Neil. Isn't that Walter Zimmerman?" asked my companion.

"You're right Billy. It is. I wonder what he's doing coming out of the club. It isn't open yet, is it?"

"Is something wrong, Mr. Zimmerman?" I asked him.

"You can say that again," he replied. "Say, you're two of the lads that I met on Woodhouse Ridge the other day, aren't you? You tried to console me when I was feeling a bit down."

"That's right," agreed Billy, "But Nicky's not with us today."

"So what's wrong then, Mr. Zimmerman?" I asked again.

"Well, in a nutshell it's the same thing that's bothered me all my life. I'll explain it to you if you like. You see, I play the harmonica, and quite well even if I do say so myself. Anyway, I've done a few turns at various working men's clubs over my time and I always include a bit of comic patter between tunes. Now, a few weeks ago, I think it was just after Christmas, I called on the steward of this particular club to see if he'd sorted out the various Turns for the following few weeks as I hadn't been putting in many appearances lately and I knew that they always had a Turn on at weekends. It's the same with most of the other clubs. I don't get paid much for each session but what I do get, along with my pension, helps me to get by."

"What did the steward say?" I asked him. I'd quite forgotten about hurrying home with my mother's polony and black pudding as I was becoming most interested in his story as, I felt sure, was Billy

"Well, he told me that the club was fully booked up right through to Easter and they wouldn't be arranging any new acts until March as there was a new steward taking charge at the beginning of that month and he didn't want to make any decisions that the new man might object to. He asked me to call back after he'd taken up the stewardship, which is precisely why you see me here now. Anyway, when I finally got to speak to him he told me that he'd been given a list of suitable artists, which included those who had appeared at the club before, plus some newer ones who had expressed an interest in performing. I asked him if my name was on the list and he told me that it was. Now, you know what's coming, don't you? He told me that, as he was new to the job and hadn't previously encountered any of those on the list he felt that the only fair way was to take them in alphabetical order and as my name was at the foot of the list he was unable to fit me in. He asked me to call again in six months time when a new list will be produced. As a matter of interest I asked him what his name was and he told me it was Charles Atkinson; so, as you can see, It's alphabeticalorderism holding me back once again. Anyway, the fact is that anyone coming to the club at the weekend will be able to see a comedian by the name of Gerry Abbot. Thank you for your interest, lads, but I'm going up to the Chemic on Johnston Street now to drown my sorrows in a glass of stout."

We watched him go and I couldn't help feeling really sorry for him. I realised, even though I'd never thought about it properly before, how glad I was that my name began with the letter 'C'.

We both hurried back home and I was scolded by my mother for taking much longer on my errand than I should have.

"I've got some news for you," she said, after she had calmed down. "You know your grandad was talking about going into a convalescent home at Ilkley?"

"Yes, mam, he said he'd be in there all over Easter."

"Yes, that's right. Anyway, he's going to be admitted there on Thursday, and he'll be staying for four weeks. So, let's hope it makes him feel a lot better then, eh."

"He said the air's a lot better on Ilkley moor so it might help his breathing," I suggested, hopefully.

"Well, we'll just have to see, won't we? I thought we might all go to see him on Saturday, by which time he'll have had a bit of time to settle in, so we might have a better idea then."

I had no wish to see Grandad Miller fall back into the state he was in when I first visited him in hospital just before Christmas and I desperately wanted to see his health get back into a more robust state.

Knowing that we were now sharing a lavatory with Mary Pearson I delayed going to the yard for as long as I could, but about an hour before bedtime I knew I could no longer delay the inevitable visit. Armed with the usual matchbox containing four matches I stepped outside. It was dark, but as I passed her house I bent down below the window sill in the hope that she wouldn't see me walking past. Was I worrying about nothing? Was I going to have to perform this ritual every time I needed to go? Fortunately, at least on this occasion, my fears proved groundless. I didn't even use any of the matches my mother had given me, but managed to ensure in the darkness that there were some square pieces of newspaper hanging on a nail on the door. With my task completed I decided to place a couple of the matches in my pocket so that I could save them to use on some future visit.

As I lay in bed that night I thought long and hard about my grandfather's forthcoming period of convalescence and I found myself being rather optimistic about the beneficial effect it might have on him and I made a point of saying so when I made the usual entry in the chronicle.

CHAPTER TWENTY FIVE

"This row get your milk," announced the headmaster, thereby interrupting his geography lesson in order to comply with the legal requirement for children of all schools to be provided with a bottle of milk halfway through the morning. He never seemed entirely happy with this arrangement as he hated any of his lessons being interfered with in this fashion. Billy and I left our seats, along with Phillip Thatcher, Wanda Aspinall and Norma Clayton and made our way to the front of the class where we each extracted a bottle from the milk crate along with a straw from the table at the side. The second part of this daily ritual consisted of each pupil sucking the milk through a straw while Mr. Rawcliffe sat at his desk glaring at each pupil as if daring one of them to contemplate blowing instead of sucking in order to create the sound of bubbles forming at the bottom of the bottle, as the consequences if anyone was foolish enough to do so appeared to be the only form of consolation he could take for having his lesson disrupted.

"My milk's sour, sir," declared Gerry Sutherland, disturbing the silence.

The headmaster directed his glare in his direction.

"Nonsense, boy" he said. "All this milk was delivered fresh today."

I was well aware that there were occasions when the milk was not as it should be, but Mr. Rawcliffe wasn't having it.

"Bring it here," he demanded.

The boy in question walked over to him and handed him the offending bottle. He examined it as if that would in some way validate his disbelief. He then took the glass that he always kept on his desk and poured some of the milk into it. After taking two or three sips he turned his face away from the class as if trying to disguise the effect it was obviously having on him, but as he turned back to face us the expression that was on his face left us in no doubt that the liquid was a long way from being as fresh as it ought to have been.

"Very well," said the headmaster, deciding to put a brave face on things. "You may as well go into the cloakroom and empty it down the sink but I'm afraid there are no spare bottles this morning, so you'll just have to do without."

"That's all right, sir," he responded.

"Is there anyone else who claims that there milk is sour?"

The classroom was silent.

"I suggest then, that if you've all finished we can get down to some serious work."

We each returned our empty bottles to the crate and returned to our seats.

"Before we return to our geography lesson," announced Mr. Rawcliffe, "I would like to speak of another matter. I doubt if there is any pupil here who has not heard of the Festival Of Britain, and if there is, I will be extremely disappointed."

Everyone remained silent.

"Good, I'm pleased that everyone is aware of one of the most important events to be taking part in this country over the past hundred years. The Festival

Of Britain is an exhibition that is designed to show everything that has made this country great. The main events are taking place in London but every school in the land has been invited to play a part in some way. I'll explain to you now how we can begin to make a contribution. It has been announced that a writing competition will take place among all the schools in the country. Each headmaster will select what he considers to be the best piece of work on a given subject written by one of his pupils. There will be several age categories. As far as this class is concerned the category will be ten to eleven year olds. The winning composition will be presented to an education panel representing the Leeds area. What they decide to be the best entry will go on display at the festival site in London. The subject that has been chosen is 'A Week's Holiday On The Coast', and you will be asked to write this tomorrow morning. Now I know that this does not give you much opportunity to gather your thoughts, but it is the same for every school in the land as the organisers wanted the entries to be totally spontaneous. However, half of this afternoon will be allocated to this project so that you can all have a serious think about what is to be the content of your composition and to jot down a few notes in your exercise book. I am aware that we have had some good compositions written in the past so I hope you do not let me down. When you go home this afternoon, put on your thinking caps and let's see what you can come up with. Are there any questions on this matter before we resume our geography lesson?"

I managed to get in first by raising my hand. I always enjoyed writing compositions and usually received good marks.

"Yes, that boy there," said Mr. Rawcliffe, pointing at me. He knew the name of every boy and girl in the class, but he always spoke in this manner when selecting someone to either answer a question or perform a particular task.

"Does it have to be about me, sir, or can it be about someone else?"

"It can even be fiction, if you like. I'm also aware that there may be pupils in this class who have not had the opportunity to experience a week at the coast. The main thing is to make it as interesting as you can but correct spelling and the proper use of grammar will play a huge part when deciding the winning composition."

His explanation suited me fine as I already knew what I was going to write about.

As Billy and I headed for home after the morning's lessons I could see from his face that he wasn't particularly happy about having to think of something to write about on the following morning.

"The only time I've been away for a week," he told me, was to Morecambe and I was only seven at the time. I can't remember much about it now."

"Well, don't forget that old Rawcliffe did say that you could make it up. Anyway, I know what I'm going to write about."

"It's all right for you. You've been to stay with your Auntie Minnie near Saltburn. You told me you'd stayed there a few times. Is that what you're going to write about?"

"I've never stayed there for a full week though, Billy. It's usually been for a few days at Easter or Whitsuntide, and I haven't been there since I was nine anyway. No, I'm going to write about something entirely different."

"What's that then, Neil?"

"I'm not going to tell you. You'll have to wait until I've written it. He's not given us much time though, has he?"

After leaving Billy, I knocked on my Auntie Molly's door and walked in. On Thursdays my mother always did some cleaning for an elderly friend and always arranged for me to have a snack at her sister's house next door, a situation that I had always found quite satisfactory. On this occasion she'd made beans on toast which she was just putting onto a plate as I arrived.

"Thanks, Auntie Molly," I said, and began tucking in.

She waited until I had finished before producing a glass of lemonade and a couple of ginger biscuits.

With half an hour still remaining before I had to be back at school I asked my aunt if she could give me the key to my house as I wanted to collect something for school.

"Well, as a matter of fact I was just about to go in myself in order to feed the dog. You can do it for me if you like."

She handed me the key and, after taking a previously opened tin of dog food from the cellar head and emptying the contents into Nell's bowl I made my way upstairs. Opening the top drawer in my room I removed the Woodhouse Chronicle and hurried back downstairs with it. Nell had already devoured all the contents of her bowl and was waiting for the two or three doggy biscuits that she usually had afterwards. As I was supplying her with her dessert I noticed Susan's red ribbon protruding from the book I was carefully carrying and realised that it might be prudent for me to remove it. I hurried back upstairs and replaced it in the drawer.

After I had returned the key next door to my Auntie Molly I realised that it was time to head back to school with the chronicle tucked inside my jacket in the hope that no one would notice it, though I thought I might mention it to Billy. I was determined that my composition entitled 'The Lucy Stone' would be the one that the headmaster would select for the competition.

"Do you remember that story I told you about when my Grandad Miller was on holiday all those years ago?" I asked Billy as we walked along the street together.

"What, the one about that gypsy girl?"

"Yes, that one. Well, that's what I'm going to write about for this competition that Old Rawcliffe was talking about."

"So, what are you carrying under your coat then, Neil?"

"I was hoping that no one would be able to notice that until I got into the classroom and put it into my desk."

"You've no chance, Neil. It's too obvious. If you don't want anybody to see it your best bet is to take off your coat and hold it underneath while you have it draped over your arm."

His words made sense and I did as he suggested, but I felt the cold seep through me immediately.

"What is it, anyway?" asked my companion.

"It's the chronicle I've been writing, the one that I told you about. I want to jot down some notes for tomorrow so that I can begin writing it straight away. If anybody finds out about it they might want to look at it, and I don't think that would be a good thing."

I was remembering the misfortune that had befallen Harry Crabtree, my grandfather's childhood friend when he took his personal jottings to school and I certainly didn't fancy the humiliation of bending over in front of the entire class with my trousers around my ankles while waiting to receive the cane.

As far as I was aware I managed to get the chronicle into the classroom and inside my desk without anyone noticing. The headmaster was as good as his word and after the first half of the afternoon consisting of a lesson on grammar and punctuation, which he no doubt thought would stand us in good stead for the composition we were expected to write on the following day, he allowed us to spend the remaining time gathering our thoughts and jotting down notes. At least that is what we were supposed to be doing, but I felt that a lot of my classmates were simply going through the motions. Fortunately, that did not apply to Phillip Thatcher who was sitting next to me, and who seemed thoroughly engrossed in using the period for the purpose that the headmaster had intended. This allowed me to keep sneaking a look at my quite lengthy account of Grandad Miller's story of 'The Lucy Stone', by lifting up the desk lid every so often. By the time the bell sounded to signify the end of school I was very happy with the progress I had made and I felt very confident that my efforts on the following morning could well result in my work being selected as the one to represent our school."

"I'm going to win this, Billy," I said as we walked back towards home.

"How do you know?" he asked. "I know you're good at writing compositions Neil, but so are a lot of the other lads, Alan Bartle for one."

"Some of the girls are as well," I replied, "Especially Dorothy Steedman, but I think I'll win because I've got the best story."

It was quite a pleasant afternoon for early March and the idea of sitting in the house until teatime didn't seem particularly appealing. I decided to see if my closest friend felt the same way. I was pleased that he agreed with my view that we played outside for a while. First of all, I thought that I'd better make sure that my mother hadn't planned any errands for me, as she often did as soon as I returned from school. On this occasion I was not required and within a few minutes the two of us were lobbing a tennis ball towards each other in the street outside.

"You keep dropping it Billy," I gloated as he failed to catch it yet again. "I've only dropped it once and you've dropped it five times."

"That's because I can't see," he told me in an attempt to defend his skill as an imagined fielder for Yorkshire County Cricket Club. I bet you couldn't catch any at all if you had the sun in your eyes like me."

"That's just an excuse, Billy. It wouldn't stop me catching it."

"Right! Let's swap places then."

I decided to do ass he suggested which left me standing outside Mrs. Ormond's sweet shop window at the end of the street. I was determined to prove to him that my fielding skills were much superior to his. Unfortunately, his first three throws resulted in the ball falling to the floor and I realised that his reason for being unable to catch the ball was correct. Each time I attempted it the sun was blinding my eyes. Billy started laughing which made me especially determined to catch his next effort.

"Right then, Billy, throw this one as high as you can. I was just unlucky before."

He did as I had suggested and, despite the sun being in my eyes again, I could tell that if I did not start moving backwards the ball would fall to the floor behind me. Suddenly, Billy began to shout.

"Look out, Neil. There's someone coming round the corner behind you."

My first reaction was to assume that he was simply trying to put me off and I started to ignore his warning. However, I found myself backing into someone and immediately turned around. This resulted in my coming face to face with my unintentional victim as we fell to the floor with me on top. The horror of the situation came home to me immediately as I heard Billy start laughing once more.

"You've done it again, Neil," admonished Susan Brown, as we lay there gazing at each other. "You're so clumsy."

I attempted to tell her that I was trying to catch the ball with the sun in my eyes, but as soon as the words left my mouth I realised that that explanation was totally unacceptable for what had occurred. It was the third time I had knocked her over in less than three months. Despite the close proximity of her face, a situation that I would normally have relished, my only thought was that she must think I was incredibly stupid.

"I'm sorry, Susan," I managed to get out, as I helped her to her feet. It was a totally inadequate response to her misfortune and to my own involvement in causing it. I could see that, although her dress did not appear to have been torn by the mishap, it was certainly dirty. She also had graze marks on her arm. What I wanted to do was to put my arms around her, give her a cuddle and say again how sorry I was, but I knew it would only make the situation worse. Feeling wretched I watched her walk to the ginnel opposite the Electra before she turned into it and disappeared from sight.

"Well, that's the end of the game," said Billy once his laughter had subsided. "The tennis ball will probably be on the tram lines in Meanwood Road by now."

"Why does it always have to be her I keep knocking over? I feel really miserable now."

"Well she didn't seem to be hurt much, did she? And she certainly wasn't as annoyed as she could have been."

I thought over what he had said. Was he right? Would she have been more annoyed if someone else had done it?

"I think I'll go back in now, Billy. I want to jot down a few more notes for this composition tomorrow."

"Well, I'm not even going to think about it until I have to."

As I began to think again about how to transfer my grandfather's account of the Lucy Stone into my own words I was struck by a disturbing thought and I grabbed hold of Billy's arm.

"The chronicle," I gasped, "I forgot to bring it home. Everybody was in a hurry to leave the classroom as soon as the bell went, so I thought it would be safe to take it out of the desk as nobody around me was taking any notice. Then you started talking to me about the picture that's on at the Astra on Friday. I forgot to pick it up, Billy. All I brought home was the exercise book that I'd been making notes in. If anybody finds it and reads it, I'll be in trouble. I've written all sorts of things in it about old Rawcliffe and especially about Tucker Lane. What if one of them reads it? I've got to get it back before anyone sees it."

"Well, you've no chance now, Neil. It's nearly five o'clock."

"The school might not be locked up yet. I'm going back to see."

I knew it was virtually a forlorn hope, but Billy decided to accompany me. The school was indeed locked and, although we found the caretaker round the back, he could see no reason to open it up again just for the sake of something that had been left behind that could simply be retrieved on the following day.

During the evening when my attention should have been on the content of the following day's composition I found my mind fully occupied by two things. The first was whether my unfortunate collision with the girl of my dreams might have lowered the high esteem in which she otherwise might have regarded me. The second was the dread that someone, at that very moment, might be reading the chronicle and all the incriminating words it might contain regarding certain individuals. I went to sleep with this niggling thought focused in my mind.

CHAPTER TWENTY SIX

"Have you found Mary Pearson hiding behind the lavatory door yet?" asked Billy as we made our way to school.

My mind was fixed firmly on my desire to find that the chronicle was exactly where I had left it on the previous day without having been disturbed. My anxiety regarding the possible consequences should it be read by the wrong person was making it very difficult for me to concentrate on the composition that I would be writing that morning. Nevertheless, I was aware that my best friend's question merited an answer.

"Not so far, Billy," I told him, "But it's bound to happen soon, isn't it?"

He didn't answer. He just grinned.

Assembly seemed to last twice as long as it usually did as I was keen to be one of the first to enter the classroom in the hope that the anxiety I had been feeling might prove to have been unnecessary. However, when I finally did walk through the door the situation was even worse than I had imagined. The object I had hoped to see was no longer on the desk where I had left it, but on the headmaster's desk was a large grey book with the words 'The Woodhouse Chronicle' emblazoned across it. As I took up my seat with a forlorn expression on my face I watched the rest of the class take up theirs. As soon as everyone had settled Mr. Rawcliffe asked me to approach him.

"You left this on your desk yesterday afternoon," he said, indicating the chronicle in front of him, "Though I didn't notice it until I entered the classroom this morning. I must say it looks very interesting. I skimmed through it without paying particular attention to what it contained, but what took my eye was the fact that it appears to be written in the style of the Anglo-Saxon Chronicle that the old English monks compiled. I can't help being pleased that you were obviously paying attention to the history lessons I've been taking."

"Yes, Sir. Thank you, Sir. Is it all right if I take it back now, Sir?"

"You can have it back after the morning lessons and I'm expecting a good composition from you today."

I walked dejectedly back to my seat. Somehow I had to try to concentrate on trying to write a winning entry for the Festival Of Britain competition and forget for the time being the horrible thought of the likely consequences of the headmaster perusing the chronicle. Once I started writing, however, I soon found myself in a world of my own as I attempted to do justice to the story that my grandfather had related to me. I could hear the occasional voices within the classroom but they sounded so faint and distant. The words seemed to fly out of my mind and onto the paper and I found myself completing the composition with twenty minutes of the allotted time remaining. I used that period to check, to the best of my ability, that I had got the grammar and spelling right. When the headmaster eventually called a halt to the proceedings I was reasonably satisfied that I had done everything that was humanly possible.

"That was awful," said Billy as we entered the playground for the morning break. "I just couldn't think what to write about. I tried putting something down about when I went to Morecambe, but that was four years ago and as far as I can remember nothing very interesting happened anyway. It's all right for you. You had something already written down didn't you?"

"Yes, but I had to write it in a different way otherwise it wouldn't have been any good. You should have made something up. He said it was all right to do that, didn't he?"

"Well I was never going to win anyway, was I? So I'm not really bothered."

I noticed Susan Brown talking to Dorothy Steedman and Eva Bentley. She kept glancing in my direction and I couldn't help wondering if she was talking about me knocking her over.

Immediately after we had re-entered the classroom the headmaster announced that he would be reading all the compositions before the midday break and that he would announce during the afternoon which one he would be sending on to the next stage in the selection process. I couldn't help noticing that the chronicle remained unopened on his desk but he made no move to hand it back to me. He asked us all to open our history books at page one hundred and eighty-four and to read the chapter headed 'King Charles And His Quarrel With Parliament', and pointed out that he would be asking us questions on what we had read before school finished for the day. This meant that all the pupils had to make at least some attempt to do as he asked. He also made it quite clear that he wanted complete silence throughout. In the main he got what he wanted. The occasional fidget was simply dealt with by a stern look in the direction of the offender. By the time the bell went to signify the end of morning lessons he looked reasonably satisfied with our general behaviour.

"By the time you all return to the classroom," he declared, "I will have finished reading all your work and I will be speaking to you about it then."

As I left the premises along with Billy, we were joined by Alan Bartle

"You like Susan Brown, don't you?" he said, addressing his remarks to me.

I was about to deny it, but I knew that that wouldn't do, especially with my closest friend beside me. Even though I didn't blush quite so much as I used to do when her name was linked with mine, I realised that if I tried to lie about it then that fact alone would set my face burning. Anyway, I was intrigued to find out why he was asking me.

"What if I do?" I said, defiantly.

"Well, I just thought I'd let you know that I think she likes you as well."

This time there was no way that I could prevent the blood from rushing to my face.

"I overheard her chatting to Dorothy Steedman and Eva Bentley," he continued, "And they seemed to be talking about which boys they liked. Anyway, I heard Susan say that she liked you, but then she said that at least she would if you didn't keep pushing her over."

Billy started laughing and I began to feel uncomfortable.

"Why do you keep pushing her over?" asked Alan.

"I don't," I replied.

"Well she said that you do."

"I don't keep pushing her over. I keep knocking her over."

"Well, that's the same thing, isn't it?"

Billy's laughter was now on the verge of becoming uncontrollable.

"If you push someone over," I attempted to explain, "Then that means that you're doing it on purpose, but if you knock someone over, then that's accidental, isn't it?"

"I don't get that. Why can't you knock someone over on purpose?"

"Stop laughing, Billy," I said, beginning to get annoyed with him.

"How many times have you knocked her over then?" asked Alan.

"Only three."

"What, you say that you've knocked her over three times and you tell me that each one was accidental?"

"Yes, why would I knock her over on purpose? The first time was on New Year's Eve. It was just outside the entrance to the ridge. The snow had started to melt and it was all slushy. I slipped as I started to walk down the hill."

"You were running, Neil," said my closest friend."

"Shut up, Billy," I said, giving him a look of annoyance for correcting me.

I continued with my explanation. "Anyway, like I said, I slipped and knocked her over as I slid down the hill. The second time was in the shop. I didn't see her as I turned round to go out, and the third time was yesterday when I was trying to catch a tennis ball with the sun in my eyes and I backed into her."

"I can't believe you've managed to knock her down three times by accident," said Alan.

"I don't care whether you believe me or not," I told him, "But it's true anyway."

As Billy and I left him and made our way home, I contented myself with my newly-acquired knowledge regarding Susan's feelings towards me. However, as we were returning to school for the afternoon lessons I became apprehensive again regarding the fact that the headmaster had still not made any comments to me about the chronicle. The first thing I noticed as I entered the classroom was that it still remained unopened on his desk.

As soon as we were all seated Mr. Rawcliffe made his announcement. "In the main," he began, "I have been quite impressed by the work that was handed in to me, though there are still a few of you who have not fully grasped the opportunity that was offered to you."

The expression on Billy's face suggested that he believed himself to be in that category.

The headmaster continued with his assessment. "I have received excellent compositions from Dorothy Steedman, Phillip Thatcher, Alan Bartle, Ernie Peyton, Valerie Trainer and Wanda Aspinall, so I would like to say well done to those pupils in particular. However, the two pieces of writing that have stood out for me are 'The Lucy Stone' by Neil Cawson and 'The Boy In The Boarding House' by Susan Brown. Now this is where I have a problem. The rules do not allow me to submit two entries and, at this moment, I am unable to decide between the two."

I felt quite exhilarated to have my name linked with Susan's in this way. Unfortunately, it seemed that one of us would have to face the disappointment of not proceeding further in the competition.

"Anyway, I think it would be a good idea," said Mr. Rawcliffe after pausing for a while, "For me to read both compositions to the class as it will give you a good idea as to the sort of descriptive writing you should be aiming for."

He began with Susan's entry, which was a very moving story concerning a five-year old boy who was staying in the same boarding house as her and her parents when they visited Scarborough in the previous year, the focal point being the fact that, not only had he been blind from birth, but also had a deformity in his right leg, which limited his ability to walk in a way that most people take for granted. The point of the story was the cheerfulness with which he accepted his misfortune and his uncanny ability to brighten the lives of everyone with whom he came into contact. The headmaster then read out my account of the Lucy stone. Both compositions were well received by the class, but I felt in my heart that Susan's was better. I have to admit to being surprised as I had no idea that she could write so well.

After we returned from the afternoon break, he chalked up some sums on the blackboard and asked us to present the answers in our exercise book. This was so he could look again at the two relevant entries and make a decision at the end of the lesson. When the appointed time arrived he dismissed the class but asked the writers of the two compositions that he considered to be the best to stay behind. As our fellow pupils departed Billy looked in my direction with a mischievous look on his face and gave me a wave. When the room had emptied the headmaster asked Susan and me to sit next to each other at the front of the class. I was eager to agree to his request and took great care that I did not knock her over in the process.

"I am still undecided about the two essays in front of me," he announced. It was the first time I had heard him refer to them by that name. It was as if his appreciation of their content had in some way elevated their status. "I would like to know, therefore, a little more about how you came to write them."

As he said this our hands came into contact between the chairs. To this day I could not say without it was involuntary or whether it was intentional on either her part or mine. All I know is that it was a wonderful moment that I knew I would never forget, and a warm feeling engulfed me.

We each did as he asked. I explained how my grandfather had reminisced about the week he'd spent at Robin Hood's Bay at the beginning of the century and Susan told him about the week she had spent in Scarborough and how impressed she had been with the little boy's cheerfulness despite his disabilities and how she thought it would make a good subject for this composition. Before the headmaster had a chance to speak I knew what I had to do.

"Susan's is better," I told him. She looked at me and the pressure on my hand increased.

"Why do you say that?" he asked.

I thought hard for a few seconds. "Because it tells you things, like those Aesop's Fables we used to read about in Miss Hazlehirst's class."

"And what does it tell you?"

"That no matter how badly you feel, there's always someone in a worse predicament, so there's no reason to let it get you down."

Mr. Rawcliffe stroked his chin. "I see," he said thoughtfully. "As a matter of fact I was about to come to the same conclusion, but I'm very pleased that you thought to mention it first. Very well then, Susan Brown's essay is the one that I shall enter into the competition."

"That doesn't seem fair," she said. She was going to say something else but I interrupted.

"It's all right, Susan. Yours was better than mine. I don't mind, really."

"Right! That's it then," said the headmaster. "Off you go home and I'll see you on Monday."

She let go of my hand as we stood up and walked out of the classroom together. The chronicle still lay on his desk but I simply ignored it. If I paused to ask for it back, Susan would have been out of the door and I would have been unable to walk back with her by my side. I was grateful to Billy for having the thoughtfulness to realise that, on this occasion, I would not have wanted him to hang around the playground and wait for me.

"I thought your story was very good," she said, as we walked along Jubilee Terrace. "It was very romantic, your grandfather keeping his half of the stone for all those years."

"But your story was better, Susan. It was better than mine."

My feeling at the time was one of elation, which became even more intense as we passed the Electra doorway and I remembered how lovely she had looked with the hailstones in her hair as we had sheltered there just before Christmas. I knew the moment would soon be over but as I neared home she turned towards me, gave me a kiss, and hurried away towards the end of the street. It was only a peck on the cheek, but it meant the world to me as it suggested that perhaps she did have feelings towards me, if only I could stop knocking her over.

That was the last day that I ever set eyes on 'The Woodhouse Chronicle'. I don't know whether he confiscated it, lost it or simply forgot to give it back to me, but I never asked for its return. I had grown weary of recording the happenings of the day night after night before I could surrender to sleep, just as my closest friend had suggested I would when I had first mentioned my intentions to him. Everything was already recorded in my memory and the most important events, like those which had just occurred, I knew I would have no problem in recalling instantly, but I was very much relieved that I had had the foresight to remove Susan's red ribbon from the book, and that night I returned it to its rightful place under my pillow.

CHAPTER TWENTY SEVEN

"Were going to see your grandad this afternoon," my mother announced immediately after breakfast. "We'll have to have our dinner as soon as your father comes home from work. I was hoping he wouldn't be working again this Saturday but I suppose in a way I should be pleased for the extra money. There won't be much time, so if you go out this morning you must make sure that you're back by twelve o'clock. I expect you to be dressed smartly when we see him, which means that you'll have to get washed and changed as soon as you get back. So try not to do anything that might get you into a filthy state."

I needed no further prompting to agree to her terms as I was very keen to find out how my grandfather was progressing. I had been with my parents to Ilkley on numerous occasions and always had an enjoyable time. To get there it was necessary to take a bus to the Headrow in town before catching one owned by the Samuel Ledgard Company at the start of its journey, which was in Cookridge Street close to the town hall. It did actually pass Woodhouse Moor which was much nearer, but my parents never preferred this option as the vehicle was often full before it arrived at the stop. I loved travelling on these buses as the seating on the top deck was totally different to the ones we usually travelled on and it was always an enjoyable journey with some really stunning scenery.

A knock on the door heralded the arrival of my closest companion, just as my mother had expected it to.

"I've got to be back by twelve o'clock, Billy," I told him as soon as we had stepped outside.

"I think I'll start calling you Cinderella," he said, laughing. "All you need is a pair of glass slippers."

"That's not funny, Billy. Anyway, the reason I have to get back for that time today is because we're going to see my Grandad Miller in the convalescent home this afternoon."

"I hope he's all right. I like your grandad."

"I think he'll be a lot better while he's there. Everybody keeps telling me that the air is a lot better on Ilkley Moor."

"What shall we do this morning then, Neil?"

"I'm not sure but I don't think I'd better go onto the ridge. My mother would go bonkers if I got home covered in muck. Why don't we go play in the schoolyard?"

It was agreed upon and we made our way along the street, passing the Electra and taking notice of the scaffolding around what was left of the roof. It was obvious, however, that no work was being done on it on this particular day. Our eyes were drawn to the large poster on the wall which proclaimed in bold letters 'RE-OPENING SOON'.

"It'll be Easter in a few more days," said my companion. "Maybe it'll open then."

"I hope so, Billy, but there isn't a poster advertising any films, is there?"

"That jungle picture we saw at the Astra last night was all right, but we had all that way to walk home when it had finished. Do you remember when we went to see the Bowery Boys? It was pouring down when we came out and we got soaked. I'll be glad when we can start going to the Electra again. Anyway, I forgot to ask you last night. Did you win the writing competition?"

"No, because Susan's was better than mine."

"Is that what Old Rawcliffe said?"

"No, I did, but I think he would have said it anyway."

"I thought you wouldn't want me to wait for you, Neil. I thought you might have preferred to walk back with someone else."

I decided not to say any more on the subject. I was not prepared to mention the kiss that Susan had given me, as I was unsure as to what his reaction might be. Having reached the schoolyard we vaulted over the low wall and walked over to the stone steps that led to the closed door of the school.

"It's a pity Nicky had to go into town with his mother," observed Billy as we sat down.

"I know. I'm forced to go on some Saturday mornings as well."

"Why does Nicky's mother want to take you along?"

"Don't be daft, Billy. It's my mother I go with, and I hate it because it's nearly all clothing shops she seems to go to and she never has enough money to buy much anyway. I think she just likes looking at dresses and things and it's dead boring."

"If you end up marrying Susan Brown I bet she'll make you go with her to a lot of clothing shops."

"I think that would probably be the same whoever either of us got married to. Girls only seem to be interested in clothes."

"I think if I had to marry one of the girls from this school," he said, "It would have to be Sally Cheesedale."

"Why Sally Cheesdale?" I asked him.

"Well I think it's because sometimes she talks about cricket and she told me that her brother plays for Woodhouse Cricket Club. That's the team that plays on that ground in Meanwood Road near the bottom of the ridge. She also said that he's been told that he has a good chance of playing for Yorkshire one day. If he did and he was my brother-in-law I'd be able to get lots of free tickets for the test match at Headingley."

I realised that my companion did not think about Sally Cheesedale in quite the same way that I thought about Susan Brown.

"I can't see that, Billy. I don't think the committee would ever allow anybody called Cheesedale to play for Yorkshire. I mean it just doesn't sound right, does it? Can you imagine the commentator saying 'Hutton and Cheesedale are just making their way out of the pavilion to open the batting for Yorkshire'? No, it just couldn't happen. It'd probably be all right for one of those soft, la-de-da southern counties where they have daft names like Ponsonby-Smythe, but it wouldn't do for Yorkshire."

After a while we left the steps and walked across the yard to the two hopscotch markings on the ground over by the wall. There were two different types of hopscotch; one where you hopped along the squares before bending down to retrieve the stone after it had been thrown and one where you kicked the stone from one square to another. In the latter case it was essential that the stone was a flat one, otherwise it was impossible to direct it where you wanted it to go. We chose the second option to begin with once we had been able to locate a stone that we deemed suitable enough. We were joined shortly afterwards by Keith Battle and Ken Stacey who had been walking along Jubilee Terrace and the competition became more intense as we alternated between the two activities. Eventually I realised that if the planned visit to see my grandfather was to go without a hitch I would need to start walking back along the street towards home.

"I'm going to have to go now," I said. "I have to be back at twelve o'clock."

I explained to the other two lads my reason for being unable to stay out any longer.

"Cinderella again," said Billy but, after saying farewell to our other schoolmates, the two of us walked back together.

We paused once more when we reached the Electra and gazed up at the scaffolding.

"I hope it does open in time for Easter, Billy. I'm really looking forward to being off school for two whole weeks, aren't you?"

"You can say that again. Winter's all right when it's Christmas or when it's snowing, but I hate all these dark nights and when the weather's bad, which is most of the time, you've got to stay indoors."

"Do you think your mam might let you go to the pictures twice a week?" I asked him.

"I think it depends on how much money she's got. It would be great if she did though, wouldn't it? Mind you, it's Woodhouse Feast over Easter as well and we'll need some money for that."

When I left him and entered my house the clock on the shelf above the fireplace showed ten minutes to twelve. My mother was already setting plates on the table even though my father wouldn't be home for another half hour.

"We're making do with egg and chips today," she announced so get your hands washed now and you can eat yours straight away."

I could tell that Nell was puzzled by this change of routine. She walked over to the top of the cellar steps, looked in her bowl and, finding it empty, walked back towards my mother and gave her accusing looks.

"As soon as you've finished eating, Neil," said my mother, "You can get a proper wash and then I want you to go upstairs while your father's having his dinner and put on the shirt and trousers I've left out for you on the bed. I want you to look really smart when you visit your grandad."

I had no real quarrel with that and by the time we all left the house I felt I would have been a credit to any family in our vicinity. We walked to the bus stop in Woodhouse Street and caught a number 60 bus, which took us to the end of Cookridge Street via Hyde Park and Mount Preston. The blue Ilkley bus, bearing the name Samuel Ledgard on the side was already parked at the stop when we arrived. The private company was based at Armley and was extremely popular among the local inhabitants.

As we climbed on board the Town Hall clock showed 1.35PM. There was no need on this occasion to ask if we could travel on the upper deck as I knew that my parents enjoyed the views on this particular route just as much as I did. I was relieved, however that, despite the fact that there was already a considerable number of passengers already seated, the front seat, which differed consider-ably from the buses operated by Leeds City Council by accommodating three people instead of the usual two, had not been taken. We took up our places and I waited with eager anticipation for the journey to begin. I was really pleased that my grandfather had chosen this particular location for his period of convalescence rather than somewhere which could have proved to be much less interesting.

The journey took us past the university and Woodhouse Moor towards Headingley and Lawnswood. Within minutes we had crossed the Leeds boundary and were out in the countryside. One particular point, at the foot of Otley Chevin, was of particular interest as it offered the first stunning view of the Wharfedale Valley. It was known locally as Surprise View because it emerged in a spectacular and unexpected manner as the bus rounded a sharp bend. This view persisted all the way to Otley at which time our chosen mode of transport pulled into the bus station. On many a pleasant Sunday or Bank Holiday this may have been our intended destination and we would eagerly make our way through the town centre and across the bridge to walk along the riverside where the swans, ducks and geese ganged up on the unwary visitor as they begged for food. The area boasted an open-air swimming facility and a café where you could sample what was on offer either inside if the weather was inclement or outside if it was warm and pleasant, which invariably seemed to be the case. There was also a substantial children's playground with its own paddling pool, which was enormously popular and beyond this was a pleasant park which gave way to a narrow footpath alongside the river where the more seasoned walkers could make there way as far as Pool Bank.

On leaving the bus station our vehicle travelled via the picturesque village of Burley-In-Wharfedale to continue along by the side of the river Wharfe to its terminus at Ilkley and we disembarked in the town centre. My mother decided that she couldn't go another step without a cup of tea so, much to my father's disapproval, we made our way to a small café in the main shopping street. By the time we left it was turned three o'clock and we knew that if we wanted to see my grandfather for what we considered to be a reasonable length of time then we would have to begin the climb up the steep hill towards the convalescent home which was situated on the very edge of Ilkley Moor. We arrived just before 3.30 and I have to admit that the imposing building that greeted us did look to be an ideal place for his recuperation. When we entered and explained to the receptionist who we had come to see, she told us that Mr. Miller would probably be found in one of the large rest rooms, probably the one in the west wing, and she pointed us in the right direction.

When we arrived at our destination it was to find Grandad Miller sitting in a corner and gazing out of the window across Ilkley Moor. There were a few other people in the room of a similar age who just seemed to be sitting around without doing anything in particular. He acknowledged us immediately, and attempted a smile.

"I wondered if you might come over today," he said.

"The journey's taken a bit longer than we expected, dad," explained my mother. Unfortunately, it means we won't be able to stay quite as long as we'd planned."

"Anyway, you're here now, so we'll make the most of it, eh."

My mother didn't mention to him how long that we'd spent in the café, but the bus ride had taken quite a long time.

"How are you feeling then, grandad?" I asked, before anyone else could get in.

"Oh, I'm right enough, lad. I'm right enough. We go out in groups for short walks on the moor. They told me the air would be invigorating, and I suppose it is, but by heck it's bloody cold as well."

"Dad, I'm sure there's no need to swear," admonished my mother. "And there's no need for you to start laughing," she added, turning towards me while raising her hand as if about to strike me across the cheek. My father remained silent, but he had a huge smile on his face.

"Oh, don't get me wrong, lass," said Grandad Miller. "I know it must be doing me good because my breathing has definitely improved since I've been in here. No, it's something else entirely that's been getting me down."

"What is it then, grandad?" I asked him.

"It's sheer boredom, son. When you arrived I was just staring out of the window thinking over my life and I seem to have been doing exactly the same thing for most of the time that I've been here. Oh, there are plenty of people willing to talk to you but there just doesn't seem to be much life in the place. There are three rest rooms and they each have a wireless inside, so I always manage to get the football results. There are plenty of books and magazines lying about to read and there occasionally seems to be a game of cards or dominoes going on. I can't complain about the meals I've been given either, but the place is just too quiet for me. I can't figure out why it should be like this. I know that most of those here are recovering from some sort of illness, but I feel that the whole place just needs something to stir things up a little. Still, it was my decision to come and I'm determined to stick it out. At least I'm breathing a lot better and that was my main purpose in being here, wasn't it?"

"I noticed a small shop just inside the entrance," said my father. "Is there anything that we can get for you?"

"Well, yes, there is as a matter of fact. I never managed to get a newspaper this morning and I always like to read the football information on a Saturday before the results are given out. So if you don't mind I'd like you a Daily Express if that's all right with you."

"I'll go for it, grandad," I suggested. "I know where it is. I remember passing it on the way in."

"Thank you very much lad, and you can get yourself a comic and a bag of sweets if you like," he said while handing me a two shilling piece.

"I wouldn't have thought that they sold comics here," observed my father. "Most of the inhabitants seem to be middle-aged or elderly."

"I know what you mean, but you'd be surprised how many visitors bring their children with them."

"Are you sure you've got enough money with you dad without giving it away," said my mother.

"Oh aye, I've got enough left and there's not a right lot to spend it on here. Right lad, let's be off with you then."

I left them to continue chatting and made my way to the shop. I felt a little guilty at buying a Captain Marvel comic as it cost sixpence which was twice the price of most of those on display and added to that a quarter of Liquorice Allsorts which, after acquiring my grandfather's Daily Express did not leave him with very much change.

I decided to explore a little before returning as I was surprised by the vastness of the place. It was much bigger than I had expected. Apart from the sound of my footsteps echoing along the corridor the place was eerily silent as I made my way in the opposite direction to the way I had approached the shop finding myself before long passing another rest room in a different wing to the one in which Grandad Miller was currently sitting. The silence was soon broken, however.

"Pardon me, lad. Have you a minute?" I was sure that the voice came from the room I had just passed. I walked back and looked inside. There were only three people in the room, all of whom were men who I would guess were in there early sixties. While two of them were sitting quietly reading the other occupant was gesticulating me to approach. I obliged him and walked across the room.

"I couldn't help noticing that you were carrying a newspaper as you walked along the corridor," he said as I stood in front of him, expectantly. "I wonder if you could do me a small favour."

"What's that?" I asked. "Do you want me to bring you something from the shop?"

"Nay, lad, it's nothing like that. No, I just wondered if you'd mind having a look at the racing pages in yon newspaper that you're carrying. You'll find them near the back in the sporting section."

I did as he asked.

"Now then, my son called a couple of days ago and I got him to place a little bet on a horse that was running yesterday. Actually, I say a little bet but it was quite a substantial one really because I'd had a tip off you see. So what I'd like you to do for me is to look at the name of the horse that won the 2:30 race at Redcar. I'd prefer to look at it myself, but I left my other spectacles in my bedroom."

I ran down the list of winners with my finger. The name of the horse that won that race is Autumn Gold," I told him.

"Yippee!" he shouted, throwing his arms in the air while startling the two other occupants of the room at the same time. "I knew it. I just knew it."

He quietened almost immediately and a suspicious look came over his face. "Now you wouldn't be playing a joke on an old man, would you?" he said. "Are you sure you've got it right?"

It occurred to me that there was no way I could have been deceiving him as he hadn't told me which horse he had wanted to win.

"Yes, it's written down here, mister." I showed him the relevant entry even though I knew that he wouldn't be able to read it.

"Tell me, lad. Can you see what the odds were? They should be written just at the side of the winner's name."

"One hundred to seven," I told him.

"That's even better," he said, triumphantly I think it's fair to say that I never saw a man so full of joy as he was at that precise moment.

"That's just what I needed," he went on. Look, here's something for your trouble, and he took a shilling from his pocket and placed it in my hand.

"Gee, thanks mister," I said, while realising that I had not really done anything to deserve it.

"I suppose you're wondering why I'm making such a fuss about a simple win on the horses, but it's the sheer boredom of being in here that's been getting to me. It's far too quiet for someone like me. I've always been a lively person ever since I was little. How old are you then, son?"

I told him.

"Eleven, eh? And I bet you've got a close friend that you do everything and go everywhere with. I bet you don't just sit around at home doing nothing."

"No, me and Billy Mathieson play outside every chance we get."

"Billy Mathieson, eh? Well I bet you get into a lot of mischief sometimes as well. Am I right?"

"Sometimes, but we never do anything really bad."

"Of course not, but the point I'm trying to make is that you're not very much different to the way I was as a child. You see, my best mate was called Sam Miller and we were known as the tearaway twins round Hunslet way at the turn of the century. You wouldn't believe some of the scrapes that my mate Sam used to talk me into."

He continued speaking to me and I continued listening for a further five minutes before I realised that I should be heading back towards my grandfather. I said goodbye and thanked him for the shilling he had given me and began to retrace my steps. I never asked his name because I knew there wasn't really any need and as I hurried back I didn't feel so guilty anymore about spending more of Grandad Miller's money than perhaps I should have.

"You've taken your time, lad," said Grandad Miller. "I thought you must have gone exploring on Ilkley Moor. We were just thinking about sending out a search party."

"I'm not sure I was," said my father with a smile on face. "I think I'd have left him to find his own way home."

"Anyway, grandad, I've got something to tell you and it's good news."

"What's that then, son?"

I looked at him, eager to see the expression that I knew would very shortly appear on his face.

"Grandad," I said "I don't think you're going to be bored anymore."

After we left him and made our way to the exit I found myself in a very cheerful mood. I knew now that when he came out of the convalescent home he would be much improved from when he went in and I found myself looking forward to two weeks away from school over the Easter period and the lighter evenings that were now beckoning. Woodhouse Feast would soon be arriving, the Electra Picture House was about to re-open and I had received my first kiss from the lips of Susan Brown. Even the school rugby matches had taken on a new significance. I felt very contented as I looked forward to the bus journey home, and as we passed the lady at the reception desk and I observed the peace and quiet of her surroundings as she sat back in the seat with a serene look on her face and her eyes half closed as she nonchalantly filed her nails I couldn't help wondering that perhaps I should have warned her that things might not be quite so tranquil now that Mr. Samuel Miller had been re-united with his old partner in mischief, Mr. Harry Crabtree.